The Incomparable Countess
by
Mary Nichols

Born in Singapore, **Mary Nichols** came to England when she was three, and has spent most of her life in different parts of East Anglia. She has been a radiographer, school secretary, information officer and industrial editor, as well as a writer. She has three grown-up children and four grand-children.

Chapter One

1817

Frances, Countess of Corringham, paintbrush in hand, looked up from her easel at her sitter. Lady Willoughby was extremely fat; she had innumerable double chins, made more obvious by a heavy necklace of diamonds, and her small eyes were sunk in folds of pink flesh. Her ginger hair peeped from the edges of a huge pink satin turban which sported a sweeping feather fastened with a diamond pin.

The picture on the canvas bore little resemblance to reality, for Frances knew that she must flatter her sitter if she was ever going to be paid for her work, and though she had caught the eyes and the shape of brows and nose, the flesh had been toned down, there were fewer wrinkles and only the merest suggestion of a double chin. But it was still undeniably a portrait of Lady Willoughby.

One day, she mused, one day she would paint what she saw and never mind the consequences. Now she had done enough for one day. She was just picking up a cloth to wipe her brush, when her ladyship spoke. 'I heard the Duke of Loscoe was come to town and intending to stay for the Season,' she said with a note that sounded uncommonly like triumph.

Not by a single flicker of an eyelid did Frances reveal any sign of agitation, though it took all her considerable self-control. 'Is that so?' She cleaned the brush with more than usual care.

'Yes, I had it from my son, Benedict, who was told by the Marquis of Risley, the Duke's son, so it came from the horse's mouth, so to speak. Benedict is at school with the Marquis, you know.'

'No, I didn't know,' Frances murmured, wishing she could add that she didn't care either.

'Oh, yes, Benedict, being seventeen, is two years older, but they are great friends.'

'You don't say!'

'Yes and Lady Lavinia will soon be making her come-out, though what the *ton* will make of her I cannot imagine.'

'Lady Lavinia?' Frances was determined to feign ignorance of the progeny of Marcus Stanmore, third Duke of Loscoe, though she was perfectly aware of the undercurrents in Lady Willoughby's words. She did not want that old scandal dragged up again. Oh, it did not hurt now; widowed and approaching her thirty-fifth birthday, she considered herself mature enough to let the gabble-grinders have their say and not mind, but she could not deny a twinge of something that might have been regret. Or was it anger? Could she still be angry?

'Oh, you know very well Lady Lavinia Stanmore is the Duke's daughter and by all accounts thoroughly spoiled by her father, especially since the Duchess died. I have heard she rides astride and drives a curricle all over the Derbyshire estate without so much as a groom beside her. And her father lets her meddle in estate business and allows her to dine with his friends and say whatever she likes to them and her not yet seventeen.'

'I am sure the Duke knows what he is doing.' Frances stood up and began gathering together her easel, canvas and paints, prior to leaving.

'Give me leave to doubt it, Countess. What that girl needs is a mother, someone to show her how to go on or she will never take. I heard that was why he had come to town—he's looking for a new wife.'

This time Frances did give a small start which she disguised as annoyance that a smudge of paint had got on to her blue jaconet gown, while her informant carried on blithely adding salt to a wound which should have healed long before. 'He is all of forty, but well preserved and still very handsome. I do believe he will be the catch of the Season.'

'I am glad my stepdaughter is already happily married,' Frances said as she packed her painting accoutrements into a large case made for the purpose. 'And I can watch events from the sidelines. Now, I must be off. The portrait will be finished in a couple of days, I think.'

'Good. Bring it round on Thursday, when Lord Willoughby will be at home, though I am sure he will approve. You have an incomparable reputation for excellence or he would never have engaged you.'

'Thank you.'

'I am having a few friends in for tea. Please do join us.'

Frances thanked her again and took her leave. A servant conducted her to the front door where another servant restored her pelisse and gloves to her and yet another carried her painting things out to her carriage and put them on the seat before letting down the step so that she could take her seat. John Harker, her groom and driver, set the beautifully matched horses to a steady trot, along Upper Brook Street, before turning into Duke Street and pulling up at the front door of Corringham House.

'I shan't need you any more today, John,' she told the groom, as a footman came out of the tall mansion and took her case, canvas and easel from the carriage and carried it indoors.

'Yes, my lady.' He drove away to the mews and she followed the footman into the house, where she took off her hat, a scrap of straw with a small brim and a large feather, and handed it to Rose, her maid, before following the footman up to the studio. He leaned the easel against the wall and put the case on a table in the middle of the room.

'Thank you, Creeley,' she said. 'Please tell Cook I will have my dinner in half an hour.'

'Very well, my lady.'

He went about his business and she was alone, alone in a room so full of memories, it was almost unbearable. But she had learned to bear them, even sometimes to welcome them. Her painting had become her life. It was not that she needed the income from it; her husband, the late Earl of Corringham, had left her well provided for, but a streak of independence, which had always stood her in good stead, had made her want to do something for herself. And besides, it kept her from brooding.

She wandered round the room, looking at the pictures she had produced over the last seventeen years. Her early efforts did not have the finesse of her more recent work, but they had a raw emotion and a realism she had since learned to suppress; ladies did not paint distasteful pictures. The tasteful ones, the ones she had been commissioned to do, were gracing the drawing rooms and boudoirs of half the *ton*; the ones in this room were those she would not sell.

She stopped to look at a painting of the Duke of Loscoe—the Marquis of Risley as he was then, for his father had still been alive—painted when he was twenty-three and she was in love with him. It was three-quarter length and showed him as a pugilist: bare-chested and wearing tight breeches. It revealed his animal strength in every line, his self-confidence, his masculinity, his handsome broad forehead and dark, copper-coloured curls, one of which hung over his forehead, as it would have done in the ring. Sparring at Jackson's boxing emporium had been a pastime of his. 'It keeps me on my toes,' he had told her between kisses.

It was a good likeness, but it was not a picture she could ever put on display; genteel ladies would be horrified that he had posed before a lady in such a state of undress and their husbands would wonder just what sort of lady she was to allow it. Besides, the dark eyes and expressive mouth said too much of the relationship between artist and subject.

Impatient with herself, she took the picture down and stood it on the floor with its face to the wall, but it left a mark where it had been hung and she began sorting through other pictures stacked around the room to find a replacement. Not all could be called portraits and not all were fashionable; there were subjects taken from nature: flowers, birds and animals, bright and lifelike and, in the case of a fox hunted to death, very bloody. And there were landscapes and street scenes too, and some of those from districts High Society ladies would never have dreamed of entering.

Taking her life in her hands, she had taken her sketch pad to some of the less salubrious parts of the capital and drawn what she saw: the miserable tenements, the squalor, the ragged children and their poverty-stricken parents, just as they were. Surprisingly no harm had come to her, possibly because she paid the people handsomely for the privilege of drawing them. Afterwards, at home in her studio, she had converted the sketches to paintings. She knew they were good, but hardly drawing-room pictures. One day she would exhibit them and prick the conscience of the *haut monde* with what was going on under their noses and which they chose to ignore.

While sorting through them, she came upon another of the Duke, a hurried sketch done on the day they had gone picnicking at Richmond, not long before that final parting. He had taken his coat off and was lying on the grass with his arms behind his head, watching her work, a dreamy smile on his face and a softness in his amber eyes which betokened his love for her. Or did it? She had never been sure.

'Drat him!' she said aloud and hurriedly picked up a portrait she had done of the Prince of Wales in that ridiculous uniform he had devised for his own regiment and hung it on the wall. Then she left the room and went to her bedchamber, where her maid was waiting for her.

She was helped out of her paint-stained gown and stood in her shift while Rose poured hot water from the ewer into a bowl. There was a full-length mirror beside the washstand and she found herself looking into it, wondering what the Duke would make of her if he could see her now. She could not describe her figure as sylph-like, but she was certainly not fat and her dark hair was still thick and black as a raven's wing. Her violet eyes were said to be her best feature; Marcus always said they were speaking eyes. Did they still give her away or had she since learned how to veil her innermost thoughts and feelings under a cloak of urbanity?

'What will you wear, my lady?' Rose asked.

The choice was vast; her wardrobe was extensive and tastefully fashionable, though she did not go in for some of the extremes that were the latest mode. She would not, for instance, be seen dead in that dreadful turban of Lady Willoughby's, nor the scant muslin that even the mature ladies of the *haut monde* considered the height of fashion.

'The pink silk with the bands of green and mauve, I think.'

'But that's old, my lady. The last time you wore it, you said—'

'Oh, I know, Rose, but it is comfortable and I am not going out tonight and shall be dining alone and perhaps later I will finish the portrait of Lady Willoughby. I do not want to spoil a good gown.'

It was unusual for her to be alone. She had many friends of both sexes, led a very full social life, was never short of invitations and entertained widely. Her guests came from a variety of backgrounds and had a wide range of interests, including politics, music, art and science, and she had the happy knack of making them all deal well together. Tonight, she was glad to be alone; it suited her mood.

Sitting over a light meal of chicken, ham and fresh

vegetables bought in Covent Garden that morning, she reviewed her life. It had not been so bad after all, though when, at the age of seventeen, her hopes and dreams had been shattered by Marcus's betrayal, she had thought it at an end. How could he? she had cried into her pillow night after night, how could he say he loved her and then marry someone else, just because his father told him to? She had accused him of having no backbone, of playing with her, leading her on with kisses and protestations of love which were as false and ephemeral as snow in summer. And she would certainly not entertain the idea of being his *chère amie* if that was what he had in mind.

She had told him she hated him, never wanted to see him again, and he had gone from her life to marry his Scottish heiress, whose dowry included a Highland castle. What had he wanted a castle for? He had been heir to a vast estate in Derbyshire, a London mansion, a house in Bath, as well as a hunting lodge in Leicestershire. It was all his now, of course, and he was one of the richest men in the kingdom. Not that she had ever considered his prospects; it was the man she had loved.

It had been her come-out year and she had wasted it sighing after a rake-shame. Most of the other young eligibles that year had found their partners and in any case could not be compared with the man she had lost. Her mother, who had spent a vast amount bringing her out, had been furious with her. 'Money wasted,' she had said. 'You are far too particular, Fanny, and without reason too. Oh, I know you have looks, but what is that to the point when you have no fortune? I cannot afford to bring you to London again next year. It has to be this year or never.'

'Mama, I cannot help it if no one has offered for me.'

'Nor will they when you have allowed yourself to be monopolised by Risley. Talk of the *ton* that has been and mortifying enough without the added humiliation of going back to the country without the sniff of a betrothal.'

To please her mother Frances had accepted the Earl of Corringham. His wife had died the previous year, leaving him with a son of seven and a half and a daughter of six to bring up, and he was looking for a new mother for them. The wedding had taken place quietly just two weeks before Marcus Stanmore had married Margaret Connaught.

There had been no love, nor even any pretence of it, but she had been comfortable with him and had learned to please him and love his children, especially when it became apparent that she would have none of her own. He had been philosophical about that. 'I have my heir,' he had said. 'And we deal well together, do we not? What do we want more brats for?'

She had been married ten years when a heart seizure had carried George off and since then she had made a secure life for herself. She did exactly as she pleased, went out and about, drove her carriage, rode in the park, attended concerts and the theatre, kept abreast of the times by reading newspapers and the latest books, and gambled in moderation but never more than she could afford to lose. She used the talents she had been given and taught young ladies to draw and paint, and was gratified when they did well. And, most important of all, she had her charitable work, the extent of which only John Harker and her banker were privy to. All in all it was a satisfying kind of life and she did not welcome anything that threatened to disturb it.

While George had been alive, she had spent most of her time at Twelvetrees, the family estate in Essex, and, on those rare occasions when she had visited the capital for a few days, she had not come across Marcus. He had rarely come to London, preferring to divide his time between his country estate and his Scottish castle. Since his wife's death two years before, so rumour had it, he had been something of a recluse. And now he was in Town. Thank goodness she had more sense than to fall in a quake about that!

She finished her meal, then went up to her studio and completed the portrait of Lady Willoughby before retiring. She was going riding with Sir Percival Ponsonby the following morning and they planned to make an early start.

Percy was a lifelong bachelor who rubbed along doing nothing in particular, but managed to be an amusing and undemanding companion and, in spite of the *ennui* he affected, was also wise and discreet. They had long ago come to an amicable arrangement to be friends and to ignore the matchmaking tattlers who did not see why they should be allowed to enjoy their lives unencumbered when everyone knows that a man with no wife and a widow with a small fortune must surely be looking for partners.

The April morning was blustery but mild. The buds were showing on the chestnut trees and there were daffodils and gillyflowers nodding their heads in the gardens, though these would soon be replaced by the flowers of summer, the roses and delphiniums, and by then the Season would be at its height. Frances wore a blue grosgrain habit with silver frogging and had secured her riding hat with a spider-gauze scarf tied under her chin. According to Percy, she looked very fetching.

They had been riding for perhaps an hour when she spotted the man she had known as Marcus Stanmore, Marquis of Risley, driving a park phaeton down the carriageway. Sitting beside him was a young lady with gleaming copper curls and a proud carriage.

'Bless me, if it ain't Loscoe,' Percy said, putting up his quizzing glass. 'And looking quite the thing too. I ain't seen him these many moons. And who's the filly, I wonder?'

'I believe it is his daughter,' Frances murmured.

'Daughter. My life, the years have flown. Wonder what he's doing in Town?'

'According to the latest *on dit*, looking for a second wife.' In spite of herself, she was curious. Would he recognise her? After all, she was no longer the gauche girl of seventeen he had known. Nor was he the stripling of twenty-three he had been.

Although he was naturally heavier and his good looks had matured, the years had dealt very kindly with him. The faint lines around his eyes and mouth gave his face character which had not been there before. His jaw was stronger than she remembered it and jutted out a little belligerently as if he did not suffer fools gladly, but he was still excessively handsome.

Percy looked sideways at her. 'Would you prefer to avoid him? It ain't too late to turn off the ride.'

'Goodness, no,' she laughed. Too many summers had passed, too many winters following one upon the other, for her still to bear a grudge. 'That would look too much like the cut direct. And I have no reason to cut him.'

'Water under bridges, eh?'

'Yes.' They were almost abreast of the phaeton and

she knew etiquette dictated it was up to her to acknowledge him first. She reined in and favoured him with one of her famous smiles, a smile which lit up her whole face and had most of the male population of London in thrall. 'Your Grace.' She gave him a small bow from the waist.

'My lady.' He pulled his phaeton to a stop and doffed his tall hat. His extraordinary hair was as thick and vibrant as ever, she noticed. She also noticed his smile did not seem to reach his amber eyes and his mouth had a slightly cynical twist, which she was sure had not been there when he was young. 'How do you do?'

'I do very well, thank you. You are acquainted with Sir Percival, are you not?'

'Yes, indeed. Good day to you, Ponsonby.'

'And you,' Percy answered. 'What brings you to the village? It must be years since you were here last.'

'Indeed, yes.' He turned back to Frances. 'Countess, may I present my daughter, Lavinia? Lavinia, the Countess of Corringham.' His tone was cool and impersonal; there was nothing to suggest he remembered that hot summer when they had been everything to each other. Everything or nothing? 'And this is Sir Percival Ponsonby.'

'Lady Lavinia, how nice to meet you,' Frances said, as Percy bowed in the saddle. 'I do hope you enjoy your visit to London.'

The only answer the girl managed was a mutter and a scowl which spoiled her prettiness and earned her a telling look from her father.

Frances was startled but, having acknowledged her, turned her attention to the Duke. 'Do you stay long in town, your Grace?'

'I think I shall be here for the Season. I have business to attend to and Lavinia needs a little town bronze.'

Frances certainly agreed with that. The child was extraordinarily beautiful and would have all the young bloods at her feet, if only she could learn to smile and be polite. Instead of attending to the conversation she was watching the horses riding past, as if the last thing she wanted to do was talk to her father's acquaintances.

'Then we shall perhaps see something of you in Society.'

'Indeed, I plan to take Vinny to some of the less grand occasions, to give her a taste of what is to come when she makes her bow next year.' He smiled suddenly and she felt the old tug at her heart and a flutter of nerves somewhere in the region of her lower abdomen and realised she was not as impervious to his charm as she had hoped. 'Lady Willoughby has already invited us to take tea with her tomorrow afternoon.'

Frances cursed under her breath. Trust Emma Willoughby to be first in the fray. And to choose the very day when she had promised to deliver the portrait. She could take the portrait in the morning and cry off the tea party, but that would be tantamount to cowardice and she had never been a coward. Besides, she could not hope to avoid him the whole Season, so she might as well begin as she meant to go on. 'How nice,' she said. 'I shall look forward to seeing you both there. Good day, Loscoe. Lady Lavinia.'

'Countess,' he answered, with an inclination of his head and picked up the reins to drive on. Frances and Percy turned to continue their ride. As a meeting it had been nothing out of the ordinary; simply a greeting exchanged by acquaintances. Had she expected anything else? Fireworks, perhaps? She smiled at her nonsensical thoughts and turned to her escort who should, after all, have her undivided attention.

It was only then, that she remembered what he had said before the encounter. 'What did you mean, ''water under bridges''?' she asked.

'I believe it indicates the passing of time, my dear.'

'I know that. I meant, what was the context of the remark?'

'Oh, Fanny, do not play the innocent. I know perfectly well there was almost a whole Season when everyone thought Stanmore was going to offer for you.'

'So?' she demanded, unexpectedly irritated. 'The tattlers are sometimes wrong, you know.'

'Yes, but I wondered how disappointed you had been.'

'Not at all,' she lied. 'I knew we should not suit.'

'And so you married Corringham.'

'I was very fond of George, Percy. Now, let us forget this conversation. It is of no import whatever.'

'I beg your pardon,' he said. 'Unless you wish it, I will never refer to it again.'

'Thank you. And I would be obliged, if you hear others mentioning water under bridges or anything of that nature, you put them right.'

'Certainly, I will, though I doubt it will be at the top of the gabble-grinders' list; it was all a long time ago.'

'You remembered it.'

'To be sure, but I am different.'

'Why different?'

'Oh, long memory and nothing else to fill it,' he said vaguely. 'Now, do we go home, or shall we have a canter across the grass?'

She laughed. 'A gallop, I think.'

It was not considered the thing for ladies to gallop;

indeed, they should do no more than walk or trot along the ride, the whole point of the exercise being to see and be seen, but Frances had never slavishly obeyed the rules and, because she was popular with everyone and considered quite beyond the marriage mart, no one took any notice when she veered off across the grass towards the middle of the park and spurred her horse into a gallop.

Sir Percival followed and half an hour later, exhilarated and free of the cobwebs in her mind which had plagued her overnight, they turned for home.

And that afternoon, just to prove her independence, she took her sketch pad and crayons and asked John Harker to drive her to the East End, where she positioned her stool and easel on one of the docks and drew a tea schooner being unloaded. Its spars and rigging were something of a challenge and totally absorbed her until it was time to return home. Marcus Stanmore, Duke of Loscoe, was banished from her mind and he did not return to it until the following afternoon.

She had taken the portrait to the Willoughby mansion and watched as her ladyship instructed a footman hold it up in one place after another in the main drawing room, undecided where it would look to best advantage. The obvious place was the wall over the Adam fireplace, but that already held a heavy gilt mirror; the fireplace recess was not light enough and the wall opposite the window too light; the sun shining upon it would spoil its colours.

'Perhaps it should go in another room,' Frances suggested when the footman had moved it for the fourth time and was looking decidedly bored with the task.

'Oh, no, it must be in here. I want all my callers to see it. Perhaps I should have the mirror taken down...'

'I think the heat from the chimney might crack the canvas in time, my lady.'

It was at this point Lord Willoughby arrived and, being asked his opinion, stroked his chin contemplatively and pointed to an empty space to one side of the room, well away from the fire. 'Leave it on its easel and put it there.'

'Not hang it?' her ladyship queried. 'Will it not look unfinished?'

'No, why should it?' He laughed. 'You can move it about as the fancy takes you. You might even start a fashion for displaying pictures on easels.'

Her ladyship clapped her hands in delight. 'So I shall.' She turned to Frances. 'Dear Countess, can I prevail upon you to let me borrow your easel until we can procure one?'

'Oh, you do not need to borrow it,' Frances said, thinking about the fat fee she had only a few minutes before put into her reticule. 'Have it with my compliments.'

'I think I will cover it until everyone is here,' Lady Willoughby said happily. 'Then I can unveil it with a flourish. It is so good and will enhance your reputation even further, my dear Countess. How you manage to produce something so exactly to life I shall never know, for I was never any good at drawing when I was young.'

Frances stifled a chuckle; the picture was undoubtedly of Lady Willoughby, but a much slimmer Lady Willoughby than the one who faced her in the flesh—mounds of it. And the good lady could not see the difference. But surely her husband could and so would everyone else. Frances began to wonder, and not for the first time, if she was prostituting her art and ought to have more self-respect, when a footman announced the first of her ladyship's guests.

They came in one by one, were greeted, asked to sit and plied with tea and little almond cakes. The easel stood covered by a tablecloth. Frances wished she could make her escape before the unveiling. She had never been happy publicising herself and her work, thinking it smacked of conceit. She was on the point of taking her leave when the Duke of Loscoe and Lady Lavinia were announced. She had been half out of her seat, but now sank back into it, feeling trapped.

He came into the room, entirely at ease even knowing that everyone was looking at him. He was dressed in a dark blue superfine coat with black buttons and a high collar. His cravat, in which glittered a diamond pin, testified to the attentions of a very good valet and his hair had obviously been cut by one of the *haut monde*'s best hairdressers. His long muscular legs were encased in pale blue pantaloons and tasselled Hessians. A concerted sigh escaped all the ladies except Frances, who refused to follow the pack.

He made his bow to his hostess. 'My lady, your obedient.'

'We are indeed honoured that you could attend our little gathering, your Grace,' her ladyship simpered. 'And this must be Lady Lavinia.'

'It is indeed.' He turned to his daughter. 'Make your curtsy, Vinny.'

Lavinia did as she was told and even managed a smile as she murmured, 'My lady.'

'Now let me introduce you to everyone,' Lady Willoughby said, and proceeded to conduct him round the room. He bowed to everyone, murmured polite nothings and moved on, followed by his daughter, whose smile was so fixed, Frances wondered what dire threat Marcus had made to produce it.

'The Countess of Corringham,' her ladyship said, suddenly looming large in Frances's vision. 'But I believe you are acquainted.'

'Indeed.' He bowed. 'How do you do, Countess?'

She managed a smile, wondering if it looked as fixed as Lavinia's. 'I am very well, your Grace.'

'The Countess is the reason for our little gathering,' Lady Willoughby went on. 'The guest of honour, you might say, excepting your good self, of course.'

'Indeed?' he said again, lifting a well-arched eyebrow at Frances, a gleam of humour lighting his dark eyes. It totally bewildered her. Had he forgotten? Or was he, like her, pretending nothing had ever happened between them? 'I am sure it is well deserved.'

Lady Willoughby appeared not to notice as she turned away and clapped her hands for attention. 'My friends,' she said. 'This is not a formal occasion, so there will be no speeches, but I particularly wanted you to be the first to see this.' And with that, she tugged the cover off the portrait. 'It is the most recent work of the Countess of Corringham.'

There was silence for about two seconds, two seconds in which Frances wished the floor would open up and swallow her, and then there was a burst of applause which was soon taken up by everyone, followed by a babble of conversation. 'She has caught you to the life, Emma.'

'The flesh tones are superb.'

'You can pick out every individual hair.'

'The hands are good too. Not everyone can portray hands.'

'I am flattered,' Frances said, rising to receive the plaudits. It brought her standing uncomfortably close to the Duke.

'Flattered?' he murmured in her ear. 'Methinks it is you who do the flattering.'

'Why not? It does no harm,' she whispered back, trying to ignore the frisson of something she refused to identify that coursed through her at his nearness. Seventeen years fled away as if they had never been. Mentally she shook herself, reminding herself that water never flowed backwards.

'I believe it harms you.'

'Fustian!' Just in time she stopped herself adding, 'And what does it matter to you what I do?' The last thing she wanted was a personal altercation with him.

'Are you so in need of funds that you must produce insipid stuff like this?' He nodded towards the portrait.

'Lady Willoughby is delighted with it. And that means others…'

'Will want to fling money at you too.'

'Nothing wrong with that.'

'No, but I thought you had more spirit.' He smiled at their hostess, who was bearing down upon them.

'Lord Loscoe,' she gushed. 'What do you think? Is it not an excellent likeness?'

He bowed. 'Oh, excellent,' he said, ignoring Frances's splutter of laughter at his duplicity. 'Lady Corringham is indeed very talented.'

'Have you ever sat for your portrait, my lord?' her ladyship asked.

'Not for very many years,' he answered carefully. 'It can be a very tedious business, and I have so little time for it.'

'Ah, but now you are in town, you must surely have

some leisure. I can thoroughly recommend her ladyship.'

'Oh, please, Lady Willoughby,' Frances put in. 'You
are putting me to the blush.'

'Oh, you are far too old to be blushing,' the woman
said tactlessly, a statement which made the Duke
chuckle. Frances felt colour flood her face, which only
proved how wrong her ladyship was. 'Now, my lord,
you must come and talk to my other guests. And
Felicity is dying to make the acquaintance of Lady
Lavinia.'

He bowed to Frances. 'My lady, your obedient.' And
then he was gone, followed by his daughter.

Frances watched his tall straight back moving away
from her and then her attention was taken by other people who wanted to talk to her about having their portraits painted. She was kept busy for several minutes,
making appointments to meet them again to talk about
their requirements, and she did not see the Duke and
his daughter leave. A few minutes later she left herself.

As a business exercise, the afternoon had been a great
success, though she was left wondering why her ladyship was so enthusiastically promoting her. Did she
think she needed the money? But she did, didn't she?
Every penny.

That evening she attended a concert arranged by Mrs
Georgiana Butterworth in aid of the war orphans, one
of her favourite charities, and enjoyed the music im-
mensely. She had not given the Duke of Loscoe another
thought and was taken aback to see him during the in-
terval talking animatedly to one of the guests. He was
wearing an evening suit of black cloth and a pristine
white cravat, simple clothes, but superbly cut, she ad-

mitted to herself, while wondering if he was truly interested in war orphans or was simply doing the rounds in search of his new wife, though the company could hardly be classed as the *haut monde* and not one of the worthy ladies present seemed to qualify. They were either married, too old, or not from the upper echelons of Society and he would never marry so far beneath him, as he had proved seventeen years before.

It was some moments before he saw her and then his eyebrows rose in surprise as if she was the last person he had expected to see. He excused himself from the matron who was engaging him in conversation and made his way over to her.

'Countess, I had not anticipated seeing you again so soon.'

'Nor I you. It is not a gathering I would have thought would interest you.'

'Why not?' he asked sharply. 'The plight of children orphaned by war is a worthy cause and you must think so, too, or you would not be here.'

'Indeed, I do.'

'Then we have a mutual interest,' he said.

She did not reply, and he looked quizzically at her. 'Do you find that unacceptable, my lady?' he asked softly.

'What?'

'That we are both interested in the orphans and wish to improve their lives.'

'Not at all.' She forced herself to ignore the swift beating of her heart. She was behaving like a lovesick schoolgirl and her thirty-five years old in a few weeks! 'The more help they have the better. Some of them are in dire straits.'

'Good. I should not like to think my presence in any way deterred you from your good work.'

'Now why in heaven's name should it?' she retorted, her voice rising a fraction. She immediately dropped her tone to add in a hoarse whisper, 'You are insufferably conceited, if you think that your presence or otherwise makes the slightest difference to me.'

'Then I beg your pardon for my presumption.'

Mrs Butterworth joined them before she could answer. 'I see you have made the acquaintance of the Duke,' she said to Frances.

'Oh, we are old sparring partners,' Marcus said, a remark which sent Frances's thoughts flying back to her studio and the painting of the pugilist. 'We have not met these many years and were enjoying a coze about old times.'

'How delightful! You must be gratified, my lady, that the Duke has joined our little band of subscribers. His name on the list will encourage others, do you not think?'

'I am sure it will,' she murmured.

'We are looking for a good property to give some of them a temporary home until we can find new permanent homes for them,' the lady told him, while Frances surreptitiously studied his face for signs of boredom and found none. But then he was always good at pretending. 'At present they are housed in a dilapidated tenement in Monmouth Street, but the lease is running out, so we must find something more substantial and comfortable very soon.'

'Then you may count on me for a donation, Mrs Butterworth,' he said with a smile which totally captivated the good lady. Little did Mrs Butterworth know,

Frances mused, that his smile hid a heart as cold and rigid as stone.

'Oh, thank you, sir. This concert has been such a success that we are thinking of holding a ball to raise more funds. May we count on you to purchase a ticket?'

'If I am not engaged on the evening in question, then I shall be happy to do so,' he said with a smile.

The orchestra began tuning up their instruments and everyone was moving back to their seats for the second half of the programme. Marcus gave Frances a thin smile and inclined his head. 'My lady.'

'Your Grace.'

Frances returned to her seat, her thoughts and emotions in turmoil. Was her every move to be dogged by the Duke of Loscoe? Was he to be everywhere she went? She had never dreamed she would come across him at this unfashionable gathering. It had been a severe shock, more than the shock of meeting him in the park, or the encounter at Lady Willoughby's. Was nowhere safe from his odious presence? But she could not hide herself away at home, could she? She had told him his presence made no difference and she must school herself to make that true.

It *had* to be true. If he had not been so long absent from London, if he had always been in the forefront of Society these last seventeen years, she would have become inured, she told herself; it was his sudden reappearance that was causing the upheaval and reminding her of that summer in 1800. One summer. One summer could not possibly be important now. She was making a mountain out of a molehill. And there was far more to life than dwelling on the past.

It was when they were all taking their leave that she saw him again. She had just taken her pelisse from Mrs

Butterworth's footman, when she felt a hand helping her on with it. She turned to thank whoever it was, only to find herself looking into the amber eyes of the Duke of Loscoe, and like amber they seemed to have a light and depth of their own, as they surveyed her face. 'Thank you,' she said coolly.

'You seem to be without an escort, my lady—may I offer my services?'

'I have my carriage, thank you.'

'Then I will say goodnight.' He took his hat from the footman and clamped it on his head before striding down the path to the road where his own coach waited. 'Take the carriage home, Brown,' he told his driver. 'I will walk back.'

It was a good walk, more than two miles through some of the less fashionable areas of London, but he felt in need of the exercise. Since coming to London he had missed the long walks and exhilarating gallops he enjoyed at his Derbyshire home; he was becoming a sloth and putting on weight. Perhaps he should take up sparring again. Was he too old for that now? It might be interesting to find out if he had retained any of his old skill.

Thinking of sparring made his thoughts turn to Fanny Randall—Lady Frances Corringham, he corrected himself with a wry smile. She had painted a picture of him stripped for a bout. He had been amazed at her skill and wanted it for himself, but she would not give it to him. 'I did it for our eyes only,' she had told him. 'I will never part with it.'

But that was before… He shrugged his shoulders as he skirted the notorious Seven Dials district towards Covent Garden. Had she kept it or had his perfidy made her hate him and the painting along with it? He had behaved badly towards her, but how was he to know she was expecting an offer? He had been in no position to make one; the match between him and Margaret Connaught had already been negotiated by their respective fathers and there was nothing he could do about it.

He should never have sought her company so assiduously that summer, should never, never have told her he loved her, however true it was. But he had been a green twenty-three and not yet clever enough to hide his feelings, nor think of the consequences. He wanted to be with her, often compromised her by taking every opportunity to be alone with her, to hold her hand and smother her in kisses while declaring he could not live without her. And her eager responses had flattered him. He had even managed to take her on a picnic to Richmond, driving her in his curricle which had no room for anyone but the two of them, so they went without so much as a maid or a groom for a chaperon.

He had not given a thought to what he was doing to her until the whole Connaught family descended on London from their home near Edinburgh and he found himself having to escort his intended for the rest of the Season and escaping to see Fanny became almost impossible. And when at last he did, at one of the Duchess of Devonshire's balls, they had quarrelled.

He had tried, after partnering her in a country dance, to explain about Margaret, telling her that it was an arranged marriage and did not in any way alter his feelings for her, but she would not listen. 'If you think that I am such a bufflehead as to allow myself to become your *chère amie*—that is the term, is it not?—then you are glaringly abroad, my lord,' she had hissed angrily.

He had been shocked at her language and tried to deny that such a thing had ever entered his head, but afterwards, in the cold light of the following day, with his head aching from the wine and brandy he had consumed, he realised that she had been right. There was no way he could marry Margaret and continue to enjoy the company and kisses of Frances, except to take her as his mistress. But one did not make light o' loves of seventeen-year-old girls only lately out of school. He wrote apologising for his behaviour and that was the end of the affair.

Had she forgotten it? He did not think so, but she had certainly made a quick recovery because she had married Corringham almost immediately, making him wonder if the Earl had been waiting in the wings all along. And now they were both free again.

It did not make any difference; they had grown up, matured, their characters had been forged on the anvil of life; they had become different people, strangers. He smiled, as he strode past the back of Carlton House towards St James's Street and home—the latest *on dit* was that he was looking for another wife, but that was far from his intention. He was enjoying being single and was in no hurry to be leg-shackled again.

If it had not been for pressing business, he would not even have come to Town, certainly not in the Season, but because he had to come and because his daughter was sixteen and behaved like a boy of twelve and it was about time she was taken in hand, he had brought her with him. He was even now awaiting the arrival of his sister from Ireland, whom he had asked to come over and give her some polish. Charlotte had been delayed by her children having measles and here he was alone in London with a far from acquiescent daughter. And he had not the faintest idea what to do with her!

What he needed was someone like Frances

Corringham. Fanny was cool and urbane, in the thick of everything, known by everyone. She was fashionably attired, knew how to conduct herself. She also had a prodigious talent. He laughed aloud, making one or two people nearby look sharply at him. They probably thought he was foxed, he did not care; it had come to him in a flash of inspiration, a way of keeping Lavinia occupied. He would ask the Countess of Corringham to paint her portrait and give her drawing and painting lessons.

He need not be present and it would leave him free to go about the business which had brought him to London. But would she do it? Was she still angry enough to turn him down? But she did not seem particular about whom she painted and was prepared to flatter her sitters for a fat fee, so why should she treat him any differently, if money was all she cared about? Tomorrow he would call on her.

Chapter Two

Frances smiled as she left the door of the rundown tenement in Monmouth Street which was home to some twenty orphans. If her Society friends could see her now, they would have apoplexy, she decided—that is, if they recognised her at all. Hatless and dressed in a grey wool dress and a short pelisse, she looked the image of a very ordinary woman, the wife or widow of a clerk or some such, respectable but nondescript.

Although, as Countess of Corringham, she was in the forefront of the charity which raised money for the orphans, it was as plain Mrs Fanny Randall that she worked at the orphanage, rolling up her sleeves to help bathe the children, or serve them the plain food which her money helped to provide. She loved the work and the children.

'A real pied piper, you are,' Mrs Thomas, the plump matron of the home, had said, adding that she must be sorry she had had no children of her own. Frances had passed it off with a smile, but her childlessness was the biggest regret of her life and something she found difficult to talk about.

She climbed up beside John Harker, who had been

instructed to come and fetch her at noon in her tilbury. He was used to her ways and made no attempt to stop her when she picked up the ribbons and drove them towards Oxford Street, which was lined with shops and businesses, its pavements full of pedestrians and street hawkers. She tooled the horses with consummate ease, weaving the light carriage neatly in and out of the medley of riding horses, carts and carriages of every description which filled the road. No one paid any attention to an unmarked vehicle being driven by a nobody, but the slight chance she might be seen and recognised led an added piquancy to the adventure.

Less than twenty minutes later she turned into Duke Street and drew up with a flourish at the door of Corringham House, only to discover the Duke of Loscoe, dressed for riding, standing on the top step, apparently having found she was not at home and about to leave. She would have driven on in the hope he would not recognise her, but it was too late; he was standing quite still, staring at her. Was it in distaste? She could not be sure.

There was nothing for it but to carry off the situation as if it were nothing out of the ordinary for ladies of the aristocracy to drive themselves about town in what was considered to be a single man's carriage. Throwing the reins to Harker and instructing him to see to the horses, she jumped down with an agility which the ladies of the *ton* would have described as hoydenish if they could have seen her, and advanced towards him, smiling.

'Your Grace, I did not expect you, or I would have been at home to greet you.'

'Good day, Countess,' he said, doffing his curly-brimmed hat and bowing, while at the same time his dark eyes appraised the simple clothes she wore and his eyebrows rose just a fraction. 'If it is inconvenient…' His voice tailed off.

She smiled inwardly to think that he was more discomfited than she was. She could easily have asked him to come another time when she was prepared to receive him, but she had to admit to being a little curious. Why was he visiting her? Surely they could have nothing to say to each other after all this time? 'It is not inconvenient, my lord. Please come in.'

The door had been opened by a footman who stood on the threshold, waiting for her to step inside. She led the way. 'Creeley, show his Grace into the green salon and ask Cook to bring refreshments.' She turned to the Duke. 'Please excuse me while I change. I will not keep you long.'

Once in her bedchamber, she stood and looked at herself in the mirror. She was a perfect antidote. The gown, although it had been clean when she left the house three hours earlier, was spotted and rumpled and some of her hair had escaped its pins and was curling about her neck. There was a smudge on her nose and a scratch on the back of one hand where the kitten they had bought to help keep down the mice at the orphanage had scratched her. It had been her own fault for teasing it.

Rose was waiting for her, clucking her disapproval. 'And the Duke of Loscoe standing on the step,' she said, pulling the gown over Frances's head. 'What must he have thought of you?' Rose had been with her a very long time and considered that gave her the right to speak her mind.

'I do not care a fig what he thinks, Rose.'

'What shall you tell him?'

'About what?'

'This,' she said, throwing the grey dress into a corner in distaste.

'Nothing. It is none of his business.'

'It will give him a disgust of you.'

'Do you think that bothers me, Rose? Do you think I lay sleepless at night, wondering what people think of me?'

'No, my lady.'

But there had been a time when she had lain sleepless because of the man who waited for her in her drawing room and that thought brought a wry smile to her lips. She had pretended not to care then for her pride's sake, but she did not need to pretend now, she told herself firmly, she did not care.

But even so, she had a feeling her ordered way of life was about to be eroded by a man she thought she had left far behind in her youth. If she had not known him before, if they were only now making each other's acquaintance, would she feel any differently? Would she find him elegant and charming? She did not know. It was not possible to rewrite history.

Marcus prowled round the room and wondered what the lovely Countess was up to. The house was furnished in exquisite taste, with carpets and curtains in pale greens and fawns. There were paintings by the masters on the walls and one or two that were unsigned and which he guessed she had executed herself. There was a cabinet containing some beautiful porcelain and vases of fresh flowers on the tables.

In his experience, when aristocratic owners of beautiful houses fell on hard times, it showed in threadbare carpets or peeling paint or walls bare of valuable paintings, but this was a room of quiet opulence, with not a hint that there was anything wrong with its owner. So why was the Countess so shabbily attired? The Earl had left her well provided for, hadn't he?

But she didn't own the house, he reminded himself. It belonged to her stepson, the present Earl of Corringham. Did he keep his stepmother on short commons? Was that why she had to paint those sickening portraits and teach young ladies to draw? Oh, poor, poor Fanny. He was glad he had decided to visit her. Teaching Vinny would add to her income and he felt he owed her something for the way he had treated her in the past.

He was standing at the window, looking out on a perfectly maintained garden when he heard her enter. He turned towards her, a smile on his lips which he only just managed to stop becoming a gasp of surprise.

She was dressed in a dark green silk day gown. It had bands of velvet ribbon around the skirt and a low-cut square neck. But what was so startling was that it showed her figure off to perfection: the trim waist, the well-rounded bosom, the long, pale neck and the raven hair, pulled into a topknot and arranged in careful curls at the back of her head. Without the least attempt to appear girlish, she presented herself as still a young woman of astonishing beauty and great poise. She wore no jewellery; her lovely neck was unadorned. He felt a sudden urge to bury his face in the curve of it.

'Countess.' He bowed towards her, realising his smile had become a trifle fixed, as if he were afraid he would let it slip and all his thoughts and emotions would be laid bare.

'I am sorry to have been so long,' she said, without explaining why. 'I hope refreshments were sent to you.'

'Indeed, yes.' He nodded towards the tray which a maidservant had put on one of the tables and which contained a teapot, cups and saucers and a plate of little cakes. 'I have been waiting for you to come and share them with me.'

'Then do sit down.' She sat on a sofa and indicated the chair opposite. 'I prefer tea at this time, but if you would rather have Madeira or sherry…'

'No, tea will suit me very well.' He lifted the skirt of his coat and sat down, his long legs, clad in buckskin riding breeches, stretched out in front of him. There was no fat on him, she realised; the shape of his calves and thighs was due to well-toned muscle.

She poured two cups of tea and handed one to him, pleased that her hand was as steady as a rock. 'Please help yourself to a honey cake.'

'No, thank you, though they do look delicious.'

She sipped her tea with what she hoped was cool detachment, but this mundane conversation was driving her mad. What did he want? Why had he come? He appeared to be sizing her up, as if he was trying to make up his mind whether she had been pining after him all the years they had been apart. Surely he did not hope to take up where they left off? If that were so he was insufferably conceited and she would soon show him how mistaken he was. 'It is a lovely day,' she said. 'I am surprised you are not out riding. I believe Lady Lavinia is very fond of that exercise.'

'She is indeed. We had a ride this morning, and I took her home half an hour since, but she finds riding in the park somewhat restricting and, as I have not brought her mare to London, she has perforce to use a hired hack.'

'She will be glad to return to Derbyshire, then.'

'Oh, I have no plans to return in the immediate future, so if she wants to ride, she must learn to bear it.' He was waiting for her to ask why he was visiting her, she decided, and she would not satisfy him on that score, even if they sat exchanging small talk all day. He put his cup down and she smiled and asked him if he would like a second cup of tea.

'No, thank you,' he said, looking round the room. 'You have a beautiful home.'

'Thank you. I have enjoyed refurbishing it over the years. Of course, it now belongs to the present Earl, my stepson, but he has said I may consider it my home for as long as I wish.'

It would be different when he came fully into his inheritance on his twenty-fifth birthday, when the Essex estate and the London house would be handed over to him. Then she would have to find somewhere to live; she did not like the idea of living there under sufferance and certainly not after he married. And before long he would. Her steady, unruffled life was about to change, but she had been putting her head in the sand and doing nothing about it. However, sooner or later, she must.

'It would be an inconsiderate son who said anything else, Countess.'

'He is far from inconsiderate, my lord. I cannot have wished for a better son, and, before you ask, I have not been so fortunate as to have children of my own.'

'I would not dream of asking such a personal question, my lady.'

She was cross with herself for allowing her agitation to show and picked up his cup and saucer and put it on the tray to give herself something to do with her hands. 'Stanmore House is said to be a very fine example of a London house,' she said, doing her best to retrieve the situation with an easy smile. 'I am told the staircase is unique and the decoration of the reception rooms superb.'

'Yes, but old-fashioned. My late wife did not like London and never came, so it has remained as it was in my mother's time.'

She longed to ask why the Duchess had not liked London, but that would be as personal a question as asking her about her childlessness and she would not give him the satisfaction of pointing that out to her.

'My daughter has never been to the capital,' he said, breaking into her thoughts. 'And until now I did not feel she needed to, but next year she will be seventeen and must make her mark on Society if she is to take well.'

'Surely there is plenty of time for that? I think seventeen is far too young for any young lady to make up her mind about marriage. Why, they are still only schoolgirls at that age and given to all manner of fits and fancies.' That is one for you to think on, she thought, as she watched his face for a sign that he understood what she was saying; that she had been fanciful at that age and had recovered from it. But the years had taught him to mask his feelings and not for a second did his expression reveal that the barb had gone home.

'I have no wish to saddle her with marriage before she is ready for it,' he said, evenly. 'But she must make her bow at court and I would not like it said she lacked polish.'

'You propose to polish her, my lord?' She spoke with the hint of a teasing smile which jerked him back seventeen years—the young Fanny Randall had had a finely tuned sense of humour—and made him stand up and go to look out of the window. The view was no different from the one he had been looking at earlier, but it was an excuse to keep his face turned from her until he had brought himself back under control. This was a business meeting and he must not allow emotion to gain the upper hand.

'No, that would be foolish in me. I shall employ others to do it.' He turned back suddenly. 'You, for one, if you agree.'

'Me?' She could not hide the surprise and dismay in her voice. 'I am persuaded you are jesting.'

'Not at all. I am told one of the accomplishments a young lady needs, besides being able to sew a fine seam, play a musical instrument and dance the latest steps, is the ability to draw and paint and I can think of no one more suited to teach Lavinia that.'

He sat down beside her on the sofa, which did nothing for her hard-won control. He was so close, she could almost feel the warmth emanating from a body which was still lithe and muscular. Her own body seemed to want to lean towards his, to feel again the contact of thigh against thigh, his arms about her, lips on lips. Shocked to the core, she stood up and went to pull the bell for the maid to remove the tray.

Because she was on her feet, etiquette demanded he should rise too. She sat down abruptly and motioned him to the other chair. He sat down again, far enough away to allow her to breathe more easily. 'It is true I have a certain facility, but...'

'You are far too modest, Countess. You have an incomparable reputation...'

'Fustian!' She smiled, remembering those were the

words that Lady Willoughby had used; she had probably repeated them in his hearing. 'You have seen my work for yourself, at Lady Willoughby's. And criticised it too.'

'I would not presume to do so, my lady. I simply made a comment that you had flattered your subject.' He smiled suddenly and his amber eyes lit up in the way she remembered; it made his somewhat sombre face come alive, the light in his eyes giving depth to his expression. 'And considering your subject, you should take that as a compliment.'

'People do not pay to see the truth, your Grace.'

'And it is important they should pay,' he murmured softly.

'Yes, it is,' she said bluntly.

'I shall pay. I shall pay handsomely.'

'I have a set fee for pupils who join my class.'

'I do not want Vinny to join a class. I expect her to receive your undivided attention.'

'I am not sure I have the time for that.'

The maid came in answer to the summons and removed the tray. He waited until she had gone and closed the door before speaking again. 'Two hours twice a week—surely you can manage that, especially for twenty pounds every time she comes.'

'Now you are being ridiculous,' she snapped, taken aback by the amount. 'No one is worth that much.'

'Oh, do not underrate yourself, Countess, it will be worth every groat of it to have my daughter properly taught.'

'And what if she shows no aptitude?' She was feeling very confused. What was he up to? She ought to refuse to do as he asked, ring for a footman to show him out, but in the back of her mind she was doing sums. Twenty pounds twice a week, that would pay for all the food, clothes and hired help at the orphanage. It might even help to furnish the new home, once they had bought it. She would be mad to turn it down.

'Drawing can be taught, can it not?' he countered.

'Up to a certain level, perhaps, but if the talent is not there, then…' She shrugged her shoulders, lifting her breasts within the bodice of her gown, so that he felt a sharp surge of desire, which he quickly stifled. 'I do not make a practice of attempting to teach what cannot be taught.'

'I do not wish to make a genius of her, nor even an artist, dependent on patronage for a living. I wish her to have a modicum of competence, no more.'

'Mediocrity is not something to aim for, my lord, whatever one's station in life and whatever one is doing,' Frances said, with some asperity. 'You would not subscribe to that for yourself—as I recall, you were always the perfectionist—so why think that a daughter should not excel? It does not preclude her from making a good marriage.'

He laughed suddenly. 'Blunt as ever, my lady. But you are right, of course. So what do you say? Will you take Lavinia on? She is a delightful child but, without a mother to guide her since my wife died two years ago, she has been let run a little wild and I can think of no one more suited to become her mentor than the incomparable Countess of Corringham.'

She refused to smile, though it was difficult when he was so blatantly trying to gammon her. 'So, I am to provide the polish, am I?'

'Why not?' He grinned at her and the hard lines of his face softened, so that he looked years younger and less overbearing. If she agreed with his outrageous suggestion, did that mean she would be often in his company? Could she bear that if, as now, he was smiling at her, trying to win her over? 'You have it in abundance. While you are instructing her, she might learn a little polite conversation, a way to conduct herself in company.'

'Twice a week. How much polish can be applied in so short a time?'

'Enough, for now. I am expecting my sister from Ireland; she is married to Lord Felmore, you know. I hope to prevail upon her to take Lavinia in hand and bring her up to the mark for her come-out next year.'

'Then why do you need me?'

'Oh, I need you,' he said softly and she wished she had not spoken, but if he thought that his flummery would have her eating out of his hand, he would have to think again. She would not be caught out a second time, but then he showed how wrong she was in that assumption when he added in a far more practical tone, 'Besides, I have business to deal with and I do not have the time to be continually taking her out and about.'

'So, I am to keep her out of mischief.'

'And be paid well for doing so.'

He would not bring his daughter himself, she decided; he would send her in the carriage with her governess and a footman, so she would not have to meet him, except every now and again to report progress and she could keep those meetings strictly businesslike. 'You think I need the money?'

'Don't you?' he asked mildly.

'Yes, but not for the reason you suppose, your Grace. And it is only that which inclines me to agree, but I would have to meet and talk to Lady Lavinia before I finally make up my mind. We may not deal well together…'

'That is understood. Let us arrange a day and time.'

'Bring her here, tomorrow, at two in the afternoon.'

'I shall look forward to it.'

She rang the bell for a footman to conduct him to the door, bringing the interview to an end.

He picked up his hat from the floor at his side and got to his feet. 'My lady, your obedient,' he said. 'Until tomorrow.'

As soon as he had gone, she sank back into her seat and shut her eyes. The encounter had exhausted her. She thought she had got over him, had learned not to care, and to remain cool in a crisis, so why was she shaking? Why had she been such a fool as to agree? Did she really want to spend hours in the company of his daughter, who could so easily have been her daughter too, if her early hopes and dreams had been realised? No one expected her to pay the whole cost of that orphanage, nor even the major part of it, she did not need to put herself through torment just for that. She could easily find other commissions which would not be anything like as stressful.

She stood up and poured herself a glass of wine from the decanter on a side table and sat down again to give herself a good scold. She was too old to let a middle-aged roué upset her. It was business, he had said so, and business was all it was, and she really ought to thank Lady Willoughby for recommending her so highly. Incomparable! She laughed suddenly and the wine spilled over her hand. She downed the rest before she could spill any more.

* * *

She spent the afternoon teaching a class of half a dozen young ladies about line and perspective and in the evening she went to a soirée given by Lady Holland. Her ladyship was sharp and imperious, and some people made fun of her, but she was still a great Society hostess and Frances knew she would enjoy the conversation of her guests, which was usually well-informed and witty and ranged from the financial troubles that the end of the war had brought with it to poking fun at the Regent. Frances returned home in a happy frame of mind, ready to take on the world.

She was not so sure about that the next afternoon when the Duke of Loscoe was shown into her drawing room, bringing with him a reluctant Lady Lavinia, but she did not let that show as she rose to greet them.

He was dressed in a dark blue superfine coat, white pantaloons tucked into tasselled hessians which would have done duty as mirrors they were so polished. His cravat of white lawn was tied in an intricate knot which undoubtedly had a fancy name but which eluded her.

'Countess, your obedient.' He swept her an elegant bow, which she suspected was more for his daughter's benefit than hers and she answered in like manner by dropping a deep curtsy.

'Your Grace.' She did not wait for him to raise her before standing up and turning to the servant who hovered in the doorway and ordering refreshments. If he wanted his daughter to be shown how things were done, then she would do her best, though this stiff formality was not to her taste. She turned to the girl. 'Lady Lavinia, what a pleasure it is to see you again.'

Her father nudged her and she curtsied and mumbled,

'My lady.'

Frances indicated the two sofas which faced each other on either side of the screened fireplace. 'Please be seated.'

Father and daughter sat side by side, so that Frances, sitting opposite, was able to assess how alike they were in looks. Both had amber eyes and thick lashes and though Lavinia's hair was lighter than the Duke's and fastened back with two glittering combs, she could detect a streak of chestnut in the gold ringlets. Both had lean faces with strong cheek bones and the finely arched brows of all the Stanmores. Lady Lavinia's mouth was thinner than her father's, more sulky, and her chin a little less prominent, though she could undoubtedly be stubborn, Frances decided.

Looking at the silent girl who seemed to be studying the toe of her shoe peeping from the hem of a pale green muslin gown, Frances was not at all sure of being able to succeed in teaching her; there was nothing worse than an unwilling pupil. But she was reminded of herself when young; she had had the same wayward streak and tendency to rebel. In her it had been squashed by a domineering mother and a broken heart and later she had channelled her energies into something more acceptable, bringing up her stepchildren, her good works and her painting.

The maid brought in the refreshments and a few minutes were occupied in pouring tea and offering sweetmeats, during which the conversation, conducted entirely between the Countess and the Duke, revolved around the weather.

'Now, Lady Lavinia,' Frances said, at last. 'I believe you are to come to me for drawing lessons.'

'So Papa says.'

'You do not like the idea yourself?'

Lavinia shrugged. 'I am hopeless at it.'

'Oh, dear. Who has told you that?'

'Miss Hastings, my governess. She loses all patience with me—'

'It is not to be wondered at,' the Duke put in. 'You do not even try.'

'I cannot see the point in trying. What use is being able to draw to me? Or dancing? Or playing the harpsichord? Or mincing about learning to curtsy?'

He sighed. 'We have been over this all before, Vinny. These are accomplishments all young ladies need in order to enter Society.'

'Then I shall not enter it. It is all a terrible bore.'

'Lavinia,' he said sharply, 'you will do as you are told. You know what we talked about only yesterday…'

'That Mama would have wished it. Yes, yes, I know, but Mama is not here, is she?'

Oh, poor child, Frances thought. She misses her mama dreadfully and he cannot see that. 'Lady Lavinia,' she said gently. 'Shall we have a trial, just to see how we deal together? If we cannot do so, there is no point in continuing; I cannot teach you if you do not wish to be taught.'

'Do not forget, I have also commissioned a portrait,' Marcus reminded her. 'I insist she sits for that.'

'We will deal with that later,' Frances said, looking from the girl to the man, her brows drawn together in annoyance. How was she to get through to the child if he continually interrupted?

He glared at her, but fell silent under her withering glance.

'Now, my lady,' Frances went on. 'Shall you come again tomorrow and we will talk some more? Perhaps you could come with your governess, so that your father may go about his business.'

'I will bring her,' Marcus snapped. 'My daughter does not go about town without a proper escort. Her governess would be useless in a tight corner.'

'Very well, your Grace,' she said, wondering what sort of tight corner he had in mind. 'I will expect you both at ten o'clock. I am afraid I cannot make it any later. I have a class at noon and an appointment for the afternoon.'

'That will serve,' he said, rising. 'Come Vinny, we have other visits to make.'

All very cold and businesslike, she told herself after they had gone, and cold was the only word to describe him, cold and top-lofty. Was he like that with his daughter all the time? Did he ever show her any affection? Whether she would break through the girl's petulance, she did not know but, for some reason she could not explain, even to herself, she wanted to try. Perhaps it was simply that she enjoyed a challenge.

She repeated that thought to Sir Percival when they were riding in Hyde Park the following morning. They had enjoyed a good gallop over the turf and had returned to walk their horses along the carriageway before returning home.

'If you do not mind my saying so, Fanny, you are a ninny,' he said, while bowing to an acquaintance in a phaeton. 'You will only invite gossip.'

'It was you who told me no one would remember the scandal, Percy.'

'Yes, but you do not have to remind them of it.'

'I am not, but if I had refused the Duke's request, he would think I bear him a grudge and that I cannot have.

The past is dead and gone and teaching Lady Lavinia will prove it.'

'How?'

'Why, because nothing will come of it. It is a business arrangement and when it comes to an end and he takes his daughter back to Derbyshire, everyone will see it is.' She smiled and inclined her head in greeting towards Lady Jersey, sitting in a carriage with one of her bosom bows.

'You should be careful you are not hoist on your own petard, my dear.'

'And what is that supposed to mean?'

'Oh, I think you are well aware of my meaning.'

'I have no interest in the Duke of Loscoe, except as a client,' she said, turning back towards the Stanhope Gate. 'He is paying me well.'

He laughed. 'And you so poor you cannot afford to turn him down!'

'No, I can't. I put the money I earn to very good use.'

'Now, I never had you down as a pinchcommons.' He sighed. 'It just shows how wrong a fellow can be.'

She laughed. 'You know me better than anyone, Percy, and you know I am not at all interested in money for its own sake.'

'Do I?'

'Naturally, you do.'

'But you know the latest *on dit* is that his Grace is looking for a second wife.'

'So?'

'Will he go back unmarried, I ask myself?'

'What has that to do with me?'

'He is rich as Golden Ball, if it is money you want. Not that you would have much of a bargain. The gabble-grinders have it that his marriage was far from content and the consensus of opinion seems to be that it was his fault. He is too stiff and overweening to make any woman happy and only his enormous wealth will make the ladies overlook his failings.'

'Percy, I do believe you are a little jealous.'

'Not at all.' They passed through the gate into Park Lane. 'But do not say I did not warn you.'

They rode on in silence while she mused on what he had said and arrived at Corringham House, just as the phaeton containing the Duke and his daughter turned into the road. This was beginning to become a habit, she thought, this meeting on the doorstep. She must remember that the Duke was a stickler for punctuality and not to be late in future. They stopped and Sir Percival sprang down to help her dismount as the carriage containing the Duke and his daughter came to a halt.

She was magnificent, Marcus decided, standing at her door in a green velvet habit that nipped her waist, and the most amazing riding hat, like a man's top hat, but with a sweeping feather and a wisp of veil to make it more feminine. He jumped down and made his bow. 'My lady.'

She inclined her head, almost haughty, except that her smile belied it. 'Your Grace, am I late or are you early?'

'I am punctual, my lady. It is the politeness of kings, so they say, and who am I to be less polite than a king?'

'I will remember that, my lord. Will you please come in? Sir Percival, will you join us?'

'No, don't think so, m'dear,' he murmured, taking her hand and kissing the back of it. 'Things to do, don't you know?'

'Of course. Thank you for your escort.'

'My pleasure, dear lady.' He turned to the Duke.

'Good day, Loscoe. Lady Lavinia.' And with that he remounted and set off at a trot towards Brook Street.

'I do not intend to stay long,' Marcus said to the groom who came round from the side of the house to lead the horses away. 'Just keep a watch on the horses for me.'

Relieved by that, Frances conducted them indoors and, once his Grace had been relieved of his hat and Lady Lavinia had been divested of her pelisse and bonnet, led the way up to her studio, where she left them to go and change out of her habit.

It took her no more than five minutes and she returned to find Lavinia standing at the window with her back to the room and the Duke prowling round looking at the pictures displayed on the wall. He had his hands clasped under the tail of his brown frockcoat.

'These are good,' he said. 'A deal better than that fribble you did of Lady Willoughby.'

'Thank you. They are the ones I have painted for my own pleasure.'

'You should share that pleasure, not hide them away.'

'They are not hidden,' she said, thinking of those she had painted of him seventeen years before and was glad she had put them on the floor with their faces to the wall. She did not want him to know that she had kept them. 'Anyone who comes into this room can see them.'

'But you have not exhibited them?'

'No, they are not fashionable.'

'I can readily see that. There is too much stark realism, the brushstrokes are too bold but, in my humble opinion, the execution is top of the trees. I am sure a more discerning public would see their merit at once.'

She laughed. 'You think someone would like to hang a picture of a dead fox on their drawing-room wall?'

'No, perhaps not that one. Why did you do it?'

'The barbarity appalled me.'

Lady Lavinia turned towards her. 'You think so too, my lady? I hate it. Papa persuaded me to join in the hunt last autumn and, though I enjoyed the ride, it was awful when the dogs caught the fox. They cut off its brush and wiped my face with it. I was dreadfully sick. I'll never go again.' It was the longest speech Frances had heard her make.

'I told you, Vinny,' the Duke put in with a smile, 'you only have to be blooded once. It will not happen again.'

'I am sure that is a great comfort to the fox,' she retorted. 'It only has to die once. Well, I tell you this: when I marry, I shall not let my husband hunt.'

He grinned. 'You think you will have the ordering of your husband, do you? Oh, Vinny, you have a great deal to learn if you believe that.'

'I shall have it written in the marriage contract or there will be no marriage.'

He laughed aloud, which made the girl colour angrily and Frances decided to intervene. 'You are evidently very fond of animals, Lady Lavinia.'

'Yes. I have a menagerie at home at Loscoe Court, but of course I could not bring them with me. Tom, the stable boy, is looking after them for me.'

'Have you tried to draw them?'

'No. Why should I? They are there to be seen and touched—why would I want to commit them to paper?'

'Now, there is an interesting question.'

'What is?'

'Why commit anything to paper or canvas? Or plaster and bronze, come to that? Shall we sit down and discuss it? We could do that while I make some preliminary sketches of you.'

'I would rather be out of doors.'

'Then let us go into the garden.' She rose and collected up two sketchbooks and a few pieces of charcoal. Then she turned to Marcus. 'You may safely leave Lady Lavinia with me, my lord. I am sure you have other calls on your time.' It was as near a dismissal as she could make without being unpardonably rude. She wanted him to leave; his presence, even when he was not speaking, was unnerving. She needed to be calm and in control, if she were going to teach her pupil anything at all.

He rose and smiled. 'I will return for her in an hour.'

They went down to the front hall together, where he retrieved his hat, bade Lavinia behave herself, and took his leave.

'Well, he did not need to say that,' Lavinia said, peevishly. 'I am not a child. Anyone would think I was going to demolish the place.'

'Oh, I do hope not,' Frances said with a laugh. 'I have only just got it looking the way I want it.'

Lavinia looked sideways at her and then, realising she was joking, smiled. Her smile, like her father's, lit her eyes, making Frances wonder why she did not do so more often. There was the promise of great beauty and a telling charm, which should be nurtured. Was that what Marcus had meant about polish? And should she still be thinking of him as Marcus, when that intimacy had long ago vanished and she ought always refer to him, even in her thoughts, as 'his Grace' or 'the Duke'?

'Come along,' she said briskly, leading the way through the main hall, past the carved oak staircase and along a corridor to a door which led into a conservatory filled with exotic plants. It was hot and humid and smelled of peat and the heavy perfume of tropical flowers. They passed quickly through it and out into the garden, where the air was dry and balmy. 'Now, where shall we sit, in the arbour or by the pool?'

Lavinia shrugged. 'It's all one to me. I would sooner be sitting a horse.'

Frances laughed. 'Do you know, so would I.'

'Then why do this?' Her arm indicated the drawing equipment.

'Because we cannot always be doing what we want to do. We all, even you, have obligations, commissions, tasks, whatever you like to call them, which must be seen to before we can think of pleasure. Your papa is paying me to teach you to draw and so I must put my efforts into that. Now, let us make a start.' She looked about her and pointed to a small wooden structure at the end of the path, which had fretted sides and a steep pitched roof with a cupola on the top. 'Would you like to draw the pergola?'

'Oh, very well.' Lavinia gave a great sigh and took the sketch-book and charcoal Frances held out to her and sat down on a bench beside the pool. She slashed impatiently at the paper, making a line here and another there, a few bold curves and some squiggles and the pergola appeared. Without taking the least trouble over it, she had the line and perspective almost exactly right. 'There,' she said handing it back. 'There is your pergola, my lady.'

Frances bit back the scolding she felt bound to deliver. Lavinia was a spoiled child who thought that being uncooperative might relieve her of doing something she did not want to do. 'Did you suppose this would persuade me that you are a hopeless case, Lavinia, and that I would tell your father we would not go on with the lessons?'

Lavinia sighed heavily. 'No, for he is paying you.'

'That is true, but it is not the only reason we will go on, I assure you,' she said, trying to sound cheerful and friendly, though she was very tempted to give the child a sharp slap. 'I am afraid I must disagree with your governess—you are not a hopeless case at all, not when it comes to drawing, at any rate.'

'How can you tell from that? It is nothing but scribble.'

'Then pray do something that is not scribble. Add some refinements while I begin my sketch of you.'

Lavinia worked with an ill grace, her face set in a scowl, which Frances transferred to her own sketchbook. Then she turned the page and began on a clean sheet. 'Lady Lavinia, do you think you could smile, or at least have some pleasant thoughts?'

'Such as?'

'Imagine you are out riding, or playing with your pet rabbit.'

'How do you know I have a rabbit?'

'Oh, no menagerie would be complete without a rabbit.'

Lavinia laughed and Frances began capturing the image, but she had to work quickly before the girl began to frown again. Both worked in silence for perhaps five minutes before Lavinia flung the pad on the seat beside her and began to roam about the garden. Frances continued to work. 'I cannot capture your likeness if you do not sit still, Lavinia.'

'Why not? It seems to me likeness has nothing to do with it. Paint what you think my father would like to see, someone demure and pretty, with hands neatly folded and empty eyes. That is what you do, is it not? Whoever pays the piper calls the tune and so you play it.'

Frances was taken aback, not only by the girl's outspokenness but by her accuracy, and it made her feel uncomfortable. She was even more discomfited when she realised that Marcus had come into the garden and was leaning against a tree watching them. How long he had been there, she did not know. She shut the sketchbook with a snap and stood up. 'I think we have had enough for one day, Lavinia,' she said evenly. 'Your papa is here to fetch you.'

'Oh, do not stop on my account,' he said, coming forward. 'I can sit and watch you both at work.'

'We have been getting to know one another,' Frances said. 'There has been little work done.'

He picked up Lavinia's book and flipped it open. 'I can see that,' he said. 'A child of six could have done this in three minutes.'

Frances smiled. 'A child of sixteen did it in one.'

'Lavinia…' he began.

'Oh, I know what you are going to say,' the girl said. 'You are going to tell me that is not what you are paying Lady Corringham for.'

Frances took the book from him. 'Your Grace, we have both learned a great deal this afternoon, though it might not be obvious. Your daughter has a natural talent, which we must encourage. Scolding her for doing what I asked her to do will not make her any more willing.'

'You asked her to do this scrawl?'

'I asked her to draw the pergola. And she did. Her imagination added the rabbit, but as she has pointed out to me, I sometimes use my imagination to enhance an image…'

He gave a wry smile. 'I heard her. It was insufferably impertinent of her and I apologise on her behalf.'

'Oh, do not do that, sir. If any apologising needs to be done, Lady Lavinia will acknowledge it and do it herself. And perhaps I should crave her pardon for being too condescending.'

'Fustian! If you are going to collude with her in her mischief, she will only become worse.'

'Let me be the judge of that, my lord. Now, if you do not wish me to continue giving lessons to your daughter, then please say so. I shall not be offended.'

'Of course I wish you to continue.'

'Then she shall come again next Thursday, if that is convenient to you.'

'It is perfectly convenient.'

She stood up and collected together the drawing equipment. He reached out to take it from her and between them they dropped the sketchbooks. They both stooped at the same moment to pick them up. Their hands touched and she felt a shaft of something akin to fire flash from his fingertips to hers and course along her arm and through her whole frame. She lifted her head and found herself looking into his eyes. His expression puzzled her. It was as if he were trying to convey something to her. Was it reproof? Sympathy? Desire, even? She held his gaze, unable to look away, almost mesmerised by those deep golden eyes.

It lasted only seconds, which seemed like a lifetime before he stood up and held out a hand to bring her to her feet. 'My lady.' His voice was perfectly normal.

She murmured 'Thank you, your Grace,' and led the way indoors.

Five minutes later, he and his daughter were gone, leaving her breathless. Never, never could she have foreseen the effect he would have on her. Had he noticed it? Had it given him a feeling of satisfaction, that, after seventeen years, he could still put her in a spin?

How was she going to deal with seeing him every time he brought his daughter to her? And if he really was looking for a second wife, he would undoubtedly be out and about, attending functions which she was also expected to attend. She could not shut herself away, her friends would wonder what was wrong with her. And why should she? It behoved her to bring all her self-control to bear and behave with indifference. She would be indifferent.

Chapter Three

Frances was called upon to exercise her indifference sooner than she expected. The Duke of Loscoe was invited to the ball which she had helped to organise in aid of the orphanage. She and a committee of ladies had been planning it for some time and it was to be as grand an affair as they could manage to which all the *ton* had been invited. He had already made a generous donation to the cause of the orphans and it would have been unthinkable to exclude him.

The choice of venue had been the subject of great debate; should it be held in Almack's Assembly Rooms, at an hotel, or in a private house? The Assembly Rooms were considered stultifying and there was hardly a hotel with large enough rooms, and besides, their owners would not wish to turn away their ordinary customers to make room for them. If it was to be a private house, then it must have a ballroom big enough to accommodate all the guests they hoped would pay for the privilege of attending.

'It had better be Corringham House,' Frances had said.

'But, Lady Corringham, are you sure?' Mrs

Butterworth had asked. 'There might be people wishing to come who might not be quite top of the trees. You never know how they might conduct themselves.'

'If they are prepared to pay, then I am sure we can handle any problems of behaviour. After all, beggars cannot be choosers.'

'My lady!' Lady Graham, another member of the committee, cried in horror. 'We are not beggars. Never let it be said that we are begging.'

Frances had smiled. 'No, but we are going to ask an exorbitant amount for a ticket, are we not? They deserve Corringham House for that.'

It was some time since Frances had entertained on such a lavish scale; usually she gave small intimate suppers at which conversation, listening to music and playing a few hands of whist were the main ways of passing time. There had not been a ball at the house since Augusta's come-out five years before and the ballroom had not been used since. She thought she would enjoy the challenge.

And so, on a warm Saturday evening in May, when London was just beginning to fill up for the Season, Corringham House was ablaze with light. Extra servants had been busy all day, polishing the ballroom floor; others were scurrying about carrying chairs, tables, plates and glasses to wherever they were needed. The dining room had been laid out with one long table covered with a pristine damask cloth, ready for the food to be set upon it, and dozens of smaller tables were arranged round the room for the guests to eat supper in small intimate groups. In the over-heated kitchen an army of specially contracted caterers were frantically preparing food, getting in each other's way and cursing

volubly. By early evening, banks of fresh flowers were
in place and the musicians had arrived.

Frances made one last tour of the rooms, including
one on the first floor for those who did not care to dance
and preferred cards, and two others set aside for gentlemen and ladies to leave their hats and cloaks and refresh
themselves. There was an attendant in each. Satisfied
that all was in readiness, she went up to her bedroom
on the second floor, where Rose was waiting to help
her dress. She felt hot and sticky and glad to soak in
the bath which had been put on the floor of her dressing
room and filled with warm, perfumed water.

Until then she had been too busy to reflect on the
possible success or otherwise of the enterprise. What
would her aristocratic friends think of being asked to
pay for the privilege of being her guests? And would
they come, knowing that others, just as rich but less
socially acceptable, might also pay and they would be
obliged to mix with them? It was too late to worry about
that now. She stood up and stepped out of the bath.
Rose wrapped a towel round her and began rubbing her
dry.

When the first carriage rolled up the drive and deposited its occupants on the doorstep, she was ready to
greet them. She had chosen to wear an open gown in
amber crepe over a silk slip in pale lemon. It had a
scooped neckline and puffed sleeves. The amber crepe
and the sleeves were sewn with tiny seed pearls and the
bodice was caught under the bosom with tiny yellow
flowers, the eye of each one studded with a pearl. Her
hair was arranged *à la Grecque* and studded with more
pearls. Apart from her rings, she wore no other jewellery.

After the ladies of the committee, who had all arrived

promptly, the first guests to arrive were Augusta and her husband, Sir Richard Harnham. Frances, always pleased to see her stepdaughter, kissed her fondly. 'I am so glad you are here. I have been thinking it will be a very poor do and no one will come.'

'Fustian!' Richard said, smiling at her and raising her hand to his lips. 'Nothing you do is a poor do. It will be a great squeeze, you see if I am not right.'

'I do hope so.' She smiled suddenly. 'Even if no one comes, they have already paid for their tickets. We have banked the money and plans have already been made to spend it.'

'Oh, Mama, please stop worrying,' Augusta said. 'Enjoy yourself.'

Considering there was only twelve years between them, Frances found it amusing that Augusta, now that she was grown up and married and had children of her own, still insisted on calling her Mama, but it did not displease her; she was very fond of Augusta.

Her stepson, James, was the next to arrive, dressed in a black evening coat, skintight pantaloons and shirt points high enough to scratch his cheeks. His muslin cravat had been tied to an intricacy that would have done credit to Beau Brummell. He had a young lady on his arm whom Frances had never seen before, but whom she immediately knew to be a very expensive *chère amie* indeed. She was dressed in a cream satin high-waisted gown embroidered all over with gold and silver thread. Her hair had obviously been dressed by someone skilled in the art and she wore a diamond necklace, diamond ear drops and several gold bracelets.

'May I present Miss Annabelle Franks, ma'am,' James said, drawing her forward.

'My lady,' she said, dropping into a curtsy. 'I am very pleased to meet you.'

'You are welcome, Miss Franks.' Then, to her stepson, 'James, Augusta is arrived, do go and speak to her.'

She watched them go with some trepidation. James had succeeded to his father's title at the age of seventeen and now, at twenty-four, was something of a scapegrace. Frances had had many a run-in with him over the coils he landed himself in, but for all that she loved him dearly. When not living at the Corringham estate in Essex, he stayed in bachelor chambers in Albany, rather than at Corringham House. She suspected it was because he did not want her to know everything he was up to.

He and the young lady had hardly passed into the ballroom when Sir Percival arrived. He looked like a peacock in his green velvet knee breeches, silk stockings and mauve satin coat. There was a froth of lace at his throat and more spilling over his wrists. He took her hand and bent to kiss it, smiling at her. 'Fanny, you look beautiful tonight.'

She laughed. 'Well, thank you, Percy. And I must say, you look magnificent.'

He preened himself in his old-fashioned clothes, unaware of the slight irony in her tone. 'I shall expect at least one dance.'

'You may have it, if I have time to dance at all. I might be too occupied.'

'Gammon! You must make time. I did not pay a ransom for a ticket to be deprived of the pleasure of dancing with you, which was the only reason I came.'

'Not to help the orphans?' she teased.

'I could have made a donation without coming.'

'I hope not too many of our guests share your sentiments or we shall have an empty ballroom.'

'No, for half London is agog to see the inside of a house they know only by repute, and observe the *haut monde* at play. They will come.'

And they did. Almost everyone who had purchased a ticket arrived in their finery and some even came without tickets, prepared to pay at the door. Richard had forecast a squeeze and he was certainly right. By nine o'clock the ballroom was crowded and noisy with music, talk and laughter, even if the different social echelons did remain in little groups, each observing the other. Frances decided that no one else should be admitted and left her post to join the throng and encourage everyone to mingle. She was immediately besieged by well-wishers and it was some time before she was free to dance herself; Percy came to claim her.

'I told you so, did I not?' he said as they took the first steps of a cotillion. 'You cannot say this is not a huge success and the Season hardly begun.'

'Yes, it was a good decision to have it early, before everyone was engaged in their own round of social events. There are to be several balls in the next three months and no doubt everyone will be exhausted.'

'Then will you please stop worrying and enjoy this dance, you are as stiff as a ramrod.'

'I'm sorry.' She smiled and allowed the music to take over and it wasn't until the end of the dance, when Percy raised her from a deep curtsy, that she saw the Duke of Loscoe, standing in the open doorway, surveying the crowd. Her earnest hope that he would be otherwise engaged on the night had gone unanswered.

He was immaculately clad in black. His superfine coat looked as though he had been poured into it, so closely did it fit his broad shoulders and narrow waist. His trousers, strapped beneath his dancing shoes, emphasised his muscular thighs and long legs and proved that, for a man who had lived in the country for years, he was very much abreast of fashion. A rose-coloured waistcoat, embroidered in gold thread, and a fantastically tied cravat of the finest silk completed a look which had all the young ladies sighing, notwithstanding he was known to be forty years old.

'Complete to a shade,' Percy remarked drily.

Frances excused herself and went, as a good hostess, to greet the Duke and make him welcome. 'Your Grace, I am sorry I left my post and was not waiting to greet you. I thought everyone who was coming had arrived.'

He smiled down at her. 'Is that a rebuke for my tardiness, my lady? If so, I beg forgiveness. My business kept me longer than I intended.'

'Goodness no, you are not late, but punctual as ever. It is I who am at fault for assuming everyone was here and beginning the proceedings too early.' That, she thought, would tell him that she had not been looking out for him and had not even noticed his non-arrival.

'Then you must make amends by dancing with me.'

There was no help for it and it was better to have it over and done with before her courage left her. She laid her fingers upon the hand he held out to her and allowed him to lead her into the dance just beginning.

Time stood still—more than that, it seemed to go backwards as they did the steps of a stately minuet, just as they had done in that Season seventeen years before. She felt a young girl again, but though the years had passed, inside she had not changed. The same things still excited and thrilled her, the same things made her sad; it was only on the outside she was older and she hoped wiser, able to meet both joy and calamity with serenity.

'Over all the years, this is what I remember most about you,' he murmured. 'The graceful way you move when you dance.'

'Really, my lord?' she said, deciding to accept the compliment as a tease and answer in like manner. 'Is that all?'

'No, it is far from all, but I doubt you want to hear what other things I remember.'

She should bring the conversation to an end, she knew that, but the seventeen-year-old inside her loved compliments and it was the seventeen-year-old inside her who was holding sway at that moment. She looked up at him and laughed. 'Are they so dreadful, these other things, that I should be ashamed of them?'

'Not dreadful at all, but delightful. The way you laugh, which is more like a husky chuckle. And the way your hair curls in your neck so lovingly and the way your eyes light up when you are animated. And your mouth. I do not think I can begin to describe that…'

She stumbled, but his firm hand held her upright and she was able to bring her steps and her swiftly beating heart under control. 'Loscoe, I do believe you are trying to flirt with me.'

'Of course,' he said solemnly, though there was a twinkle in his eyes. 'And you are not indifferent, are you?'

She wished he had not used that word. The years rolled on and the seventeen-year-old faded to be replaced by the mature woman, the cool Society hostess 'Every woman likes compliments, but she would be a ninny to take them seriously, especially when they are delivered by someone so obviously skilled in the art.'

'You think I am skilled? My goodness, that must mean your swains are singularly inept for I have been buried in the country for years and am sadly out of practice.'

'Then I should hate to be one of this Season's innocents, if you are going to practise on them. Heartbreak does not come easy when you are seventeen.'

'I have no intention of breaking anyone's heart,' he said, serious now. 'I cannot think why you should imagine that I would.'

'It is said you are looking for a new wife and that is why you are come to London.'

'Now, do you know, that is news to me.' He laughed suddenly. 'And you speak of being seventeen. Is that significant?'

She, who prided herself on the way she could guide a conversation, keep everything light when it needed to be light and serious when seriousness was called for, seemed to have lost control of this one. 'Not especially, but I think you are expected to make your choice from this Season's debutantes.'

'Am I indeed? I wonder what Lavinia would say to a stepmother who is little older than herself.' He smiled. 'Can you imagine it?'

Frances smiled to herself. Lady Lavinia would make short work of anyone who could not master her. 'I am only twelve years older than my stepdaughter and we are very fond of each other,' she said.

'Ah, but you are you.'

'And what does that mean?'

The dance was coming to and end and he did not answer, as she dipped into a deep curtsy and he bowed with a flourish and offered his arm to escort her from the floor. 'I shall come back for the waltz before supper,' he said, as he relinquished her.

She could not help it; she had to have the last word. 'My, how can someone buried in the country for goodness knows how many years know the steps of the waltz?'

His smile, as he turned from her, faded almost to a grimace. She still had the power to make him tremble with desire, but she was so elegantly detached, so cool, that even her banter was meant to put him in his place, inform him that she, just as well as he, could flirt and mean nothing by it. But his compliments had been genuine; he had surprised himself when he uttered them. Had he really been harbouring such memories for seventeen years?

He shook himself and strode across the floor to where Lady Willoughby guarded her daughter and bowed before them. 'Miss Willoughby, may I request the pleasure of this country dance?'

Felicity, prompted by her mother, sank into a deep curtsy, her face red with pleasure, then laid her hand upon his arm to be led onto the floor, which set the mamas a-twitter again.

Frances watched them, feeling drained. He had been arrogant seventeen years before and he was arrogant now. He had enjoyed making her squirm, enjoyed the buzz of conversation which followed him wherever he went, positively glowed with satisfaction when he was surrounded by sycophantic mamas, all trying to put forward their daughters. Surely he would not marry one of them?

It was not beyond the bounds of possibility. After all, she had married George and he had been older than Marcus was now. It often happened when a widower needed heirs or someone to be a second mother to the heirs he already had: he chose a very young lady. Wives who were young were usually also strong, able to bear children and look after elderly husbands when they became frail. They did it for the jointure they would receive on becoming a widow. And widows had more freedom than spinsters. As she did. She valued that freedom.

Smiling, she mingled with her guests, thanking them for coming and engaging them in light conversation before moving on. She looked in on the card players, but they hardly noticed her so absorbed were they. When she returned to the ballroom, she found Percy leaning nonchalantly against a pillar, surveying the scene through his quizzing glass.

'What are you looking at?' she asked him.

'His Grace, the Duke of Loscoe,' he said. 'Already there is speculation about which he will choose.'

'And what do you think?'

'I think he has more sense than to shackle himself to one of those ninnyhammers, though he is wise enough to leave the door open.'

'That sounds so cold-blooded. You'd think he was buying a cow at market.'

He smiled and let the glass drop on its ribbon to dangle on his chest. 'Well, he is, isn't he? Nothing so commonplace as love comes into it. And they cannot see it. Or perhaps they do not care to.'

'Percy, I do believe you are envious.'

'Not while he confines his attentions to those empty-headed chits, though if he were to turn his eye in another direction, I might not be so easy about it.'

She was intrigued. 'What other direction?'

'Oh, it is of no consequence,' he said airily. 'Come,

they are making sets for the Sir Roger de Coverley. Let us take to the floor and show how it is done.'

It was not easy to converse during the country dance, but she was puzzled. Sir Percival Ponsonby, the confirmed bachelor who always maintained that marriage was nothing more than enslavement, in love! She could not imagine it. 'What did you mean, another direction?' she demanded as they left the floor at the end of the dance. 'I cannot believe you are in love. You have always been outspoken against marriage. Leg-shackled, I believe is the word you are wont to use.'

'Being in love has nothing to do with marriage, Fanny. It is only women who insist on linking the two.'

'Oh, you are talking about a light o' love,' she teased. 'Who is she this time?'

He turned to look down at her, smiling. 'Now, you do not expect me to tell you, do you?'

'No, of course not, you would be too much the gentleman.' She laughed. 'Go and dance with someone else or you will have the gossips talking about us and that I will not have.'

'Very well.' He bowed and left her with Mrs Butterworth, whose plump face was wreathed in smiles.

'It has been a wonderful evening,' that good lady said. 'Of course we have yet to deduct your expenses, but I think we can safely say the orphans will benefit by a considerable sum.'

'I will cover the expenses,' said a voice.

Frances whirled round to find the Duke at her elbow. 'Your Grace, I did not know you were there.'

'I came to claim my waltz and overheard. Please allow me to meet the cost of the ball. It will mean all the money you have taken will be profit.'

'My lord, I cannot allow that,' she said.

'Surely it is not for you to refuse,' he said, looking past her to smile at Mrs Butterworth. 'I am sure the ladies of the committee will urge acceptance.'

'Indeed, yes,' Mrs Butterworth said, simpering up at him. 'How very generous you are, your Grace.'

Why, Frances asked herself, did everyone fall over themselves to toady up to him—he was conceited enough as it was? 'But, sir, it was never my intention to ask for expenses,' she said.

'No, I am sure not, but that doesn't change the fact that tonight has been a costly business and it will please me to help. You are, after all, a widow…'

'An independent widow,' she said tartly.

He bowed in acquiescence. 'Just as you please, my lady.'

'Oh, please do not quarrel over it,' Mrs Butterworth put in. 'Can you not share the charges?'

He laughed and looked at Frances. 'A capital solution, do you not think so, my dear?'

'Very well.' She gave her answer reluctantly, not because they could not use the money but because it somehow belittled her, made it seem that she needed a man's protection.

'Now that is agreed, let us have our dance,' he said, unaware of her rancour. 'I have to prove to you that I know how to waltz.' And without waiting for her to protest, he took her hand and led her onto the floor.

Not only did he know the steps, he was very accomplished and she was soon whirling round with his hand on her back guiding her. And if he held her a little closer than the regulation arm's length, she was too immersed in the conversation they had just had to notice. He was insufferably top-lofty. What Mrs Butterworth must have thought she dare not think.

'Your Grace, you will have the whole room talking about us,' she protested. With his arm about her waist and his face only a few inches from hers, her determination to be indifferent to him was slipping badly.

'Why?'

'That business with Mrs Butterworth. You did it to humble me.'

'Why, in heaven's name, should I do that?' He sounded genuinely astonished. 'I simply wish to help the orphans, the good lady knows that. You are not the only one to care about them, you know.'

'I do know, but she thought we were quarrelling. And I am sure other people thought so too.'

'Are we? Quarrelling, I mean.'

'No, of course not.'

'Then there is no case to answer. And I am the last person to allow a little tattle to bother me.'

'Yes, I know that,' she said, thinking of the Season when she had been seventeen and he had humiliated her so badly. The whole town had been whispering. She would not let him do it to her again. No man would ever hurt her like that again.

'Then there is nothing to worry about. I assure you I have no intention of marrying again, not this Season anyway. If the *haut monde* chooses to amuse itself by speculating, then that is up to them. You are quite safe.'

'Me?' she queried, only just managing not to shriek it. 'You cannot possibly think that I—' She stopped and took a deep breath. 'Loscoe,' she said as firmly as she could manage, 'I was not asking for reassurance on that subject. I am completely indifferent to your intentions.'

'Good.' He laughed and whirled her round in perfect time to the music. 'It is strange that it does not occur to the gabble-grinders that I am in the capital to do exactly as I said I was, to see to some urgent business and give my daughter a little experience of town life before her Season next year.'

She stopped herself asking what that business was; he must not think she was curious, or even cared. She did not and his conceit did not need curiosity from her to feed it. 'Lady Lavinia is very talented,' she said, determined to change the subject. 'You must be very proud of her.'

'Am I?' he said, as if it needed some thought. 'Yes, I suppose I am.'

'You do not seem very sure.'

'Of course I am sure. She is my daughter, but she was always with her mother more than me. I am only now getting to know her.'

'That is a sad thing to have to admit.'

'Perhaps, but…' He shrugged and decided not to explain that he and Margaret had been so badly mismatched they could agree on nothing, not even the raising of their daughter. His wife was happiest and so, evidently, were his children when he was from home and so he had spent more time than was strictly necessary at his other properties. In a way, it was a pity he had, for he might have prevented the trouble which had culminated in his present visit to London.

They were silent for the rest of the dance, each trying to analyse how they felt and failing utterly. He was puzzled, she confused. But there was something about the way they moved together, the expressions on their faces, the sadness in their eyes which made those who watched them begin to wonder. And remember.

'I was thinking of taking Lady Lavinia to an exhibition at the Royal Academy the next time she comes to me,' she told him when the dance ended and they were walking side by side to the supper room, not touching, but close enough to feel each other's warmth and know that the lifting of a hand would bring them into contact. Uncomfortably aware of it, she had to find something mundane to say, a safe subject to discuss. 'With your permission, of course.'

'You think she will benefit from such a visit?'

'Yes, there are some fine paintings there, not only of the Old Masters, but from today's artists too. Lady Lavinia would gain an insight into how the very best have been executed. Do you not agree?'

'Oh, I agree, but my daughter might not and, when she is determined, she can be very difficult.' He paused for a moment as they found seats in the dining room and a waiter brought a selection of dishes over to them. 'I should not like you to have to deal with the sulks.'

She chose chicken in a mushroom and caper sauce, some glazed ham and a small piece of partridge pie. 'Oh, I think I can win her round, my lord.'

'Really?' He piled his plate. 'This looks delicious. Your cook has excelled herself.'

'Thank you, I shall tell her.' She paused, watching the waiter fill their glasses with punch, a speciality of her butler's which, though refreshing, had a hidden kick. 'Then you give your permission for the outing?'

'Yes, yes, but I will accompany you.'

'That is not in the least necessary.'

'Oh, but it is. The daughter of one of England's foremost dukes cannot be too closely guarded...'

Frances laughed. 'My goodness, do you imagine someone will try to kidnap her between Duke Street and the Strand?'

'Such things have been known,' he said drily. 'But I should like to come. It is many years since I was in

Somerset House. It might be very interesting to see what new works of art they are exhibiting.'

What could she do but accept with a good grace? But it meant one more occasion when she was going to be thrown into his company. It was strange that the business he spoke of was not so urgent it prevented him from being available whenever the fancy took him. She smiled to herself as they returned to the ballroom for the second half of the evening's entertainment.

He could not ask her to dance again without causing comment and even he would not be so indifferent to that as to flout convention. He excused himself and, taking one look at the expectant faces of the young ladies turned towards him and the scowls of the young men, decided to take himself off to play cards.

The card room was occupied by several elderly gentlemen and an inveterate gamester or two who were playing for the highest stakes Frances would allow in her house, which were modest. Marcus, not a true gambler, declined to join them and instead sat with the other men who were doing no more than gossip. And they were every bit as dedicated to it as their wives. He soon learned the latest *on dit*, who was dangling after whom, who was having an affair, who was the latest favourite with the Prince Regent and news of more unrest among the cotton weavers and stocking makers.

'The suspension of *habeas corpus* seems not to have dampened their ardour,' a Mr Coleman said. 'They are as determined as ever to congregate. You come from that part of the world, your Grace, have you heard anything of a new uprising?'

'Not since they stopped the Blanketeers,' he said, referring to a protest begun by the cotton weavers in Manchester with the intention of marching to London and putting their case to the Prince Regent. The march would inevitably have taken several days and so the men had equipped themselves with provisions and a blanket each, hence their name. The march had been broken up by militia before it reached the capital, but there were some who compared it with the Bread March of the women of Versailles at the beginning of the French Revolution and that was still very much alive in the memories of many. 'But you can hardly blame them. They are hungry and hunger is the sharpest weapon of all.'

'Surely you do not condone lawlessness?'

'No, certainly not, but I can still sympathise.'

Sir Joshua Barber, a fat man with a florid countenance, whose wealth came from cotton manufacture, gave a snort of derision and Marcus, afraid that an argument was about to ensue which he had no wish for, was wondering whether to rejoin the dancers or make his excuses to leave, when Sir Percival came in and joined the group.

'It's deucedly warm downstairs,' he said. 'And I'm getting to old for prancing about all night.'

'Know what you mean,' Lord Willoughby said. 'Wouldn't have come m'self except Lady Willoughby insisted, couldn't be seen to ignore the Countess's pet cause, so she said. The whole *ton* would be here and it would look odd if we cried off.'

'She was right,' Percy said. 'Anyone who is anyone is here.'

'And a great many more besides,' his lordship said. 'I never met such a queer set.' Whether he included Sir Joshua in their number, Marcus could not be certain.

'Her ladyship has a great talent for organisation,'

Percy said. 'She has only to smile and everyone falls over themselves to please her.'

'Whether they will or not,' Sir Joshua muttered, referring to his wife, who was on the organising committee.

'Oh, come, sir,' Marcus said. 'You are surely not admitting to being under the cat's paw? Wives, in my book, should obey their husbands.'

Percy laughed suddenly, making Marcus look at him in surprise. 'I doubt the Countess would agree with that last remark,' he said.

'That why you never married her?' Sir Joshua asked. 'No wish to live under the cat's foot?'

'Question never came up,' he said loftily.

Marcus knew, as clearly as if Sir Percival had said it aloud, that he was in love with Frances. Had Frances rejected him, or had he never found the courage to ask? He tried to imagine her married to this outdated fop, but all it did was make him smile. And that was followed by a strange sensation in his chest, a sudden tightening of the muscles which made breathing difficult. Concluding it was because he was out of condition, he decided to pay a visit to Jackson's boxing emporium the following day and have a few rounds with whoever happened to be there. It would do him good.

'Used to know her, didn't you?' Sir Joshua queried. 'Years ago.'

Marcus smiled. 'In my green days, yes.'

'Not so green now, though, eh?' he said, tapping the side of his nose with a claw like forefinger.

'Neither is she,' he said coldly and stood up. 'Gentlemen, I bid you goodnight.'

'Going home?' Percy asked.

'Yes. Like you, I have danced enough for one night.'

'You will disappoint the young ladies.'

'Oh, I do not think so. There are any number of more attractive young bloods to divert them.'

Marcus sketched a brief bow to the company and left the room. He was surprised, as he walked along the corridor towards the stairs, to find Sir Percival right behind him.

'What is your game, Loscoe?' he asked.

'Game, Sir Percival? Do you mean cards? I play a little whist and chess…'

'I did not mean that and you know it. What I want to know is why, after all this time, you are come to the Village. Are you looking for a second duchess?'

Marcus stopped and turned towards him, fixing him with a cold stare. 'That, sir, is my business.'

'Oh, I do not dispute it, so long as you leave Countess Corringham alone. Hurt her again and I will make it my business too.'

'Are you threatening me, Sir Percival?'

'Not at all, Duke,' Percy said blandly. 'But Fanny was badly used when she was too young to understand the ways of young men and since then she has been too afraid to allow anyone to become close. It has affected her whole life.'

He could not believe what the man was saying, did not want to believe it. Frances Corringham did not give the impression of a woman wearing the willow. 'You mean she holds herself aloof from you and you have been disappointed by it.'

'Not at all. As I said before, the question has never arisen.'

'Because you are afraid of being given a right about?' Marcus laughed. 'You should have more bottom, my friend. Faint heart never won fair lady.'

He turned and proceeded down the stairs with every appearance of nonchalance, though Sir Percival continued to dog his heels.

Frances had gone back to her hostess duties, though there seemed to be little to be done now; everyone was having a grand time and, under the influence of the punch which did seem to have a strange effect on people not used to it, even some of the stiff-rumped aristocrats who had condescended to grace the occasion had unbent enough to converse with those beneath them on the social scale. Not that anyone could be classed as coming from the lower orders, but there were a few doctors, lawyers, artists and literary people among the guests, even a few manufacturers and industrialists who had money enough to buy their way into society and who hoped to marry their daughters to a title. To Frances they were all interesting people and she conducted animated conversations with them all, finding some common interest to keep the talk flowing before moving on.

She was well aware of the matrons sitting on the sidelines, tearing everyone to shreds, but took no notice. If their lives were so barren it amused them to deride others, then they were to be pitied. But she did wonder what they were saying about the Duke. Whatever it was, it was his own fault for allowing it to go on without refuting it. For a moment she considered dropping a hint herself that the gentleman in question was not planning to marry, but discarded the idea immediately. They would think she had an ulterior motive, a wish to have him for herself, and that would never do.

'Mama,' she heard Augusta's voice behind her and turned to smile at her. 'We are leaving. Andrew has not been well and I told Miss Speedan we would not be late home.'

'Why didn't you say?' she asked in alarm. 'What is wrong with him?'

'It is only a head cold, but he does like to have his mama beside him when he is unwell. He will be better in a day or two.'

'Then bring him to see me. And Beth. She is not ill too, is she?'

'No, she had the cold last week, and now she is getting better she is a handful. Poor Miss Speedan is finding it difficult to manage.'

'Then you must leave at once.' She reached forward and kissed her stepdaughter, then turned to Richard. 'Take care of her. Take care of all of them, they are very precious.'

'I know.' He smiled and took her hand. 'As soon as Andrew is well again, Gussie will bring them to visit you.'

She went with them to the hall where their outdoor garments were returned to them and watched as they made their way to their coach before turning back indoors. She loved her little family dearly and it made not the slightest difference that they were not her own flesh and blood.

She paused in the hall, knowing she ought to return to the ballroom, but she was feeling exhausted. It had been a long day and she had been working for most of it, and the presence of the Duke of Loscoe had not helped. That he could still set her limbs quivering and her heart fluttering she was obliged to concede and the effort not to let it show had taken every ounce of her energy. She was tempted to go up to her room and rest for half an hour, and even had her hand on the newel post of the banister, when she saw Marcus descending the stairs.

She paused while he came down to the last step and stopped. She raised her eyes to his and found herself trapped in his gaze. His eyes darkened from amber to brown, as his glance flickered over her and came to rest on her face. His mouth twitched slightly as if he wanted to smile but could not quite manage it. There was irritation there, and something she could not quite define. Was it pain?

They were facing each other; he could not come down and she could not go up without one or the other moving to one side and it seemed for an interminable time that neither was going to do so, so locked in contemplation of each other were they.

'Are you going stand there all night, Loscoe?' She was startled to hear Percy's voice; she had not seen him in the dimness of the staircase behind Marcus. 'Can't you see her ladyship wishes to pass you?'

Frances tore her eyes away from the Duke to look up at Sir Percival, then stepped back, though she still clung to the newel post as if to a lifeline. 'Oh, no, Percy, it is unlucky to pass on the stairs. The Duke knows that and is simply saving me from ill luck.' She forced a smile. 'Your Grace.'

He nodded and stepped down to the hall floor. 'My lady, I was about to find you to bid you goodnight. It has been...' He paused, wondering what the evening had been and how best to express it without being untruthful. A pleasure? Not exactly. 'An interesting evening.'

'Thank you for coming.'

'I shall call on you the day after tomorrow for our little outing. Will two o'clock be convenient?'

'Quite convenient, my lord.'

He bowed, received his hat from a footman and made his way out of the house. He could not have come in his carriage for Frances perceived him striding off towards Brook Street and concluded he was probably going on to White's or perhaps Boodles to finish the evening's entertainment, playing cards for higher stakes than she would allow in her salon. She turned back to Percy, who stood beside her watching the Duke disappearing into the night.

'An assignation, eh?' he said, looking at her quizzically.

'Assignation?'

'Two days hence at two o'clock in the afternoon.'

'Good heavens, no! We are going to take Lady Lavinia to the Royal Academy. It is part of her instruction.'

'It seems to me the tabbies have a point,' he said slowly. 'Loscoe is using his daughter as a means of being often in your company.'

'Percy, how can you say that?'

'It is not what I say that matters. It is other people who have remarked on it. I only repeat what I have heard.'

'And I wish you would not. The Duke has no interest in me, but what I do for his daughter. It is a business arrangement.'

'Are you sure?' It was unlike him to be so serious and she looked up at him, puzzled.

'Percy, are you just a little bit jealous?'

'I am a whole lot jealous. Why, I had come to look on you as a companion when I fancy riding in the park and a happy partner on those occasions like balls and supper parties when to go alone would incommode my hostess. You know how women like everything neatly in pairs.'

'I know at least a handful of ladies who would happily fulfil those functions.'

'No, you do not. I am considered an object of amusement by almost everyone, even you, but you are good enough not to allow it to show.'

'Goodness, sir, whatever has got into you? Naturally you amuse me, but that is what you set out to do in the first place.' She reached out and put her hand on his sleeve. 'Percy, let us not quarrel over the Duke of Loscoe. He is not worth it. I find you infinitely more comfortable to be with.'

'Comfortable.' He gave a huge sigh. 'Damned with faint praise.'

'Oh, Percy.' She laughed. 'How can you be such a ninnyhammer?'

'It was the way I was made, my dear.' He bowed over her hand. 'Now, having been cut to the quick, I will take my leave. Shall you ride tomorrow?'

'Percy, I truly think I shall be too fatigued to rise early enough. And there will be a great deal of clearing up to do here, and the committee must meet and go over the accounts. The next day perhaps. We can go in the morning before the Duke calls with Lavinia.'

He smiled agreement, relinquished her hand and, taking his hat, disappeared after the Duke. The departure of the two men seemed to signal a general leave-taking and it was not until everyone had gone and she was alone in her bedchamber, sitting before the mirror brushing out her hair, that she was able to reflect on the events of the evening.

As a fund-raising exercise it had been an outstanding success, but it was not its success or otherwise that occupied her thoughts, it was the Duke of Loscoe and the strange effect he had on her. He had only to be in the same room and she was aware of him. She did not need to see him or hear him; she could feel his presence, knew when his eyes were on her, seeking her out.

And if that were not enough, he had only to speak to her and her insides turned to quivering jelly and she could hardly breathe. It was missish behaviour of the silliest kind. And what made it more foolish was his arrogant assumption that she wished for his attentions. Why should she be at all bothered whether he intended to marry this Season or next, or at any other time? And to have taken the trouble to tell her she was safe was the outside of enough!

Did he think she had spent the last seventeen years wearing the willow for him and he had only to drop the handkerchief and she would pick it up? Arrogant, conceited, impossible man! She must disenchant him of that idea at the first opportunity.

Chapter Four

'Stanmore! By all that's wonderful, haven't seen you in goodness knows how many years.'

Marcus looked up from stripping off, ready for a sparring match with Gentleman Jackson, to find himself face to face with a huge red-headed man, whose ruddy countenance was beaming at him in joyful recognition.

'Donald Greenaway!' He held out his hand, which was grasped and pumped vigorously. 'How are you? Haven't seen hide nor hair of you since you went off to the Peninsula.'

'Well, I am back home now, complete in wind and limb. A major no less but, for all that half-pay is not going to keep me in shirts...'

'Looking for something to do?'

'Yes, but there's no great rush to settle down. How are you? Heard about your wife, can't recall now who told me, but sorry for it.'

'Thank you. It happened over two years ago, but I am still trying to come to terms with being a widower.'

'Not for long, I'll wager. You'll have no trouble finding a new wife.'

'Not sure that I want one.'

'Oh, playing the field, eh? Can't say I blame you. What are you doing in Town if not to look over the fillies?'

'I had to come on family business—'

'Sir,' Mr Jackson interrupted them. 'Do you wish to postpone our bout?'

'No, no, I am coming. Donald, meet me at White's in an hour, have a bite of breakfast with me.'

'Glad to.' He feigned a playful punch towards Marcus's nose, but the Duke easily avoided it. 'I've had my time in the ring today or I would take you on. An hour it is.'

Jackson did not spare Marcus and for a good half-hour he was forced to defend himself, though he was not slow in returning punches, which the maestro easily avoided.

'You are out of condition, your Grace,' he said, when the bout finished and a breathless Marcus stood heaving at the side of the ring.

'I know. I have been too much occupied to spend time sparring. I will make amends while I am in Town.'

'Good. You never know when being able to defend yourself will come in useful, not to mention handing out the punishment yourself.'

Marcus left him to wash and dress and a few minutes later, once again the gentleman about town, he climbed into his phaeton and set off for St James's and a good breakfast. As usual the place was crowded with men who had been gaming all night and were in want of sustenance, but Donald was waiting for him, having secured a table.

'There's pork chops on the bill of fare,' he said. 'Or boiled ham or woodcock pie. Which will you have?'

'The pork chops, I think,' he said, seating himself opposite his friend. 'And a large pot of coffee.'

'I believe I am to address you as your Grace nowadays?' Donald said, after they had been served and the waiter had left them.

'No, you clunch! I am Stanmore or Marcus to you as I always was.'

'You do not care for your elevation?'

'I am of the opinion that an aristocratic title and an inheritance often bring more pain than pleasure.'

'Now, I would never have believed it. Why should that be?'

'The responsibility, the putting aside of one's own inclination for the good of the estate and the furtherance of the family name, weigh heavily. I have sometimes envied my brother his freedom...'

'Oh, you mean *noblesse oblige* and all that.'

'And all that,' Marcus said with a wry chuckle. 'I am become used to it now, but there was a time...' He shook himself; memories of his youth had been tumbling over themselves to give him pain ever since he had come to London and met Frances again, and he wanted to change the subject. 'Now, tell me, what do you propose to do with yourself now the war with Bonaparte is ended?'

'I could find another war, but to be honest I am sick of it all and would find some more peaceful occupation. My family were farmers, I might try that. I fancy sheep. The people will always want their mutton and wool, don't you agree?'

Marcus laughed. 'Indeed, though it is hard to imagine the daring Major Greenaway in a shepherd's smock and carrying a crook instead of a rifle. I have heard of your exploits, you know.'

'All puffed up,' Donald said. 'I did no more than my duty. Now, I fancy a little diversion before I settle down. How about joining me for a trip to Newmarket next week?'

'Can't be done, old friend. I am tied up in Town. I came on business and brought my daughter...'

'Is she old enough to come out? How time flies!'

'No, next year, but since Margaret died I have been trying to spend more time with her and decided that she should see a little of what to expect when she comes out.' He paused, wondering whether to tell his friend something of his reason for coming to the capital. 'I find she is taking up so much of my time...'

'You have no time for enjoyment?'

'No, not that. I have so little time for the project which brought me here.' He stopped, wondering whether to go on, but Donald Greenaway had been his friend since they were at Cambridge together and he felt he must confide in someone. 'I am searching for someone...'

'Oh, a defaulter?'

'No, a woman.'

'Oh, I see,' Donald said knowingly. 'A little bit of muslin slipped through your fingers, has she?'

'Nothing like that,' Marcus said sharply. 'If that were the case, I could shrug my shoulders and find someone else with no trouble. Mrs Harriet Poole was the wife of my head groom at Loscoe Court. At least, he was a groom before he decided to join Wellington's army. It behoved me, as a large landowner, to supply some troops from the estate and I made a promise to my men that if any of them volunteered, I would look after their women, though I never ordered anyone to go. It never occurred to me that my groom would be such a buffle-head. He had a good job and I paid him well...'

'Mayhap he had other reasons for going? Men have been known to enlist to escape a nagging wife. This Harriet Poole, what manner of woman is she?'

Marcus shrugged. 'Comely enough. About twenty-five years old. Joseph Poole enlisted in 1811 and was reported killed in 1814, but a few months ago, we heard he had survived as a prisoner of war and was now re-leased and on his way home. The trouble was, Mrs Poole had had a child nearly three years ago and, hearing the news, she disappeared rather than face him with it. You may imagine Joseph Poole's reaction when he came home and heard the unwelcome news.

'He left again swearing vengeance on her and on the man who had fathered the child. I must find her before he does. According to her mother, Mrs Poole went to live with her sister in London, but knowing it would be one of the first places her husband would look for her, she stayed only a few days and now no one knows where she is.'

'Surely your responsibility ended when the man came back?'

'No, it did not. There are other reasons which I cannot go into.'

'Well, it seems to me that, whatever your reasons are, you should leave well alone. The woman brought her troubles on herself. I would not consider any light o' love worth the effort you are putting into this.'

'No, except for the child. I cannot abandon it.' He had made promises before, to Margaret and to Frances, and there had been no possibility of being able to keep both and that had resulted in prolonged misery for at least two people; he could not be sure if Frances had been unhappy beyond those first few weeks. And now he had made another pledge and he would keep it if he had to move heaven and earth.

'Oh.' Donald, still labouring under a misapprehension, smiled. 'In that case, my friend, I am at your service. I have always fancied myself at detection. Tell me what you have discovered already.'

'I had not thought to involve anyone else.'

'You cannot search the whole of London alone. And you may rely on my discretion.'

Marcus hesitated only a moment before smiling and holding out his hand. 'Done, my friend.'

They had been talking quietly, but certainly not whispering, and most of what had been said had been overheard, making the eavesdropper smile with satisfaction. Leaving the club, side by side with Donald, Marcus did not even see him.

'I have my phaeton here,' he told Donald. 'Can I take you anywhere?'

'Yes. First to speak to Mrs Poole's sister and then to those people you have questioned so that I may hear what they have to say for myself, and then to my lodgings, I think.'

'You mean to start straight away?'

'No time like the present and the longer we delay, the colder will grow the trail.'

They climbed into the phaeton and Marcus picked up the ribbons, feeling more cheerful than he had for days, simply because he now had some help and the task seemed infinitely less daunting. 'If you find them, you will have my undying gratitude,' he said, weaving his way in and out of the traffic towards Lincoln's Inn Fields where he knew Mrs Poole's sister resided. 'Nor will you find me ungenerous.'

'Let us find them first.'

They made their calls, questioned Mrs Poole's sister and all the acquaintances that good lady could recall Harriet having in Town, though these were very few. 'She would have to have some way of earning a living,' Donald said when they left. 'She might have had to resort to—'

'No, no, I do not think she would do that,' Marcus put in hurriedly.

'Maundering, then. The constables would know of any beggars on their patch.'

'Which patch?'

'Any or all. You may drop me off on the corner of Covent Garden. I will begin there.'

Marcus did not think the lady would resort to that either, but as he had no other suggestion to offer, he complied and they were soon in the square beside St Paul's. He pulled up to allow Donald to climb down. 'Shall I wait?'

'No, my friend, leave it to me. You go back to your daughter.' He waved a hand and disappeared down a side street.

Marcus sat where he was for a minute, looking with unseeing eyes at the busy market scene before him. Finding one woman in a city the size of London was like looking for a needle in a haystack and he did not hold out much hope of success. But then surely Joseph Poole might be having equal difficulty? And the child? What would become of that child, if anything happened to his mother? It did not bear thinking of.

And he must not forget there was another child to consider. His first-born, who was becoming ever more difficult to manage; he cursed himself for leaving her to be brought up almost exclusively by his wife. She had been thoroughly spoiled, her every wish gratified. He preferred to think it was indolence on Margaret's part rather than vindictiveness, though sometimes he wondered. He was thankful that Duncan, who had been sent off to school at an early age, seemed not to have been affected to quite the same degree.

Now, he had to pick up the pieces and try to mould them all into a family again, and that was further complicated by his unexpected re-acquaintance with Frances, whom he had once loved so fervently he had been prepared to give up his inheritance for her, though she had never known it. How did he feel about her now? He was not at all sure. Seventeen years was a long time to hold to love, however deeply felt, if there is nothing to feed it on.

They had both changed and, as she had pointed out to him in no uncertain terms, she was independent; she did not need him. Sir Percy Ponsonby had more claim on her than he had and he must suppose that sooner or later that fop would pluck up the courage to propose. Would she accept? He realised, with a sudden constriction of his chest, that he would not like that at all.

His reverie was interrupted by the noise of a disturbance and he shook the images of Frances from his mind and looked towards it. He blinked and blinked again and then he was jumping down and running forward, pushing aside everyone who impeded him.

Frances had slept fitfully and at half past ten the next morning, unable to lie abed any longer, had rung for Rose to bring her hot water and a cup of chocolate. Once dressed, she went down to try and eat a light breakfast for which she had no appetite and then set about supervising the work of the servants. Not that supervision was needed, they were already hard at work restoring the house to its usual calm orderliness. She paced about the rooms, directing an operation here and there, but her presence was superfluous and she decided to go up to her studio and work on Lavinia's portrait. Perhaps, in the ordered chaos of a room where she had always felt comfortable, she would be more at peace with herself.

She pulled out her sketches of the girl, set up a canvas and began mixing paint, doing the work methodically as she always did, but there was no fooling herself; she was not comfortable at all. Her insides were churning and her hands shook. If she had not known differently she would have blamed the fact that she had drunk too much wine the night before and was slightly foxed. She had had very little to drink and her present malaise was due entirely to the Duke of Loscoe.

Even now, she could not think of his effrontery without shaking with rage. To suppose that she was waiting for him to take up where he left off seventeen years before and that she cared as little for her good name as he did for his, was the outside of enough. He might dismiss the gabble-grinders as of little importance, but she could not. It had taken ten years of marriage to a worthy, but dull, aristocrat, followed by years of uneventful widowhood to establish her unsullied reputation.

There might not have been any scandal about it if her mother, in anticipation of an offer, had not gone round her bosom bows dropping boastful hints. A young girl's disappointment had become common knowledge when his engagement to Margaret Connaught was announced in the newspapers. There were even those who said it served her right for puffing herself up beyond her station.

Only her innate sense of dignity and stubborn pride enabled her to put her bitter disillusionment behind her, to make the most of her life and become generally known as someone to whom not a breath of scandal could be attached, who could be trusted to teach the daughters of her friends to draw and paint, who always respected a confidence and knew exactly the right amount of deference to give to her subjects. In short, someone who never put a foot wrong. If the coming to London of the Duke of Loscoe changed any of that, she would never forgive him.

But did that also mean she had not forgiven him for what happened seventeen years before? Did it mean she still cared? Had all those years of trying to forget been a waste of time? What was his game? What was he trying to achieve? Her discomfort? He had certainly managed that. But why would he be so vindictive? She had done him no wrong, had been prepared to put the past behind them and deal civilly with him, had agreed to teach his daughter and paint her portrait. That had been a mistake, but if she had refused he would certainly have been confirmed in his belief that she still harboured some feelings for him. And it was not true. It simply was not true!

She looked down at the sketch of Lavinia laughing. The daughter was so like the father, she could not look at it without bringing him to mind. Those laughing eyes were the exact copy of the eyes which had looked so lovingly and happily at her seventeen years ago. She put the sketch down and went over to the stack of pictures against the wall and fetched out the one she had painted after their picnic at Richmond. She took it to the window and rubbed the dust off it with the back of her hand. Here he was as he had been, young and handsome, carefree and open-hearted, his eyes shining with adoration. Looking down at the portrait, her heart was swamped with memories.

They had gone in his curricle, which in itself was a greatly daring and very risky thing to do. But she had been too much in love to hold out against his entreaties and promises that no one would ever know. She had told her mother she was going to visit a friend and her mother had simply smiled knowingly and asked no questions. Frances, who had never lied to her before, had congratulated herself on how well she had done it. It was only afterwards she realised that her mother was fully cognisant of what she was up to and was hoping her daughter would be so compromised that Marcus would have to offer for her. She had even confided in one or two of her friends that she knew where they had gone.

It would have been a triumph to match a young girl with no more background than a distant relationship to a baronet to the heir to one of England's premier duke-doms. Her mother's hopes before that summer had been that, given a Season, she would take well enough for an offer from a baronet or perhaps the younger son of a minor aristocratic family and it was to that end she had borrowed money from her cousin, the baronet, to bring her out.

Instead of that Frances had caught the eye of Marcus Stanmore, Marquis of Risley, who had made a point of being included in any outings she attended and dancing with her at the numerous balls to which her mother managed to obtain invitations. It had been a wonderful Season, with no foreboding, no unease to mar it. She had thrived on his attention, unaware of the gossip, though it was doubtful if she would have taken any notice if she had known about it. He had paid her pretty compliments, sent her flowers and contrived somehow or other to spend a few minutes alone with her whenever they were at the same function. Like everyone else, she had lived in anticipation of an offer. So where was the harm in going on a picnic with him?

It had been a wonderful, wonderful day. The weather had been warm, the sky blue as the blue of her muslin gown, the grass green and luxuriant. The hamper he had ordered to be put in the box had been full of good things to eat and the champagne had tickled her nose and made her laugh. And she had found time to make a sketch of him, telling him to sit still while she did it.

He had stretched out on the grass, his hands behind his head and said, 'That is no hardship if I can sit and look at you. I could do that for hours on end, except...' He had paused and smiled. 'I might feel the need to reach out and touch you, to know you are not a dream, not an angel or some fairy figure that will disappear into the clouds if I blink.'

'Oh, but I am not about to disappear.' She had laughed. 'Solid flesh and blood, that's me.'

'Beautiful flesh and blood. Each drop, each feature, nose, eyes, lips, put together in such perfection my heart is bursting.'

'Gammon!' She had been at bursting point herself, bursting with happiness that this handsome, desirable man loved her.

He had remained still only long enough for her to sketch in the outline of his face and form before reaching forward and grabbing the sketchbook from her, to fling it beside them on the grass. Then he had taken her into his arms to kiss her. He had attempted to kiss her once or twice before, but they had always been inter-

rupted or in too public a place and it had been no more
than a brushing of his lips on her cheek or against her
hair and that had been enough to set her limbs in a
quiver and turn her insides to liquid fire. She had been
too young and innocent to understand what it was all
about, but she knew she ought to protest. Her protests
had been feeble and easily silenced. 'I love you,' he had
said. 'How else am I to show you?'

But when he had taken her in his arms on that picnic,
she was aware of some new dimension. He did not con-
fine his lips to her cheek or her hair, he demanded her
mouth. And she had given it gladly, allowing the kiss
to go on and on, while his hands roamed over her back
and crept forward to her breasts. She could feel the heat
of his fingers through the thin muslin of her gown and
her own heightened response, could feel his thighs
against hers as he lay alongside her.

To her eternal shame, she had done nothing to stop
him, had even wriggled herself closer to him and put
her hands about his neck. The love they bore each other
carried them forward into transports of recklessness. He
began undoing the little buttons on her bodice and slid-
ing his hand inside to cup her breasts and run the ball
of his thumb over her nipples. She held her breath, un-
sure of what was to happen next and a tiny feeling of
apprehension found its way to that part of her mind
which was still functioning.

She had pulled away, suddenly fearful and embarrassed. 'No,' she said, sitting up and hurriedly trying to
fasten the buttons again. 'I am sure we should not be
doing this. It is wrong.'

'Wrong? How can it be wrong? We love each other
as much as two people can love, have we not already

agreed to that? Have I not told you over and over that I cannot live without you?'

'Yes.'

'And you love me too?'

'Oh, yes.'

'Then what is troubling you?'

She did not know exactly. 'I have been thinking. I know that it is not considered correct for two people such as we are to be alone together and the reason has now become clear to me.'

'Oh, and what is that?'

'It is to keep us from temptation, that we may not be pitched by our emotions into indiscretion. Such intimacies should be postponed until after the wedding.'

He had smiled and reached for her hand, speaking earnestly. 'Nothing would please me more than there should be a wedding very soon, my love, but there are difficulties to be overcome...'

'Difficulties?' she had queried, a little frisson of alarm coursing through her. 'You mean your parents do not consider me suitable?'

'They know nothing of you, so how can they consider you at all? I have yet to tell them.'

'But you will tell them?'

'Of course I will. As soon as they come to London in two weeks' time.'

'Two weeks is not so very long to wait,' she had said.

'It is an eternity.'

'For me too.' She had leaned over to kiss his cheek, intending to soften the blow of her rejection, but he had pulled her to him again, renewing his kisses.

'Dear sweet Fanny...'

'No, you must not. Marcus, please.' She pushed him

away and reached for her bonnet which lay discarded on the grass. 'You frighten me.'

'Frighten you? Oh, my darling, that is the last thing I would wish for and I am truly, truly sorry. I do not know what came over me.'

'Don't you?' Safely back on her feet and far enough away not to be seized again, she had recovered a little of her lost composure and was inclined to tease, for he had been a very serious young man. Or so she had thought.

He had laughed and snatched at her hand to put it to his lips. 'Oh, I do. Love is what came over me. And love can be very demanding, but you know I would never do anything to upset or hurt you.'

'I know.' Never on that day had she considered him anything but sincere. Nor, young as she had been, did she realise that he, too, was very young and, though perhaps not as inexperienced as she was, was certainly out of his depth.

Two weeks later he had broken her heart.

She looked up from the picture to the view of the garden from the window and was surprised to find she could not see it. She was blinded by tears. She had not even realised she was crying. The mature woman of the world, the poised Society hostess, the portraitist whose reputation was one of cool competence, was weeping as if she were still seventeen and had only then learned of the perfidy of man. One man.

Impatiently she replaced the picture, scrubbed at her eyes with a handkerchief taken from the pocket of her petticoat and stood looking about her. Her easel and canvas, the paints and the sketch of Lady Lavinia, were still where she had left them, almost accusing her of gross self-indulgence. Determined to return to work, she sat down before the easel and picked up a brush. But it was impossible. She could not concentrate, not on this particular subject. She snatched up a new sketchbook and crayons and left the room.

Stopping only to slip on a pelisse and bonnet, she left the house and walked with determined step towards Covent Garden. Here was noise and bustle. Women porters were scurrying about, with tiers of baskets upon their heads, men were calling their wares or guiding huge draught horses pulling loaded wagons and hundreds of children ran among them, shouting and squabbling, some of them hardly old enough to toddle. None seemed to have shoes nor seemed to notice the want of them. Their clothes were little more than rags. Occasionally a carriage passed from which the occupants looked out on the scene with distaste.

Frances perched herself on the end of a cart which, judging by the smell, had once contained chickens, and began drawing, her charcoal crayon moving swiftly over the paper, a line here, a curve there, capturing the moment as it was. She made no concessions to nicety; she did not put shoes on the feet of the urchins or smiles on the faces of the men, nor beauty on the countenances of the women. She did not make them look clean and wholesome, for the truth was that they were indescribably filthy.

'Here, what you doin'?' one man demanded, coming to look over her shoulder. His tone was belligerent, but she turned with a disarming smile, which she had always found to serve her best, and held out the picture without speaking.

'My, but that's me missus to a T,' he said, apparently pleased. 'And that's my Daisy and old Rob's boy, Henry. And is that me?'

'Yes. Do you not recognise yourself?'

'But what you want to make a picture of us for?'

'Because I find you interesting. If I could prevail upon you to continue with what you were doing, I could finish it.'

'I don't know about that. I reckon you ain't up to no good. Taking the likeness to the Runners, I shouldn't wonder.'

'No, why should I do that?'

'Get us off the street. Not that we ha' done anything wrong. A man has to mek a livin' where 'e can.'

'Yes, that is what I must do too. I paint for a living.'

The man stopped staring at the picture and turned towards her, openly appraising her. 'And a fine living it must be by the looks of you, lady, and all on account of poor folks like us.'

She had taken the precaution of bringing a purse with her and now she opened it and extracted a guinea. 'Here, sir, this is yours if you will be so kind as to allow me to continue…'

He grabbed it and shouted to his wife and daughter to come and look and they crowded round Frances, overwhelming her with the unwashed smell of them and she was tempted to tell them to buy soap with some of the money. In moments she had attracted an even bigger crowd and became aware that there was some dispute going on between the first man and another.

The second man, in a greasy leather jerkin and trousers stiff with grime, pushed his way towards her. 'What d'you mean by giving that hog grubber a yellow boy?'

'I only wished to recompense him for his trouble. If he lost business because he was posing for me…'

'Business! He ain't got no business 'ere. Got no licence to trade, yer see. Now, if you was to tell the watchmen about him, you'd oblige yours truly, that you would. He'd see 'im in chokey.'

'And have me wife starve!' the first man shouted. 'I ain't done you no 'arm.'

'Takin' the bread out of me nippers' mouths, that's what you a-doin'. Chickens at sixpence apiece and ten cabbages for tuppence ain't fair tradin'.'

Frances felt the situation slipping from her and stood up to leave, but she was not going to be allowed to escape so easily. They crowded round her, demanding that she draw them all and give them all guineas in payment. She opened her purse, which was knocked from her hand and its contents spilled on the greasy cobbles. They fell upon the coins, pushing her to one side to get at them.

She was suddenly aware of a different commotion and saw a tall figure in a beaver hat push his way through the crowd as if they were so many puppets and not big strong men with volatile tempers. They fell back before him, leaving a path clear by which he strode towards her. 'Fanny, are you hurt?'

She was so unaccountably relieved to see him that she hardly noticed his use of her given name, though she could not be certain of his mood. His dark eyes were certainly sombre, but that might be to intimidate the people who crowded round her. 'No, your Grace.'

He grabbed her arm and propelled her forward, pushing his way back through the crowd who were looking decidedly hostile. He flung them another handful of coins and, in the ensuing scramble, extricated them both. 'What on earth did you think you were at?' he demanded angrily.

She could see his phaeton standing on the corner and supposed it was from the high seat of that he had been able to see over the heads of the crowd and perceive the coil she was in. She ought to be grateful for her deliverance, but the anger in his voice generated anger in her own. 'Drawing them.'

'Are you run mad? They could have trampled you underfoot and not even felt it.'

'I was in no danger. I have done it before and your interference will not have stood me in good stead for their good offices in the future.'

'In the future,' he repeated through gritted teeth, 'there will be no future outings of this nature.'

She stopped in her tracks and turned towards him, eyes blazing. 'I am not your wife, nor yet your daughter or servant, that you may give me orders, my lord.'

'No, but while you have any hand in the instruction of my daughter, you will take instruction from me as to your conduct.'

'My conduct!' She was almost beside herself with fury. 'And I suppose you think your own conduct so blameless that it gives you the right to dictate. But let me tell you, I have been too long independent to welcome orders from anyone, least of all you. Look to your own conduct.'

They had arrived at the phaeton and he put his hands about her waist to help her up, giving no indication that her barb had gone home. She shrugged him off. 'Let go of me, sir! I will not be handled in so familiar a fashion. I will take a cab or a chair.'

He looked around and stepped aside. 'Then do so, Countess.'

She had taken two steps from him when she realised that not only was there no such thing as a cab or a chair in that part of the city, but she had no money to hire one if there were. Her purse lay on the cobbles some distance away and she was not inclined to go and retrieve it. Besides, it was empty. She turned, retraced her steps and climbed onto the seat unaided. Without speaking, he jumped up beside her and picked up the reins.

They were silent for some minutes. The steady clop of the two perfectly matched greys was a muted accompaniment to treacherous thoughts on both sides. She was furious at his assumption that she needed rescuing and that he had only to say the word and she would never go again. His agitation derived not from anger that she was making a spectacle of herself, but from fear for her safety.

When he had glimpsed her in that evil throng, he had imagined himself too late to save her, that before he could descend from his carriage and reach her she would be dead or so badly injured that recovery would be impossible. The thought of his lovely Fanny being injured, mutilated, even dead, had stopped his heart and when, seeing her alive and well had set it beating again, he had nothing to say but harsh words. His anger covered more than his relief, it disguised his true feelings. And even as they sat side by side on the high seat of the phaeton, his wrath was still in the ascendancy.

'Countess, I must insist you do not repeat this indiscretion,' he said, trying to soften his voice. 'If I had not come along…'

'If you had not come along, I should have walked home in perfect comfort, your Grace,' she said, not thinking to question why he should be in that particular district. 'I have been among the poor on many occasions and made drawings of them. They are perfectly amenable when I pay them. It is a way of earning money not previously open to them.'

'It is too dangerous and unseemly. You will earn the reputation of being eccentric.'

She laughed. 'I am no more bothered by that than you are about the tattlers who will have you married to Miss Willoughby.'

For a moment he forgot their quarrel. 'Good God! Is that what they are saying?'

'Well, either Felicity Willoughby or Constance Graham,' she said, glad of the distraction. 'I have heard there are wagers being taken on the outcome.'

'You do not say. And who is favourite?'

'I believe it is Felicity by a whisker, simply because you went to Lady Willoughby's tea party and you have not yet been seen in Lady Graham's drawing room.'

'Then I had better remedy the situation as soon as maybe. I think I will give them a run for their money.'

'I wish you would not—the poor girls are hardly out of the schoolroom and do not understand the ways of gentlemen such as yourself. They will take seriously something you only intend as a hum. And that would be cruel in you.'

Her inference was not lost on him; she still bore a grudge. 'I should have thought that with the onset of maturity and proper reflection, you would have come to look on me in a less pugnacious light, my lady. Have you, in seventeen years, not grown up at all?'

'I do not know about me, my lord, but it seems to me you certainly have not.'

He sighed heavily. 'How are we to deal together, if you cannot converse in anything but rage, I cannot conceive.'

'We do not need to deal together at all. It will be simple enough for you to find someone else to teach your daughter.'

'And have the tabbies speculate on why the arrangement came to such an abrupt end? I think not, my dear.'

'I am not your dear anything.'

'No, of course not, my lady. I apologise for what was only a friendly form of address, but if you find it offensive, then I will not repeat my mistake.'

'Good.'

They were drawing up at Corringham House and she hardly waited for the enormous wheels to stop turning before scrambling down and making for the door.

'Tomorrow at two,' he called after her. 'I shall be punctual.'

The footman who had been watching out for her opened the door. She brushed past him and started up the stairs, too upset and confused to speak. She stopped when she reached her bedroom and looked about her. The room was beautifully furnished, its carpet and the matching curtains on the two large windows in pale blue, the bedspread and tablecloth a subtle rose pink. Her maid had been in since she left it, for there was not a thing out of place. The orderliness of the room contrasted oddly with the tumult inside her. What a mull she had landed herself in!

She looked down at her bedraggled gown and was surprised to discover she was still holding the sketch she had done. It calmed her more than anything else could have done. It conveyed very simply the poverty of those poor people's lives, their struggle to scratch a living and she wished she could do more for them. But perhaps she was being impossibly condescending; from the height of the luxury she enjoyed, how could she understand their problems? She ought to concentrate on helping the war orphans and not indulge herself with misery on her own behalf. She had nothing to be miserable about.

She heard the front door knocker and, going to look over the banister, perceived Creeley admitting Mrs Butterworth, Lady Graham and Mrs Harcourt. Smiling, she made her way down to greet them.

A light nuncheon was served and they spent the afternoon on a post mortem of the previous evening's entertainment, counting the money and discussing the prospects of finding a house suitable for a new home for the children. Their requirements were so particular that finding such a property at the price they had fixed on was turning out to be more difficult than they had imagined.

'We need more events like last night's,' Mrs Butterworth said, 'particularly if we can persuade patrons like the Duke of Loscoe to stand buff for the outlay.'

'Yes, a very generous man,' Mrs Harcourt said, 'though I can but wonder at his interest in other people's children, when by all accounts he has never taken notice of his own.'

'How can you say that?' Lady Graham put in. 'He has brought his daughter to London, you met her at Lady Willoughby's only last week, and he was most particular towards her.'

'So he may be, when it is too late. I have been at Loscoe Court at the Duchess's invitation and she intimated that his Grace hardly saw his children and would not recognise them as his if he met them in the street…'

'Well, I find it difficult to believe he would not know them,' Lady Graham said, quite missing the point. 'They all have that widow's peak on their foreheads and brows that always seem to convey a look of astonishment.'

'Astonishment?'

'Yes, you know what I mean, sharply raised and very clean cut.'

'So what is that to the point?'

'Why, that he must know his own children.' She laughed suddenly. 'It is to be hoped he has not strayed, for any child of his would be instantly recognised.'

'Ladies,' Frances said, wanting more than anything to change the subject. All this talk of the Duke was not helping her nerves at all. 'I think we should not be speaking of his Grace in those terms, not when he has been so very generous.'

'Quite right,' Mrs Butterworth put in. 'I have always found him most attentive and polite. I cannot believe he is anything but a doting papa.' She turned to Frances and added to her discomfort by appealing to her. 'Don't you think so, Countess? You have seen him more often than any of us. He brings his daughter to you to be taught to draw, does he not?'

'Yes,' she said guardedly, remembering Percy's report that the gossips said he used his daughter to visit her. The last thing she wanted to do was to feed the flames of that particular *on dit*. 'He brings her, but he does not stay throughout the lesson. He comes to fetch her when it is finished.'

'And how does he seem to you?'

How could she answer? She could say he was a monster, who still held her in thrall even when she professed to hate him. She could say he was conceited and arrogant and expected everyone to bow to his bidding simply because he was blessed with a title. She could say he was a gallant gentleman who was prepared to risk life and limb to save her from making a cake of herself. She smiled. 'He is a considerate father, though doting is hardly the word I would have used. At any rate he means to prepare Lady Lavinia for her come-out as well as he is able.'

'Oh, you would defend him, my lady.' Mrs Harcourt said. 'You have reason to.'

It was as much as Frances could do to remain civil. 'I am sure I do not understand you,' she said coldly.

The silly woman looked about her and, finding no support from the other stony-faced ladies, gave a trill of a laugh. 'Why, I meant only that he must pay you for teaching his daughter...'

'So he does, and if you were to look at the charity accounts, which is one of the reasons we have met here this afternoon, you will realise those payments go directly to our funds, which make us doubly indebted to the Duke.'

She hated herself for her defence of the man, but her inbred honesty forbade her to do anything else, and if it meant an end to that particular rumour, so much the better. She wished she knew why Mrs Harcourt seemed so antagonistic towards her; she had never, to her knowledge, done or said anything which could have upset her. It did nothing to soothe her troubled mind.

'Oh, you have not upset her,' Percy told her the next morning when they were riding. 'But she was a particular confidante of the Duchess of Loscoe and she sees any slight to the duchess as a slight to herself.'

'But I never met the Duchess in my life.'

'No, but I have no doubt she felt wronged by you.'

'Why, for goodness sake? If anything it was the other way about, though I have long recovered from it.'

He reined in a little to turn and look at her. 'Are you sure?'

'Most decidedly. I wish I could convince you.'

He smiled and moved on. 'Oh, it is not me that needs convincing, my dear.'

'Who, then?' And when he did not answer, 'You mean those abominable tattlers?'

'Those too.'

'Percy, you are speaking in riddles.'

'I do not think so. If it were only the brewers of scandal-broth, I would have a solution.'

'Oh, and what is that?'

'Why, to marry me,' he said offhandedly. 'That would silence them, would it not?'

She looked up at him in surprise. He was looking straight ahead, his chin tucked into the high points if his collar. 'Percy, I am persuaded you are roasting me.'

'Why, of course I am.' He gave a short chuckle. 'I had to make you smile somehow, didn't I? Your mood is far too sombre for such a lovely day.' And with that he spurred his horse into a canter, so that she had perforce to follow.

But was he joking? As a jest it was not at all funny. But he would never consider marriage, not even to her, and certainly not to fetch her out of a bumblebath which was none of his making. But she ought to have at least pretended to take him seriously. Making fun of him must surely have dented his self-confidence. Her usual tact seemed to have deserted her since the Duke of Loscoe came to town. Drat him!

Chapter Five

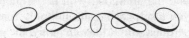

By the time the Duke's barouche, bearing his Grace and Lady Lavinia, rolled up to her door at exactly two o'clock that afternoon, Frances had talked herself into a more sensible frame of mind. She waited in the drawing room, wearing a day gown of pearl grey jaconet, with a high neck and long sleeves buttoned at the wrist, its only decoration a deep flounce at the hem. It was, of course, superbly cut, but for all that, very plain and almost matronly. Her matching pelisse and bonnet of straw ruched with lilac silk were both becomingly simple. It was the image she intended to convey.

'His Grace, the Duke of Loscoe,' Creeley announced in ringing tones, and almost before the last word was out, the Duke was in the room, had swept off his high-crowned hat and was executing an exaggerated leg, which made her want to laugh, but his formality set the tone, and so she rose to make a deep curtsy.

'Your Grace.'

'My lady, your obedient.' He was, she noted as he handed her up, the picture of elegance. His superbly tailored green superfine coat, which could only have been crafted by Weston, his aquamarine waistcoat, cambric shirt, close-fitting white pantaloons and tasselled hessians, proclaimed him the very top-of-the-trees man about town, even without his mathematically tied cravat. He was awesome.

'Where is Lady Lavinia?' she enquired, wondering if he had left his daughter at home, for she had not followed him into the room. The thought that he might want to spend the afternoon with her without a chaperon, made her catch her breath, but only for a moment before she dismissed the idea as ludicrous and was securely in control again.

'She remained in the carriage. I saw no point in bringing her in, when we are to set off again immediately.'

'No, you are right. Let us go, then.'

With a straight back and her head held up, she led the way out to the carriage. It had been finished in dark green with the Loscoe arms emblazoned on each door. The horses were perfectly matched and shining with good health. Seeing his passengers approaching, the coachman left their heads to open the door and let down the step.

'I took the liberty of asking Mr Turner to be our guide,' Marcus said, putting his hand under her elbow to help her up the step. 'We are to meet him at the Academy. I hope you approve.'

Joseph Turner! She could hardly believe the great man would deign to act as a guide, but then, if you are the Duke of Loscoe, all things are possible. 'Naturally, I approve. It will be a singular honour and I am sure Lavinia will benefit from his wisdom,' she said, settling herself beside her pupil. 'It was very thoughtful of you to think of it.'

He took the facing seat, aware that his knees were

almost touching hers, and though she tried to hitch herself back, there was no room to do so. She was very cool, he noted, almost frosty, as if any kind of intimacy with him was repugnant. Well, icicles could be thawed with a little warmth, though why he felt he had to melt this one he could not say.

He smiled at her as the carriage moved off, and though her lips curved a little in response, it was not exactly a smile and it certainly did not reach her eyes, which remained wary, as if she were a small wild creature suspicious of the hand of friendship. She had no reason to be suspicious of him, he thought, he meant her no harm, never had done. He had once truly loved her and, though that could not signify now, it must surely have meant something to her at the time. Had she still not forgiven him? And if she had not, why had she accepted his commission? Was it for money? She had admitted she needed it. Or was there something else, the wish to revenge herself, to make him squirm? If that were so, she would soon learn her mistake; he was not the squirming kind.

The journey took no more than a few minutes and they were soon standing together on the footpath outside the Academy. Marcus bade the coachman return in two hours before escorting the ladies into the gallery, where Mr Turner came forward to meet them.

He was an elderly gentleman, not very big, with a swarthy complexion and piercing dark eyes. He was dressed in a black tailcoat which looked too big for him and old-fashioned black breeches. His fingers were paint-stained, as if he had only recently been at work on one of his masterpieces. 'Have you anything particular you wish to see, your Grace?' he asked, after Marcus had introduced his companions.

'No, we are in your hands.'

Under his tutelage, they moved from room to room, studying portraits, landscapes and examples of still life executed by artists from Holland, Belgium and Italy. He extolled the virtues of each, explaining how and why they came to be painted and why they had found a place on the walls of the Academy. His comments were pithy and Frances listened in fascination to all he had to say.

When they moved on, he paused before one of a pair of hers, which had been so fortunate as to be hung on a wall in one of the upper rooms.

'Now this one is called *Autumn*,' he said, pointing at one of them. 'You will note the splendid colouring of the leaves, russet and yellow and gold, all hues to be found at that time of year; one can almost feel and smell the decay in the air and on the ground where the dead leaves have fallen among the toadstools. And see the clever way the wind is depicted, how the branches of the trees strain against it and how the swirl of the clouds presages a storm.'

'And the artist?' Marcus asked, though he was fairly sure he knew. The brushstrokes were so very much her own.

'It is one of Frances Corringham's,' he said, peering short-sightedly at her signature. 'Some say the better of the two, though many prefer this one.' And he pointed to *Winter*. 'It is the same scene, you will note, but now we are in the depths of winter. There is snow upon the ground and one's eye is drawn to the footsteps of an animal…'

'A fox's,' Frances said, realising, with some amusement, that he had not been listening when Marcus introduced her and had no idea who she was.

'Quite,' he agreed. 'A fox has been through the wood

and his trail leads off into the distance. The perspective and attention to detail are truly remarkable. The trees are bare and you can almost see the individual crystals in the frost on the branches. Now there is no wind, all is still and silent.'

'How do you know it is silent?' Lavinia demanded suddenly. 'The fox could easily be howling somewhere.'

Their guide did not like having his flow interrupted and gave her a withering look. 'The painting itself is all silence.'

'Naturally it is,' she said with a laugh. 'Paint and canvas cannot utter a sound.'

'Lavinia!' her father muttered. 'You are being disrespectful.'

'You do not think a picture can speak?' Frances asked her.

'No, such a thing is absurd.'

'One must feel it, here,' their guide said, putting his hand to his chest. 'The heart of the artist is in the paint and it is the heart that speaks.'

'And what does this say to you?' Marcus asked, with a smile. He could have been humouring their guide, but Frances felt he was more likely trying to tease her into saying something about the picture herself. But as Mr Turner was saying enough for both of them, she remained silent.

'It speaks of cold and death, but also of renewal. There is beauty even in death and a promise of new life in the tiny snowdrops you see blooming under the trees. The week before they were not there, the week after they will be gone along with the snow and then spring in all its glory will colour the landscape. So it is with all our lives.'

'Did I mean to say all that?' Frances whispered to Marcus and watched his lips twitch.

'Apparently you did,' he murmured. Aloud he asked, 'Is there one of spring?'

The picture of winter was indeed cold, he mused, cold as she was. All the time they had been slowly moving from room to room, painting to painting, she had hardly spoken, certainly had not smiled. He longed for spring, its rebirth, the burgeoning of new life, new beginnings. My God! he thought, was that really what he wanted?

'Alas, no,' Mr Turner answered him. 'Perhaps the artist is engaged on it now.'

'Pity. I should have liked to see it.'

'Let us move on,' Frances said, more embarrassed than ever. 'Let us see what other exhibits have to tell us.'

'Very well,' their guide said, leading the way to another series of rooms. 'Let us consider the English masters.'

They stopped to admire the works of Romney, Lawrence and Constable, pictures of horses by George Stubbs which managed to engage Lavinia's attention for a short time, portraits by Sir Joshua Reynolds, Francis Coates and Gainsborough and the street scenes of William Hogarth, whose striking images were more like caricatures than representative of real people. But the message they conveyed was self-evident.

'Ugh! How horrible!' was Lavinia's comment on coming before one which depicted a mother, drunk on gin, dropping her baby on its head. 'Poor child!'

'Ah, then you will admit that the picture speaks to you?' Frances queried with a smile.

Marcus laughed. 'Her ladyship has you there, Vinny,' he said.

'No, I did not admit to it speaking, only that it makes me think. Either the artist was a man with a very strange imagination or such things really happened. But if they did, why paint them? Are pictures not meant to be for the enjoyment, not the disgust, of the beholder?'

'Not necessarily enjoyment, Lady Lavinia,' Frances answered. 'They can also be used for education and enlightenment. One picture is worth a thousand words.'

'Oh, to be sure, I have already deduced that much,' she said. 'Why else am I brought here?'

'And what have you learned?'

'I have learned to question,' she said.

'Good,' Frances said. 'That is all I ask.'

'Then let us repair to Grillon's for tea,' Marcus put in. 'We have been here above two hours and my head is spinning.'

And so they returned to the carriage which took them to the hotel in Albemarle Street, where Marcus ordered tea with honey and almond cakes.

Frances was surprised how pleasant an interlude it was. Though Lavinia had little to say, her father made up for it with a joviality he had not exhibited before. He was polite and amusing and several times had Frances laughing with some tale of the *haut monde* or the story of a farrago at Risley, involving the local inhabitants. He was an unexpectedly good mimic and could take off most of the well-known characters of the *ton* with tolerable ease and his command of the Derbyshire dialect was remarkable.

He was, she realised with a jerk on her heartstrings, more like the Marcus she had known and loved seventeen years before than the stiff-necked aristocrat who had rescued her from the ruffians in the market and who thought he could hand out orders and would be instantly obeyed.

Tea over, they returned to the carriage and were driven to Corringham House, where he bade her good-bye on the step, explaining when she invited him in for further refreshment that he had an evening engagement and must reluctantly return home to change before going out again. She said she quite understood and thanked him civilly for his escort, before confirming that she would expect Lady Lavinia for her next lesson two days hence.

She watched him climb back into the carriage and shut the door before turning slowly and entering the house. What a puzzle he was turning out to be! From being a sombre and bad-tempered man, throwing his orders out and bullying his daughter, he had, in the space of a few hours, turned into a model of everything a gentleman escort ought to be. After she had determined to treat him with cool disdain, he had quite spiked her guns.

But it would make teaching Lavinia easier, she decided, as she went up to her room to change, ready for a visit to the theatre. She was going to the theatre with Percy and she was looking forward to it. With Percy she could be at ease, did not have to watch every word she uttered lest it be misinterpreted. True, he did not make her limbs ache with longing, but he could make her laugh. She was reminded of his proposal. Was that meant to be a jest? Or did he really expect her to give it some serious thought and give him an answer?

She wondered if Marcus might also be at the theatre, but when she was settled in her seat and had time to look around her before the curtain went up, she decided he was not one of the audience and chided herself for continuing to think he must, of necessity, be everywhere she went. The play, a musical satire set in the time of the Regent's grandfather, was perhaps not to his taste and his engagement was probably at his club or some gambling hell, though she had never thought of him as a gambler. But then, did she know him at all? Did she know the real man, the one who dwelt beneath the façade he showed to the world?

One short summer, when you are seventeen and in love, did not constitute a basis for good judgement of a man's true character. Why, she had been married to the Earl of Corringham for ten years and she knew very little more of him at the end of that time than she had at the beginning. Oh, she knew his preferences for food and that he liked orderliness, but not much more. A man used to keeping himself close could hide his real nature very easily. She shook herself as the orchestra began the overture and the curtain was raised.

Concentrate on the performance, she told herself sternly, and took her own advice. Percy was an amenable escort and he did not mention his proposal again and she hoped he had forgotten ever making it. At the end of the evening he escorted her home and bade her goodnight on the doorstep, urbane as ever.

She was surprised the following afternoon, on returning home after a visit to the orphanage, to receive a letter from the secretary of the Royal Academy telling her that both her pictures had been bought and that the anonymous buyer, who had paid what was asked without a quibble, desired her to paint *Spring* and *Summer*.

'He is in no great hurry,' the letter concluded. 'You may do it at your convenience.'

At any other time she would have been gratified by the commission, but when was she ever going to find time to do it? The orphanage, her commitment to Lady Lavinia and her classes took up almost every spare moment. She would have written to turn down the offer but for that last sentence and the fact that the new orphanage was going to cost a great deal more than had originally been budgeted for. Since the war, everything had gone up in price, including bread, which was the staple diet of the children in their care. She would find time for it, *after* she had completed the portrait of Lady Lavinia Stanmore.

By the time the Duke brought Lavinia for her next lesson, the portrait was beginning to take shape and, while Lavinia did an exercise she had set her, Frances continued with it, but it was not easy, for the laughter which had occasioned the first sketch was more often absent than present and trying to paint what was not there was very difficult.

'Lavinia, do smile,' she said. 'Why are you so Friday-faced?'

'Oh, Papa is the outside of enough. I only wanted to be taken to the park in the phaeton, but he said he did not have the time; he was up in the boughs about it, as if I had asked for something quite out of the way. I cannot think what it is that engages him so much. He is never at home, except to convey me here and leave me.'

'He did say he had business to conduct,' Frances said mildly. 'And it is to be supposed that is important.'

'I do not believe it is. Mr Chapman, his man of business, called the other day when he was out and I received him…'

'Should you have done that? Surely the butler could have told him the Duke was from home?'

'So he could, but Papa had said just before he went out that he was going to visit his man of business and that was obviously a whisker and I was curious.'

'Surely Mr Chapman did not reveal your father's business to you?'

'No, of course not, but he confirmed that he had not seen Papa in a se'nnight and had been waiting on him. Papa is up to something havey-cavey, I am certain of it. Either that or he is seeing a lady, though if he is, he spends an unconscionable time with her. I have heard him come home at breakfast time on more than one occasion.'

'Lavinia, I am quite sure you should not be telling me this.'

'But who am I to tell? I see no one else but servants and they are as close as wax…'

'Lavinia! I beg you say no more. I do not want to know.'

'Are you not also curious?'

'Not at all,' she said firmly. She did not want to hear about Marcus's nocturnal adventures, certainly not from the lips of his daughter. 'Now, tell me what you thought of the Royal Academy.'

'I thought there was little to admire.'

'How can you say so? They are the best works of art to be collected together for public scrutiny.'

'Those at Loscoe Court are better.'

'Very likely. I own there are private collections that are its equal, but they are not open to the public.'

'Grandpapa was an avid collector and Papa has added to it, though I do not think he has any of yours.'

'That does not surprise me. I am not of the first water.' She would have been astonished if the late Duchess would have allowed any of her work to be hung at Loscoe Court, even if they were considered to be good enough to hang beside the Great Masters, which she was sure they were not.

'You have seen the collection?'

'No, sadly I have not.'

'Would you like to?'

Lavinia had somehow twisted the conversation so that she was the one doing the quizzing and Frances was beginning to feel uncomfortable. 'One day, perhaps.'

'You know, my lady, I was wrong about you. You are not all you seem.'

'Do you say so?'

'Yes. I don't know what it is, but you are not my idea of a Society lady. You are so down to earth, unafraid to depict unpleasantness. I was looking at those sketches you did of those poor children. Do they really live that?'

'Yes, they do, some far worse.'

'I never knew that. I never knew such conditions existed…'

'No reason why you should have. They are usually hidden away in stews and alleys where respectable people never go. They do not want to know about them, it pricks their consciences…'

'But you think their consciences should be pricked.'

'Yes, I do.'

'Like Hogarth did?'

'In a way, yes.'

'Then why do you not have an exhibition? You could ask Papa to sponsor it…'

'Oh, I do not think so, Lavinia. The Duke has a great many other calls on his purse and he has already been very generous to the orphanage.'

'But he admires your work, I know he does, or he would not ask you to paint me.'

'And he expects results, Lavinia, so shall we go on with our work?'

Lavinia fell silent, but the scowl had returned to her face and after a few minutes, she began to fidget. 'Lavinia,' Frances said in exasperation, 'do sit still. I cannot paint you if you are continually moving about.'

'I cannot sit still. I have had no exercise today at all—not even a ride, if you can call it riding when one is obliged to *walk* one's horse like some new mounted toddler. He would not take me out in the phaeton and there was no one to accompany me on a walk, not that there is anywhere interesting to go to even if there were.'

'Oh, dear, you are in the dismals.'

'Well, wouldn't you be, in my shoes? Papa promised me when we came to London he would take me out and about and all he has done is bring me here and take me to the Royal Academy, and he would not have done that if you had not suggested it.'

'You had tea with Lady Willoughby.'

'So I did—how could I have forgot such a *diverting* afternoon?' she said with heavy sarcasm. 'Oh, I am bored beyond redemption.'

'Put on your pelisse and bonnet,' Frances said, suddenly making up her mind. 'We will ride in the park in my tilbury.'

She did not pause to ask herself what the Duke might

say to that or she might have reconsidered; she was simply thinking of Lavinia and how she would treat her if she were her own daughter. It was the work of a few minutes to order up the carriage, pack up the paints and don outdoor clothes and only a few minutes more had passed before they were bowling along Brook Street towards Brook Gate where they turned into the park and joined the parade.

Here were carriages of every description, from stately barouches, old-fashioned landaulets, curricles, tilburys, gigs, park phaetons and those of the high-perch variety such as the Duke of Loscoe owned, all being driven in stately convoy. Frances joined them and the horses were soon neatly trotting along the carriageway. They pulled up every now and again to speak to acquaintances of the Countess, passing the time of day and comparing notes about the various entertainments they meant to attend and who had invited whom to what.

In the course of this, Frances presented Lavinia to a great many people who had not yet met her. As soon as the ladies discovered who she was, they preened themselves like peacocks and asked her to convey their respects to the Duke, promising to send him invitations to this, that and the other.

'Toadeaters, all of them,' Lavinia said, when they reached the end of the carriageway and were turning round to go back. 'As if Papa would be the least interested in their little entertainments.'

'How can you tell? Besides, some of them are very influential, especially Lady Jersey,' Frances explained after they had parted and were proceeding on their way again. 'If she is seen to stop and speak to you, then you are in favour, and more invitations are like to come your way.'

'You are gammoning me.'

'Not at all. Her ladyship is one of the committee of ladies who hold sway over the weekly balls held at Almack's Assembly Rooms. A voucher for one of those is almost as much prized as an invitation to one of the Queen's drawing rooms. Next year, when you have your come-out, you will undoubtedly receive one.'

'And if she decides she does not like you?'

'Then beware, for you are about to be ostracised by all.'

Lavinia laughed. 'Then you must hold yourself in readiness for a veritable barrage of invitations, my lady, for everyone stopped for you. Except that strange woman in the huge black bonnet; you could hardly see her face.'

'I think it may have been the bonnet at fault,' Frances said mildly. 'For how she can see anything not immediately in front of her I cannot imagine.'

'Do you know her?'

'Yes, I am acquainted with her. Her name is Mrs Harcourt.'

'Goodness, I did not recognise her. She was always coming to Loscoe Court and she and Mama would sit together in Mama's day room and coze away for hours. I think she thought Papa might ask her to take Mama's place after she died. She came to stay after the funeral and began toadying up to him, telling him that she understood just how he felt and she would help him to get over his loss by having everything in the house exactly as he liked it. He was very rude to her. He told her if she truly was sincere in wanting to make everything as he liked it, she would take herself off and leave him alone.'

'Oh, dear.'

'She climbed on to her high ropes and said he was ungrateful and a great many other things I did not understand. He simply agreed with everything she said in the politest fashion and then had Clayton, the butler, show her the door.'

'Lavinia, I am quite sure you should not be telling me this.'

'Then who am I to tell?'

'Why, no one. People twist things, you know, they make a Canterbury tale from the smallest thing and puff it up until it becomes a prodigious scandal.'

'Would you do that?'

'No, of course I would not, but others might.' The girl was making her feel uneasy again and something had to be done to bring the confidences to an end. She pulled the horses to a stop. 'I collect you have often driven your papa's curricle in the country.'

'Yes. I am considered a nonpareil with the ribbons.'

'Lavinia, how absurd you are! Nonpareil, indeed!'

'Oh, well, I would be if I were a man.' She laughed. 'Papa has said I am every bit as good as Duncan and easier on the horses than he is. I should like, above everything, to drive his high-perch phaeton, but he will not allow it.'

'I should just think not!' She paused. 'Would you like to drive now?'

'May I? Oh, I should just think I would!'

'Then you may, but go easy on the horses. And do not try to overtake anyone.'

She relinquished the reins to a bright-eyed Lavinia and the next minute the horses were trotting sedately along the carriageway, back to the entrance. Frances would have taken over at the gate but Lavinia was doing so well, she allowed her to tool them all the way back to Corringham House, where a groom came forward to take the equipage back to the stables. Frances began to think it might be the beginning of a better understanding between them. All the girl needed was a little attention and affection.

Even before Creeley opened the door, Frances knew she had a visitor; her stepdaughter's carriage was waiting in the street, the horses being led up and down by her coachman. 'Lady Harnham is here with the children, my lady,' the butler told her. 'I did not think you would be long and I was sure you would want them to wait. I have shown them into the small salon.'

'You did right, Creeley,' She took off her hat and handed it to him. 'Come, Lavinia, I will introduce you to my stepdaughter and her children.' She led the way past the main reception rooms at the front of the house and down a corridor to a smaller room that looked out on the back garden.

As soon as she opened the door, she was besieged. Two little pairs of plump legs ran helter-skelter to meet her and two pairs of equally plump arms hugged her knees, nearly bowling her over. She knelt to put her arms about the children. 'Oh, my little loves, it is so good to see you are well.'

'I's been sick, Gra'ma,' Beth said.

'So's I,' Andrew chimed in.

'But you are better now, I see.'

'Oh, yes,' Andrew said solemnly. 'In plump currant.'

Frances laughed. 'Where did you learn that phrase?'

'Oh, his papa said it to him and he's been repeating it ever since,' his fond mama said. 'I told Richard he would have to be more careful of his tongue, Andrew seems to pick up everything so quickly nowadays.'

Frances stood up and took the children by the hand.

'Now, you two imps, there is someone here I should like you to meet.' She turned to Lavinia, who was smiling for the first time that morning. 'Lady Lavinia, may I present my step-grandchildren. This is Andrew. He has recently had his fourth birthday, so he is becoming quite the little gentleman.' And to Andrew, 'Make your bow, love.'

He had obviously been taught his manners for he stood to attention and, laying his arm across his waist, bowed towards Lavinia.

'And this little scrap is Elizabeth, known to all as Beth.'

'Beth,' her mother said. 'Show Lady Lavinia how well you curtsy.'

The tiny child made an attempt at it, but promptly sat on her bottom. Lavinia scooped her up before either her mother or Frances could reach her. 'Oh, what a clever puss you are. I am Vinny. Can you say that?'

'Course she can,' Andrew said. 'Vinny is easy to say. Go on, Beth, you say it.'

'You are big enough to address Lady Lavinia properly, Andrew,' his mother said.

'Oh, do not let him be stiff with me, Lady Harnham,' Lavinia said. 'I prefer Vinny when I am with friends.' She turned to Andrew. 'Shall you and I take Beth into the garden and see what we can find?'

The boy slipped his hand in hers and she took the children away, watched by the two ladies who had been so taken by surprise, they could find nothing to say.

'Well, the tattlers are way off the mark with her,' Augusta said at last. 'I had heard she was surly and downpin all the time, but she is a delightful young lady.'

'You would say that of anyone who praised your little darlings, Gussie.'

'Not if I thought they were doing it to curry favour with me, but she cannot be at all concerned what I might think of her and she seemed to take to the children so naturally.'

'Perhaps there is hope for her yet, though if you had seen her earlier this afternoon…' She stopped herself and went on. 'No, I must not decry the girl; she has yet to learn to conduct herself that is all.'

'Why did you take on the commission?'

Frances laughed. 'It was a challenge, I suppose, and you know me, I have never learned to say no when appealed to.'

They were interrupted by Creeley throwing open the door and announcing the Duke of Loscoe. 'Come for his daughter,' Frances murmured.

He strode into the room, swept off his hat and bowed. 'Ladies, your obedient.'

'Your Grace,' they said in unison, bending slightly at the knee.

'Creeley,' Frances said, as that worthy retreated. 'Ask for refreshments to be sent, if you please.' Then, to Marcus, 'Please be seated, my lord.'

'Where is Lavinia?' he asked, looking about him as he threw up the skirt of his buff coat and folded his length into one of her chairs.

'She has taken the children into the garden,' Augusta told him, leaving Frances to examine her hands in her lap and note that her fingers were covered in paint. What would he think of her? She tried to hide them in the folds of her gown, but imagined she saw a smile flit across his face.

'We had, in any case, finished our lesson,' she said primly.

'And have you examined her on our visit to the Royal Academy, my lady?'

'We discussed it, certainly.'

A footman arrived with the tea tray and put an end to the questions, to Frances's immense relief. She did not want to have to relay the discussion she had had with Lavinia; he would undoubtedly think her wanting and might ring a peal over his daughter. If she were ever to make headway with Lavinia, she had to do it in her own way by gaining her trust.

Lavinia returned with the children while Frances was pouring the tea. Her muslin gown was grubby, her hands dirty and her hair was tangled.

'Vinny, what have you been doing?' Marcus asked, as the children ran to their mother. 'You look as if you have fallen into the shrubbery.'

'We found a rabbit,' Andrew said, so eager to tell his story he forgot to be shy with the new arrival. 'A poor little rabbit not in plump currant at all.'

'It has a broken leg,' Lavinia said, as the adults fought to hide their smiles. 'I expect it was chased into the garden by a dog. I heard one yapping only a few minutes before.'

'Vinny put a stick on it, so, and bound it up with her handkerchief,' the boy went on, winding an imaginary bandage about his own arm. 'Then Simpson put it in a box.'

'Did he, love?' Frances asked. 'Whatever for?'

'Who is Simpson?' the Duke demanded.

'The gardener, your Grace,' Frances answered.

'We left it in the potting shed until it is time to go

home,' Lavinia said. 'I promised the children I would look after it until it mends…'

'No, Vinny,' Marcus said with a heavy sigh. 'We are not having sick animals at Stanmore House. It is bad enough having a menagerie at Loscoe Court, but in town…'

'But, Papa…'

'No, Vinny.' He turned to Frances. 'I am afraid my daughter thinks she can cure every injured and sick animal she comes across. At Loscoe Court she has dogs, cats, rabbits, owls, blackbirds, foxes and heaven knows what else.'

'You cannot let them die,' Lavinia said.

'That is nature's way,' he said. 'They become well again or they die and it is not for humans to interfere.'

'Why not? Just because *you* have no feelings—'

'Lavinia!' he commanded. 'That is enough.'

Frances knew by the fierce look on his face and the set of his jaw that Lavinia would be in for a severe scolding the minute they left the house. She could almost feel sorry for her, except one should not allow an impudent child to go unpunished.

He turned from his sullen daughter to his hostess. 'My lady, may I trouble you to ask your gardener to dispose of the animal—no doubt your cook can make something of it…'

'No, no.' Andrew began to cry. 'Gran'ma, you must not eat it.'

Frances gave the Duke a telling look and took the child in her arms to soothe him. 'No, of course we will not eat it, love. The Duke did not mean that at all. He meant Cook should take care of it in the kitchen until it is better.'

'Yes, yes,' Marcus said, hurriedly. 'That is exactly what I had in mind.'

'Andrew, do stop crying.' Frances reached out and took a sugar plum from a dish on the table. 'Here, dry your eyes and you may have this.'

Mollified, the boy stuffed it into his mouth, as Beth left her mother to come and beg one for herself.

'I nearly forgot why I came,' Augusta said, deciding it was time she took the children away. 'Shall you be coming to the opera at Covent Garden next Friday, Mama? Richard has promised to obtain seats. I hear it is outstandingly good.'

'I should love to.'

'I am glad you feel able to recommend it,' Marcus put in. 'I had planned to take Lavinia and hoped it was a suitable performance for her to see.'

'Oh, there is nothing in the least objectionable in it,' Augusta said.

'Then please join us in our box. There will easily be room for all of us.'

Frances wanted to decline; she had no wish to spend any more time in his company than she had to, but before she could find a plausible excuse, he had added. 'It is the least I can do after being such a jobbernot.'

'Jobbernot,' Andrew repeated. 'Jobbernot. Jobbernot. Jobbernot…'

'Hush,' Augusta said, although everyone was laughing, including the Duke. 'It is exceedingly impolite to repeat what people say. You are not a parrot, you know.' She turned to Marcus. 'I am very sorry, your Grace.'

'Think nothing of it,' he said. 'Only say you will join us at the theatre.'

'I shall be delighted, my lord, on one condition. You have supper with us afterwards. Isn't that right, Mama?'

Thus appealed to, there was nothing for Frances to do but agree. 'I shall look forward to it.' It was the performance she was looking forward to, she told herself, the drama on stage, the costumes and the sets, which particularly interested her; it had nothing to do with the Duke of Loscoe.

'Then allow me to call for you in my carriage.'

'I have my own carriage…'

'Oh, I know that, Countess, but there will be a dreadful crush at the door and it will save your groom having to harness up your horses and keep them out late.'

She decided it would be churlish to refuse and besides, she did not want to have to explain to Augusta why she had. 'Then, I accept your kind offer.'

'Seven o'clock, then,' he said, bowing his way out. 'I shall look forward to it.'

'He is nothing like as stiff-rumped as people would have him,' Augusta said when the door had closed on him and his daughter.

'Stiff-rumped,' her son chanted.

'Andrew, you must stop this at once,' she said severely. 'I shall not bring you to see Grandmama again if you cannot behave. Now, take Beth to the kitchen. I am sure Cook will find something for you to eat. That is if you do not mind, Mama?'

Frances was not really paying attention, being busy wondering who it was had said the Duke of Loscoe was stiff-rumped. Was he? When she had met him a week ago, she would certainly have agreed, but he had shown no sign of it in the last few days. Perhaps it had been his business which had been worrying him and now he had brought it about and was able to relax a little more.

But in spite of what she had told Lavinia, she *was* curious about it. But that did not mean she would allow him to disrupt her life, not now, not ever. Allowing him to take her to the opera meant nothing at all.

'Mama?'

'What? Oh, yes, of course. Run along, children.'

They scampered off and Augusta went on, 'Mama, have you seen James lately?'

Frances had been so taken up with her own affairs that she had to stop and think when it was she had last seen her stepson. 'Not since the charity ball and then I hardly spoke to him. He is not in a scrape, is he?'

'Not exactly a scrape, but I think he has got himself into dun territory.'

'So? Young men, especially young men who think themselves of consequence, often get into debt. James is no exception.'

'Mama, I am worried about him. He confided in Richard that he did not know how he was to come about.'

'Why did he not come to me?' Frances knew it irked James to have to apply to her when he was pinched in the pocket but, until he was twenty-five in a few months' time, his fortune was managed by trustees. He lived on an allowance which should have been ample to keep him in clothes and pay for his leisure pursuits, his horses and a little moderate gambling. But that was the trouble, James seemed not to know the difference between moderation and excess.

'Richard told him to apply to you,' Augusta said. 'But it is only two months ago since you stood buff for him and he is ashamed of himself.'

'Did he tell you how much he owed?'

'He did not say anything about it to me at all, but he

told Richard he thought it was in excess of three thousand, but he was not at all sure of the exact amount.'

'Good heavens!' Frances was reminded of the young lady James had brought to the ball and wondered if her extravagant tastes had contributed to his problems. It was either that or he had gone in too deep at cards. But three thousand! The trustees would throw up their hands in horror and imply that, if she had not indulged him, he would have grown up with a better understanding of the value of money.

'Will you speak to him?'

'Of course I will, if you think it will do any good.'

'I believe he is to be at the opera on Friday and he will surely come to see you during the intermission.'

Frances did not think that would serve. How could she discuss such matters with her stepson in the Duke's box? She could hardly ask everyone to leave so that she might speak to him alone and the last person she wanted to hear of her private affairs was the Duke of Loscoe. How could she condemn him for his handling of his daughter when she could not influence her own stepson?

At exactly seven o'clock on Friday evening, Marcus rapped at the door of Corringham House and was admitted by Creeley. 'Her ladyship will be with you directly,' the butler said. 'Will you wait in the drawing room?'

He was about to agree when a slight sound from above made him lift his head and he saw her standing at the top of the stairs, about to descend. She was a picture of loveliness. Her gown of green silk showed off her figure to perfection; it fitted closely to her curves, no longer gauche as they had been at seventeen, but softly rounded with maturity. Released below her bosom the material flowed like water, rippling about her body, hinting, oh so subtly, of what was beneath. He found himself visualising her smooth white body, her long legs and firm round breasts, and desire sprang in him so forcefully that he could hardly breathe.

Slowly she came down the stairs and it seemed as if she was prolonging the descent, one foot, in its white stocking and green satin shoe, peeping out from beneath the hem of her skirt as she took each step, revealing a neatly turned ankle. Was she aware of the effect she was having on him? Was that smile one of pleasure at seeing him or of mockery that she could reduce him to a palpitating moonling? Was she triumphant, amused or simply being charming?

He let out his breath in a sigh as she finished her descent and held out her hand to him. He took it and bowed over it. 'My lady, your obedient.'

His voice was husky, she noticed, and there was a tremor in her own as she answered. 'Your Grace, you are punctual as ever.'

He was clad all in black, except for a white frilled shirt and a white cravat tied in a knot James had described as *trône d'amour*. He had shown her how to tie it too, but she had been all thumbs and the starched muslin had been like a limp dishcloth when she finished. She was almost tempted to ask the Duke if he had tied it himself or if his valet had done it for him, but decided that would be too familiar and familiarity was not what she wished to cultivate with him.

But, oh, how handsome he was, with his dark locks cut so that they curled about his ears, his fine Stanmore brows and straight nose. Lady Willoughby was right, she decided as he escorted her to his carriage; he would be the catch of the Season. He had said he had no plans to marry, but when did a man ever have plans to do that? Not before they were forced into it by circumstance, so James had told her when she had mentioned it was time he thought of matrimony and setting up his nursery, not when they could enjoy the favours of their mistresses and pursue their interests unencumbered.

And thinking of mistresses made her remember what Lavinia had told her. Did the Duke of Loscoe keep a mistress? And from that question another was engendered; did she mind? No, she told herself as she settled herself beside Lavinia and he took his seat opposite, so close her skirt was brushing his knees. Whatever had been between them had died long ago. But who was not to say a new fire could not be kindled from the ashes of the old?

The thought, coming to her so suddenly, made her gasp and it was all she could do to stifle it under the pretence of a little cough. She was glad it was dark in the coach and he could not see the colour flare in her face, for she was sure it was there; she could feel the heat in her cheeks. How could she? How could she have such improper thoughts about a man who could hide himself so completely behind a veneer of politeness— he was an enigma, a stranger. But he was no stranger. She knew he could be passionate, if not caring, and that his mistress would want for nothing. Until he tired of her. That was the trouble with being a mistress; there was no security. Mistresses had to rely on the generosity of their protectors.

What, in the name of heaven, had set her thoughts along that track? Was it the fact that once, seventeen years ago, when he told her he was to marry Margaret Connaught, he had as good as suggested she become his *chère amie*. Even now, after all these years, she burned with the memory of her humiliation. She had no wish to become the Duke of Loscoe's paramour and he was not looking for a wife; he had told her so. It was marriage or nothing. She was so taken aback by that thought, she almost cried out. She must be mad!

As the carriage passed beneath one of the street lamps in Piccadilly on its progress towards Covent Garden, Marcus looked across at her and wondered what thoughts had brought that flush to her cheeks. It made her look like a young girl again and his heart contracted painfully.

Chapter Six

Marcus had been right about the press of carriages. The street outside the theatre was packed with vehicles, but they were eventually set down at the door and made their way into the foyer, where Richard and Augusta were already waiting. By the time they had taken their seats in the Duke's box, Frances had composed herself sufficiently to take an interest in the audience, bow and smile to acquaintances, and, when the curtain went up, to pay attention to the production. Not for nothing had she taken seventeen years cultivating a quiet poise to stand her in good stead when things went wrong.

As Augusta had predicted, James came to the box during the intermission. With his fair curly hair and clear blue eyes, he was a handsome young man, though Frances wished he would not act the exquisite so blatantly. He wore a deep blue evening coat, pantaloons of a slightly lighter shade, and a brilliant waistcoat of blue and yellow stripes with pearl buttons. His cravat, tied in a complicated knot, filled the space between the top button of his waistcoat and the high points of his collar which were starched within an inch of their lives. Flounced lace peeped from beneath the end of his cuffs and fell over his hands, one of which held a quizzing glass.

'Ma'am,' he said, dropping the glass on its ribbon and attempting to execute a flourishing leg which in the confines of the box, nearly had Augusta's plumed turban off her head. 'Your obedient.' Then he bowed to Marcus, grinned at his sister who was adjusting her hat, said, 'How do you do, Dick?' to Richard and turned to Lavinia, one eyebrow raised.

'James, I collect you have not yet met Lady Lavinia Stanmore,' Frances said.

'No,' he answered, openly appraising Lavinia. 'I should most certainly have remembered if I had.'

'Lady Lavinia, my stepson, the Earl of Corringham.' Lavinia was actually smiling, Frances noted, though the change in the girl's expression did not fill her with unalloyed joy if the cause of it was James's undoubted charm. 'Lady Lavinia is the *Duke*'s daughter,' she added with heavy emphasis, as if to tell him that he had better beware. 'She is to have her come-out *next year*.'

'My word, I shall look forward to that,' he said, seizing Lavinia's hand and bowing over it. 'Lady Lavinia, your most obedient servant.'

'Good evening, my lord,' she said, returning his appraisal with her own. 'Are you enjoying the performance?'

'Oh, indeed, I am.'

'Now that you have succeeded in disrupting the whole box,' Augusta said to her brother with some asperity, 'will you sit down?'

'No, thanks, Sis, I just heard the bell.'

'Then join us at home for supper,' Augusta went on, blithely unaware of the misgivings in her stepmother's breast. All she was trying to do was make it easy for

Frances to tackle James about his debts and she was determined that he would not slip through her fingers. 'Cook won't mind an extra cover.'

'Delighted.' He bowed to everyone, gave Lavinia a knowing smile and took his leave.

Frances risked a glance at Marcus and became uncomfortably aware that he had also noticed the looks which passed between the two young people and knew he would hold her accountable if James did not behave himself.

The meal turned out to be far more convivial than she had expected it to be. Richard and Augusta were very good hosts and their cook, knowing the Duke was going to be one of the guests, surpassed herself with turbot in a shrimp sauce, sole bonne femme, saddle of lamb, roast goose and fruit pies and syllabub, all washed down with a selection of fine wines. Marcus did justice to the meal and found himself envying Frances her family. Though they were not blood relations, they were obviously very fond of her and not above teasing.

'When we were children we called her Little Mama,' James told him. 'She was such a little scrap of a thing when she came to us and so anxious to please. I am afraid we did not make it easy for her, we were always into scrapes—'

'You mean you were,' Augusta put in. 'I am sure *I* did nothing to upset Mama.'

'Oh, no? Who was it put sugar in her paints? And all because she would not let you have that hideous pink dress you saw in the Pantheon Bazaar.'

Frances laughed. 'Hideous though it was, I bought it for you, but no sooner did you have it than you hated it.'

'Oh, she was only seeing how far she could tease you,' James said. 'Wicked stepmothers had to be put in their place.' He sighed dramatically. 'But the trouble was, Loscoe, Little Mama was hardly more than a child herself and anyone less wicked it would be hard to imagine. So we became her friend and she ours. It has remained so every since.'

'James, you are putting me to the blush,' Frances said, acutely conscious that Marcus was drinking in every word, smiling at her in that slightly mocking way of his which made her want to hit him.

'I am only telling the truth.'

'Then it is a great shame you do not think of Mama more often,' Augusta put in. 'You have been nowhere near Corringham House for a month. If it had not been for the charity ball, you would have no idea how she was.'

'I know very well how she is. She is in prime kilter as always, busy with her little orphans, painting antidotes with more blunt than looks, teaching untalented schoolgirls how to draw. I hear her praises wherever I go, such a fine woman, so generous, so gifted...'

'James, do be quiet,' Frances said.

'He is toadying up to you, Mama,' Augusta put in. 'So watch out.'

'Oh, I know it very well, and I am curious as to the reason, but you do not need to tell me now, James. Call on me at home tomorrow morning. Ten o'clock.'

'Ten!' he exclaimed, aghast at the thought. 'You cannot mean it, ma'am.'

'I do. If you are going riding in the Park, it is not so far out of the way to pay me a morning call.'

'Oh, very well,' he said. 'But you know you will be depriving me of much-needed beauty sleep.'

'Then go to bed earlier,' she retorted.

Marcus smiled at the banter. It *was* banter and not meant to be taken seriously; he could tell by the soft way James spoke to his stepmother even when he was pretending to be affronted, and the sparkle in her eyes as she answered him. There was a great deal of love there, as there was between Frances and Augusta and the two small children he had met earlier in the week. They were a happy and united family. It was a pity Frances had never had children of her own. Had the old Earl been capable? Was she barren? He felt infinitely sad on her behalf; she would have made an excellent mother.

But she did not appear sad. In truth she seemed very cheerful, as if she had had all she wanted from life: good husband, loving family, a talent that was appreciated and staunch friends all round. He envied her. He, who had vast estates, influence in high places, money enough to buy anything he wanted, envied her. Money could not buy the only thing he lacked, a woman who loved him. For, assuredly, Margaret had not loved him, had even told him once that she held him in aversion. It had not been her fault; they had been pawns in a game played by both sets of parents. Given a free choice, Margaret might have met and married a man who might have loved her and he would not have lost Frances.

'You will forget her,' his father had said, making it sound like a command. 'You are too young to know what is best for you. Be guided by me and your mama, as we were by our parents.'

In the old Duke's day, parents often arranged the marriages of their offspring without any reference to them; it was a matter of lineage and inheritance, still was in some quarters. If a man wanted love, he did not go to his wife for it; there were always others... Oh, but how unsatisfactory those others had been! And however unfashionable it was, he had wanted a wife he loved. Was it too late? Did he even want to risk a second try?

'Don't you think so, your Grace?' He heard Augusta's question but had no idea what had gone before and could not answer it.

'I am sorry, Lady Harnham, I was in something of a brown study...'

'I was speaking about the opera we saw tonight. I own the costumes were very fine, but I thought the singing not so good and the story a little weak. What did you think?'

He smiled ruefully; he had paid scant attention to the opera, being too aware of Frances sitting not three feet away. She was even more lovely than she had been at seventeen, but now it was the loveliness of an ice maiden, unapproachable. 'I agree wholeheartedly,' he said, for want of anything else to contribute.

'Then all I can say is that you have no soul,' Frances said.

He turned his head to look at her and it seemed there was a message in his eyes, a message she could not interpret. 'Oh, Countess, I assure you that I have.'

'Then you must allow the soprano had a magnificent voice.'

'It was certainly very loud and my Italian is wanting for I could not make out a single word.'

'Did you not make the Grand Tour, my lord?' Augusta asked.

'No, I came unexpectedly into my inheritance before I could go and the tumult in Europe soon put an end to travel for all but the army. Now, of course, we have peace and the young men are able to go again. My younger brother, John, is in Italy at this moment.'

'Do you think the peace will last?' Frances asked, anxious to move away from personal issues. 'It seems to me that this carving up of Europe between the victors can only lead to more trouble—'

'Talking of trouble,' Lavinia put in, 'What do you suppose will happen to the framework knitters? I read in a pamphlet—'

'Lavinia, where did you come across a pamphlet?' her father asked. 'Their publication has been suppressed.'

'That won't stop people printing and reading them. The framework knitters are being driven to starvation right on our doorstep. Loscoe Court is not so very far from the unrest.'

'Lavinia,' he said sternly, 'you do not understand and it is hardly a fitting subject for a young lady to introduce at the supper table.'

Lavinia fell into her usual sullen silence after this put-down and, the meal being finished, Augusta decided it was time the ladies withdrew and left the men to their port. She rose and led Frances and Lavinia to the drawing room.

'I hope they are not going to prose on all night,' Augusta said, after the tea tray had been brought in. 'It is very late.'

She had her wish, for the men wandered in fifteen minutes later, smelling of port and cigar smoke and soon after that James took his leave, saying he would wait on his stepmother the following morning. 'Though I ain't going to promise to be there on the dot of ten,' he said as he kissed her hand. He bowed low to Lavinia. 'Perhaps, my lady, we shall meet again soon.'

She smiled at him. 'Perhaps we shall, my lord.'

'We must go too,' Marcus said. 'Countess, if you wish to stay, I will send my carriage back for you.'

'No, I am ready to leave. I have a busy day tomorrow.'

Augusta laughed as she rose to summon a servant to fetch hats and capes. 'When do you not?'

A few minutes later, the Loscoe carriage was bowling away in the dark. No one spoke for several minutes. Lavinia, still resentful, sat in the corner, her head lolling on the upholstery which padded the back of her seat.

'Vinny is half asleep,' he said, as they turned from the Strand into Pall Mall where the new gas lamps shed little pools of yellow light, revealing a drunken dandy getting out of a chair and falling to the ground from where he had to be helped by the link boy, who was seventy if he was a day. 'If you do not object, my lady, I will take her home first then we will go on to Duke Street.'

If Frances was dismayed at the thought of being alone in the carriage with him, she did not betray it, but answered evenly, 'I have no objection, your Grace, but you do not need to accompany me. I can easily send your coach back...'

'Oh, I do not doubt it, but I am not so lacking in manners that I could allow a lady to return home alone from an evening spent in her company.'

'I am used to travelling about alone, your Grace.'

'What is that to the point? Besides, I need my coach, I have to go out again.'

'If I had known that, I would have taken my own carriage to the theatre rather than inconvenience you,' she said, remembering what Lavinia had told her about his nocturnal excursions and wondering where he was going after he left her. To more congenial company than she was, she did not doubt.

'You are not inconveniencing me.'

They fell silent, and yet there was so much they could have said. The right words, spoken softly, might have healed the hurt of so many years; gentle explanations might have bridged the gulf that lay between them. He knew it. She knew it. But, perhaps because they had a witness, the silence remained unbroken. Or was it that too much time had passed? When they reached Stanmore House in St James's Street, she remained in her seat while he saw Lavinia safely inside.

A few minutes later he returned; this time he sat beside her. They were so close her gown was brushing his pantaloons, his arm against hers. She could feel his warmth, imagined she could hear the beat of his heart. Or was it her own?

'Vinny is exhausted,' he said, as he gave the coachman the office. 'I gave her into the hands of her governess and no doubt she will sleep until noon.'

'I doubt it, your Grace, she is young and resilient, but had you forgot she is engaged to sit for her portrait again tomorrow? I can easily postpone it, if you wish.' It would be better if he did, she thought, because she had just remembered James was going to call on her and they would be there at the same time.

'I do not wish. And do you think you could refrain from all this "your Grace" nonsense? You used not to be so stiff.'

'I did not know you as a duke then.'

'True, but even so, I recollect you dispensed with using my title.'

'That was a long time ago and I was young. I knew no better.'

He turned to look at her, though he could see little in the gloom of the carriage, even though they were passing beneath a street lamp. All he saw was her profile, looking straight ahead. She had taken off her hat and it lay on her lap. 'No better than what?'

'No better than to assume a familiarity I had no right to. You were far above my touch and it is a pity I did not realise it at the time.'

'Oh, Fanny, have you still not forgiven me?'

'There was nothing to forgive. We were friends and then we went our separate ways. That is life, your Grace.' She was surprised at how calm her voice sounded.

'Marcus, please,' he corrected. 'Or, if that is too much for you, Stanmore will do. That is what my friends call me and I wish us to be friends.'

'Friends?'

'Indeed, yes. You are teaching my daughter and painting her portrait. We are bound to be thrown together a little, especially if we attend the same functions, and...' He paused, knowing he was going too fast; there was no sign that she was softening. The ice was still solid, though she had turned a little towards him. 'I do not want to be at odds with you.'

'I was not aware we were at odds, sir. I have not quarrelled with you, nor do I intend to. You are, after all, my employer.'

She meant that as a set-down, he knew, but it only served to inflame him. How could she remain so cool, so unconcerned, when he was burning with a desire he found hard to control? Did she not know it? Could she not hear it in the tone of his voice, the quick intake of his breath? She was not a schoolgirl, not missish; she had been married and should be able to sense how he felt and meet him halfway. Unless she was truly indifferent. And could he blame her for that?

The carriage drew to a stop outside Corringham House, but neither moved. The coachman, who had no doubt learned to be discreet and not be too quick to open the door and let down the step when his master escorted a lady home, sat waiting for a signal to do so. Marcus was in no hurry to give it. He smiled gently and picked up her hand to kiss the back of it.

The touch of his lips on her skin made her shudder with a desire she could not stifle. He could still do that to her, even after the passing of years, and she was very much afraid that he had seen it, or felt the trembling of her fingers. 'Fanny, I have missed you. All the years…'

'Too many,' she murmured.

'Not enough to erase memories of how you were, your love of life, your fire…'

'The fire of youth,' she murmured, wondering if she ought to open the door herself and jump out before she gave herself away and something happened she would later regret. 'You had it too, as I recall.'

He turned her hand over and kissed the palm. 'Fire is not specific to youth, my dear.'

She sat unmoving, afraid to move, afraid to utter another word, tense with a longing she had not felt since he had walked out of her life seventeen years before. Before she could withdraw her hand, he moved his lips to the inside of her wrist, and then kissed her fingers one by one. The passion she was trying so hard to subdue coursed from her fingertips to her whole body and set her in such a quake, she thought she would explode. She certainly could not speak.

When she did not protest, he lifted his head and looked into her face. He could see little but her eyes, wide open, bright with surprise, and then her eyelids flickered and the pupils darkened with an ardour so intense he could have sworn he felt the heat of it. The ice was melting. Encouraged, he twisted in his seat so that he could cup her face in both his hands. She opened her mouth to object, only to have it covered by his own mouth. Her protest, if indeed it was a protest, died as she felt herself respond.

Her whole body was crying out for him and she clung to him, allowing the kiss to deepen, feeling his hands shift from her face to shoulders. Her hat fell to the floor and her cape fell back as he slipped one arm about her and drew her close against him. She put her hands into the hair at the nape of his neck, drawing his head even closer. Seventeen years of hunger went into that kiss.

Want of breath forced them to draw apart. 'Oh, Fanny, how I have longed to hold you like that again.'

'Have you?' She was breathless, her breasts heaving under the thin green silk of her gown. He saw it, saw the creamy mounds rising above the low neckline, and though he wanted to touch, he knew he must not.

'You know I have.'

'I know no such thing.'

'Oh, come, you are a woman of the world, not a green girl…'

With a supreme effort she pulled herself together and was once more in control of her turbulent emotions. 'I have seen nothing of you for seventeen years and suddenly you are here, expecting me to fall into your arms…'

'Oh, but you did, my sweet, my incomparable Fanny, you did.'

His voice held a note of triumph, but what he had said was so palpably true she could not even pretend to be affronted, and she certainly did not want a war of words with him; she had a fair idea she would lose it. 'You took me by surprise.'

'Did I? Now, I thought otherwise. I thought you, too, were remembering…' He wondered whether to tell her he still loved her, that he wanted to make up for all the wasted years, but as he had already told her he was not contemplating marriage, she would make the same assumption she had made seventeen years before, that he was looking for a *chère amie*; better to leave it unsaid.

'A kiss. What's a kiss?' She was scornful. 'Something and nothing. What passed between us seventeen years ago was a pleasant interlude which we, as mature adults, can look back on with amusement. And trying to resurrect it can only lead to disappointment, don't you agree?'

'Yes, of course,' he said, hastily picking up his cane from the opposite seat and tapping on the roof to remind the coachman of his duty. 'A pleasant interlude, nothing more. I beg your pardon for my presumption.'

She picked up her hat, adjusted her cape and bodice as the coach door was opened and the step let down. 'Goodnight, your Grace,' she said, stepping down.

She did not hear his answer as she walked, back stiff, head held high, towards the house. Creeley had been watching for her and the door was flung open as she reached it. In a dream she thanked him and went past him, up the stairs to her bedchamber. In a dream she flung her hat on the bed and kicked off her shoes, before crossing the room to stand looking out across the rooftops of London, silhouetted against a starlit sky. Away in the distance she could hear a carriage, the sound of its rumbling wheels and the clop of the horses' hooves diminishing into silence.

He had gone and she must pretend that kiss had never happened, just as she had pretended his kisses had never happened before when she was young and heartsick and it was the only way she could make herself go on. She had promised herself no man would ever hurt her like that again, and that, if she ever saw Marcus Stanmore in the future, she would remain aloof. And what had she done, almost the minute he had come back into her life? Fallen for that silky charm, dropped her guard, allowed him to kiss her. What a ninny she had been!

Would he, too, pretend it had not happened? Could they meet and converse, could she go on calling him 'your Grace' and talking about art and orphans and parenthood like the friends he spoke about? What a strange way he had of showing friendship! He had once before hinted she should become his mistress—was that what he was dangling after, a pleasant interlude? She had been the one to use those words, not him, though he had been quick enough to agree, as if she had given him the opening he desired.

She had to disabuse him of that idea. But how? Could she refuse to receive him when he called? It would also mean that Lavinia would no longer have lessons and he would cancel the portrait. And what would her friends say to that? In no time it would be all over the *ton* that the Duke of Loscoe and the Countess of Corringham had quarrelled so violently that she would not let him into her house. And why they had quarrelled would be the subject of endless speculation.

She turned as Rose entered the room to help her undress. 'Did you enjoy your evening, my lady?'

Frances took a deep breath and smiled. 'Yes, Rose, I did, very much.'

And that was no lie, she told herself, as Rose helped

her off with her clothes and slipped her nightdress over her head. Regret it she did, most heartily, but she had enjoyed that kiss. George had never kissed her like that, not in ten years of marriage. In spite of her dilemma, she smiled wryly as she climbed into bed. Wanton, that's what she was. Frances, Countess of Corringham, was a wanton. She was also in love.

Marcus did not go home but ordered his coachman to take him to White's. 'I shan't need you any more tonight,' he told him when he set him down outside the club. 'I'll walk home.'

He had arranged to meet Donald Greenaway; though they might have a hand or two of cards, the purpose of the meeting was to exchange information and very possibly go on with their search for Harriet Poole. If he had known that Frances and his daughter were speculating about his nightly excursions and drawing their own conclusions, he would have chuckled. Far from enjoying himself, he had been combing the great city for a woman and child who seemed to have disappeared.

Donald was convinced that finding her husband first would serve them best and that he would be found among the low life of the city, the harlots and petticoat merchants, thieves and vagabonds, and they were creatures of the night. It was certainly the time when informers could be found and bribed for information. And so night after night, they had patrolled the streets, entered filthy taverns, questioned the people who lived in the rookeries. But so far they had had no success. Were the Pooles still in London? If not, where should he be looking?

Donald was waiting for him in one of the smaller

rooms, watching a game of faro. He rose when he saw him and came over to shake his hand. 'I'd nigh on given you up.'

'I had an evening engagement.'

'Oh, accommodating, was she?'

He smiled crookedly, remembering that kiss. She had been asking for it, wanting it as much as he had, or so he had thought. Had he misread the signals? Had it really meant nothing to her? If she was telling the truth when she said it was something and nothing, then she was an accomplished flirt, a tease. Perhaps he was not the only one to enjoy the favour of her lips. What about Sir Percival Ponsonby? Were there others? Why did it matter so much? He shook himself. 'You are off the mark, my friend, it was a visit to the opera with friends, nothing more.'

'You know, Stanmore, you are becoming a dull old fellow. This Mrs Poole seems to have taken your wits as well as your heart. I said you could leave the finding of her to me and I meant it. You should learn to enjoy yourself. I know a curvaceous little Cyprian...'

'No, thank you.' He looked about the room at the card players. 'Do you want to play?'

'No, for then we cannot talk. Come into the corner and I'll tell you what I've learned.'

Marcus called the waiter over to order two bumpers of brandy, and they settled themselves into armchairs, facing each other and close enough to converse in low voices.

'Poole is definitely in London,' Donald went on, after the waiter had gone. 'I had it from a Bow Street Runner...'

'What business has a Runner with him? Has he broken the law?'

'Not yet, but they are watching him. They think he is involved with the frameworkers' agitation.'

'Fudge! He was my head groom, nothing to do with frameworkers.'

'I'm only telling you what I have been told.'

'And Mrs Poole? And the child?'

Donald shook his head. 'The Runner didn't know anything about a woman and child. He was only concerned with Poole. It seems he's become something of a tub thumper, inciting the mob to join in with the knitters' grievances. There's to be a meeting tonight in a tavern in Seven Dials. I thought I would be there.'

'I can't see how that will help us to find Mrs Poole.'

'It will if I follow him home afterwards. At least we will know then if he has found his wife.' He paused to take a mouthful of brandy before going on. 'If Mrs Poole is with him, what then? Do you intend to separate her from him?'

'Good God, no! The child is my only concern.'

'You would forcibly drag it from her arms?'

'No, but I am convinced Poole would not countenance the child, even if he forgave his wife. He would accept money to be rid of him and I doubt she would object.'

'So, you agree we should find out how the land lies?'

'I cannot go in these clothes,' he said, indicating his evening coat and tall hat lying on the table beside him. 'Come home with me and I'll change.'

'I do not think you should come at all. You are too well known, even by the lower orders, and if Poole sees you…'

'I can disguise myself. I used to love charades as a boy. My brother and I would often dress up in clothes we had found in the attic.'

Which was how Lavinia, hearing her father come home and then go out again only half an hour later, went to the window and saw a shagbag walking away from the door. If it had not been for his gait, she would not have recognised him and even then, she was not sure because he suddenly developed a bent back and a limp. Puzzled, she went back to bed and did not hear him return.

However, he was in his place at the breakfast table when she went down next morning.

'The Countess was wrong,' he told her with a smile. 'She said you would be at the breakfast table before me.'

'She was not to know you would not even go to bed.'

'Of course I went to bed. Whatever gave you the idea I did not?'

'I heard you go out again.'

'Oh. I was not gone for long. I had to meet a friend.'

'Are we going riding this morning?'

'No, we have to go to Corringham House and there isn't time. Tomorrow, perhaps.'

'But I am not in the mood for drawing or sitting still.'

'Nevertheless we will go. We are expected.'

'You only take me there to save you from having to take me out and about with you.'

'Fustian!' He was dog-tired and in no mood for arguing with a recalcitrant child. 'You know I would spend more time with you if I could, but I have important business—'

'Business that keeps you out all night.'

'That is enough, Vinny. I can see that I have allowed you too much freedom to express yourself. Children, especially daughters, should not question what their par-

ents do, it is unbecoming and shows a lack of breeding…'

'And breeding is all, as Mama said.'

'Vinny, be silent when I am speaking to you.' He
wondered in what circumstance Margaret had spoken to
their daughter about breeding, but he would not ask, for
that would only encourage her outspokenness. 'The next
year or two are going to be very important for you and
I want you to be up to the mark and that means adopting
the social graces, learning to curb your tongue, as well
as being proficient in dancing, music and drawing.' He
drained his coffee cup and stood up. 'Now, finish your
breakfast and fetch your pelisse and bonnet. We do not
want to be late.'

His daughter went off, muttering about the politeness
of kings. He smiled ruefully. She was a handful and he
was dog-tired, but he loved her.

Dearly as she would have loved to plead a headache
or fatigue in order not to receive Marcus and his daughter, Frances knew it would not do. She must at least
maintain the appearance of normality, she must hold her
life together, to be the calm, mature widow everyone
believed her to be.

As soon as she had breakfasted she went up to her
studio to prepare for the lesson. Somehow she must engage Lavinia's attention, give her something to do
which interested her so that she could finish that portrait. It was beginning to be something of a burden and
she was not satisfied with it. It was flat, the animation
was lacking and, though the features were certainly
those of Lady Lavinia Stanmore, the personality, the fire
were missing.

Fire! That was a word Marcus had used about her. It

was apt, because she had been on fire with love and in those days she had made no attempt to hide it. She had been so confident of the outcome, encouraged by her mother. How could she have been so gullible? And now he was back and her brain and her heart were at war with each other. Sleeping or waking, she could not get him out of her head and it did not help to keep reminding herself of how he had hurt her, that he would do so again if she let him.

She heard the door knocker, counted the seconds as Creeley went to open it, more as he admitted the callers, more as he progressed steadily up the stairs and scratched on the studio door. She took a deep breath and settled her face in a welcoming smile, as Creeley entered. 'Lady Lavinia Stanmore, my lady.'

He had not come! His daughter was alone. She let out her breath, relieved and disappointed at the same time. She smiled at the girl. 'Lavinia, how prompt you are!'

'Papa brought me and he is never late. He asks pardon for not stopping. Pressing business, he said. He will fetch me at noon.'

'Then let us begin,' she said, becoming businesslike. The confrontation had been averted for the time being and she must put him from her mind. 'Shall we start with a lesson or the portrait?'

Lavinia shrugged. 'It is of no consequence.'

'Then we will begin with the portrait.' Lavinia could not be relied upon to sit still for more than a few minutes and it would be best to take advantage of it while she could. 'Take up your position.'

After a few minutes, it became obvious it was not going well. Frances was ready to give up for the day when she had an idea. 'I have it,' she said. 'Wait here a moment.'

She hurried down to the kitchen and took the rabbit out of its box. Its leg had healed and it would soon be time to set it free but, in the meantime, it could be useful. She carried it up and put it into Lavinia's lap.

'Oh, you kept it!' The girl's face lit up with delight. 'I thought you would do as Papa said and have it killed and cooked.'

'No, I promised I would not, didn't I? Andrew will want to see it next time he comes. Now, if you would hold it…'

She did not need to pose the girl. Lavinia sat perfectly still with the rabbit in her arms, stroking it gently and murmuring softly. The animal seemed to understand and did not struggle. Indeed, it seemed soothed by the quiet voice. Frances dipped her brush in paint.

An hour later, nearer eleven o'clock that ten, Creeley came to announce the arrival of the Earl of Corringham. Absorbed as she was, Frances had forgotten he was coming and was almost resentful of the interruption. It was the best sitting they had had and the portrait was really beginning to take shape, but an hour was long enough; she was surprised that Lavinia had remained still so long. She stood up to clean her brushes. 'Tell him I shall be down directly,' she told Creeley.

When he had gone she told Lavinia to put the rabbit back in its box and finish an exercise she had given her the previous week and then went down to the drawing room where James was waiting for her, dressed in full frockcoat, nankeen breeches, yellow stockings and high-heeled, buckled shoes.

He executed a flourishing leg. 'You see, ma'am, I am come as a dutiful son at your command.'

She smiled and indicated a chair with a gesture of her hand, seating herself opposite it. 'And why do you have to wait for a command?' She paused to watch his face. 'Especially as I know you to be in dun territory.'

He flipped up the skirt of his coat and sat down. 'How do you know that?'

'Never mind how I know. Is it true?'

'A gentleman is always in debt, you know that. It is the nature of the beast.'

'Maybe, but it is profligate of you to allow it to reach such a pass that everyone is dunning you. What is it— gaming, or a little bit of muslin?'

He sighed. 'A little of both. But I shall come about.'

'How? More gaming. That is a downhill road, James. I have told you so before.'

'Yes, and said I was not to apply to you again, so why ask me about it?'

'How deep are you in?'

He shrugged. 'Can't say exactly.'

'Then try a guess.'

'There are gaming vouchers out to the tune of two and a half thousand—'

'James! I cannot believe it.'

'Why not? You gamble, ma'am, you know how it is, the next hand is always the one which will recoup. Only, of course, it does not.'

'What else? Tradesmen?'

'Well, debts of honour have to come first, don't they, so the tradesmen have to be left. I owe Weston for a coat and Tattersall's for my new hunter, a real goer that is. Then there is Rundell and Bridge for jewellery...'

'Which I saw about the neck of Miss Franks, if I am not much mistaken.'

'Well, you have to give presents, it is expected.

Trouble was, I had bought a watch and a bracelet the month before and they were dunning me like mad. The only way I could put them off was to give them more business on expectation…'

'James, you have not been giving out post-obit bills?'

'Why not?' He stood up and began to pace about the room. 'I am already the Earl and everyone knows I am to come into the whole inheritance before the year is out.'

'If you go on like this, by the time it is in your hands, you will owe the whole amount,' she said with a heavy sigh. 'Then what will you do?'

'Oh, it is not as bad as that.' He stopped to face her. 'All I need is something to tide me over, just to get them off my doorstep…'

'I seem to recollect telling you not to apply to the trustees again. They already think I am too lenient with you. And where am I to get nearly three thousand pounds?'

'Oh, that's doing it too brown. You are earning a mint of rhino with your painting, especially now the Duke of Loscoe has become your patron. Everyone will be flocking to have their portraits done.'

'I am not paid in advance, James.'

'Ask the Duke for a down payment.'

'I cannot possibly do that,' she said, aghast at the suggestion.

'Too proud?' he suggested with a quirky smile. 'Or too independent. Everyone knows he is dangling after you…'

'James, it is not true. And I'll thank you not to repeat rumours like that when you hear them.'

'It is not the only rumour I have heard, Mama. It is all over the *ton* that his mistress has run out on him and taken their child with her and he is combing London to find them…'

She was so taken aback, she could not speak for a moment. She remembered thinking only the day before, when Lavinia had spoken of the Duke's nocturnal excursions, that he might have a mistress tucked away somewhere, but she had assumed it was a simple dalliance. But a child!

'Wherever did you hear such fribble?'

'Oh, it is not fribble, I do assure you. He was overheard telling a friend all about it.'

'Some friend!'

'Oh, it was not the friend who squeaked, but the listener. Sir Joshua Barber—do you know him? A big fat man, made his money from cotton…'

'I have met him. He was at the charity ball. I did not know you were acquainted with him.'

'Now, why should I be acquainted with a mushroom like that? No, he told Mrs. Harcourt and she told Lord Graham and he told Annabelle.'

'So, you share your mistress with Lord Graham.'

He shrugged. 'He has more blunt than I.'

'Is she worth getting into debt for, James?'

He sighed and sat on the sofa beside her. 'I knew you would somehow bring me round to that again. Is it any wonder I do not visit as often as I ought?'

'Well, is she?'

'Probably not.'

'I will find the money for you, but there are conditions.' Her jointure had been invested to bring in a fair return; she would draw on that until she had finished the portrait of Lavinia, and she would take the commission from the Royal Academy she had been offered. If the worst came to the worst, she would have to give a little less to the orphans. After all, her own stepson must come first.

'I must give her up.'

'Yes, she is too expensive. And stop gambling.'

'The first is no hardship, there are plenty more fish in the sea, but as to the second... How is a man to pass the time if he cannot play a hand of cards, now and again?'

'I am sure you will find a way. Take a repairing lease to the country, pay more attention to the working of the estate. After all, in a few months' time, you will have the running of it.'

'I suppose so,' he muttered morosely, just as the door opened and Lavinia came tripping in with the rabbit in her arms.

He shot to his feet, his face creased in a huge smile. 'Why, Lady Lavinia, I did not know you were here. How do you do?' And he swept her a bow.

She responded with a slight bending of the knee and an answering smile. 'My lord.'

'What are you doing with that rabbit?'

'I found it injured and Lady Corringham has been looking after it for me. Is it not beautiful? Look at its eyes, they are so blue. Stroke its fur, see how soft it is.'

Frances watched in alarm as he reached out and did as she asked and their hands came into contact. She saw them look up and their eyes met and held, just as they had in the theatre. Much as she loved James, she was not at all sure she trusted him with the highly charged emotions of a sixteen-year-old.

'Lady Lavinia,' she said sternly. 'I left you with an exercise to do.'

'Oh, I have done it long ago. And I was bored.'

'You could have found something else to occupy you.'

'There is nothing in your studio, my lady, but pictures. Besides, the rabbit is hungry. I was taking it to the kitchen to beg food for it.'

'Then do so, while I say goodbye to the Earl. Then return upstairs to the studio.'

Lavinia turned to James and curtsied, he bowed and, with a last lingering look at him, she left the room.

'My word, Mama, she is a fetching chit, is she not?'

'Yes, but too young for you and too well nurtured.'

'Whatever I am, I am not a rakeshame, ma'am,' he said in offended tones. 'I do not seduce innocents. How can you think I would?'

'No, of course not. I am being too sensible of my responsibility when she is in my care. Now, you may take your leave and I will settle your pressing debts for you.'

'Oh, Little Mama, you are a sweetheart! I will be good, I promise.'

He left the house with far more alacrity than he had entered it and she smiled, knowing he had turned her round his thumb—that was nothing new. Sighing, she made her way upstairs to her studio. Marcus would be here soon to collect his daughter and she did not know how she was going to survive the encounter.

Chapter Seven

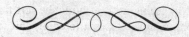

It became evident as soon as Frances entered the room that Lavinia had been moving the portraits stacked against the wall. The girl was standing at the window, holding the picture of her father as a young pugilist.

'What are you doing with that?' she said sharply, annoyed that her privacy had been invaded.

'I was bored and wanting something to do, so I began looking at your pictures. I thought I might learn something from them.'

'And have you?'

Lavinia smiled as Frances took the picture from her hands. 'Oh, yes, I have learned you knew my father before this year. That is a picture of him as a young man, is it not?'

'It could be any young man.'

'It could, but it isn't. My lady, you are too good a portraitist for your sitter not to be instantly recognisable. Besides, no one could mistake the way Papa's hair grows from his brow. Mine is the same.' And she pulled up the curls that fell on her forehead to reveal a pronounced widow's peak. 'Not to mention the shape of the brows. Like little wings, they are, outspread to fly.'

Even in her anger at the girl's impudence, Frances appreciated the imagery. It was, she realised, very apt. 'So, the picture is of the Marquis of Risley as he was then,' she said, putting it back against the wall. 'What is that to the point? You should not have moved it.'

'Why was it turned to the wall?'

'It is not the sort of picture young ladies should be looking at.'

'Me, you mean? Because he is my father?'

'Not at all. Any young lady. You are not my only pupil, you know.'

'It is very intimate. How well did you know him?'

'I do not think your papa would be pleased to hear you quizzing me, Lavinia.'

'Oh, do answer me. It is the only way I shall find out about him. Duncan and I hardly saw him when we were children; he was almost a stranger to us.'

'You had your mama. Questions like that should have been addressed to her.'

'Oh, she was never in good health. We had to creep about the house like mice so as not to disturb her. Miss Hastings looked after us, but she was not very fond of exercise, so Duncan and I used to go off on our own, until he went away to school. I miss him.'

'I am sure you do.'

'I suppose that's why I am such a hoyden. Mama despaired of me. Papa has tried to be kind to me since Mama died, but he is so distant and so strict, as if that will cure me. It would be nice to know that he can be human.'

'Of course he is human, Lavinia, how can you say he is not?

'Then tell me what he was like.'

'A young man like any other. A nobleman. Athletic.'

'Yes, I can see that,' his daughter said, with a smile. 'How did you come to paint the portrait? Where did you do it? In your studio?'

'No, I had no studio then. I went to Gentleman Jackson's boxing establishment.'

'You never did! Oh, how daring of you.'

It had been very daring. In their efforts to be alone together she and Marcus would dream up the most extraordinary places to meet. And one day, when he told her he was going to box, she had begged to watch him. How she had managed to slip away from her mama she did not remember, but manage it she had, and taken her sketchbook with her.

'It was commissioned,' she told Lavinia, and that was only half a lie, for Marcus had asked her to do it. 'But the gentleman changed his mind and so I was left with it on my hands.' Changed his mind about other things too. From being everything to him, so he had said, she had become nothing.

'I think it is very good, much better than that horrible thing you did of Lady Willoughby.'

'They are two different styles and subjects and should not be compared.' Frances felt easier discussing the merits of works of art, than the foibles of the Duke of Loscoe. She could not get out of her head the titbit of gossip James had told her. Could it possibly be true? How much did Lavinia know? 'The one is a fashionable portrait, the other an action painting, full of movement. At least it is meant to be.'

'Oh, I can see that. The one of Papa has such strength, every brushstroke is bold and telling. It says, "I am a god, I am invincible."'

'Oh, Lavinia, how whimsical you are!'

'Am I? But you have not answered my question. How well did you know Papa when you were young?'

'Not very well. We met at the usual Society events when I had my come-out. I was just seventeen and he was twenty-three. I never saw him again after the end of the Season.' True, all of it. For how well did she know him? Not well enough, or perhaps too well, to avoid the heartache that followed.

'Oh. I thought there was more to it than that.'

'Well, there was not and why you should think there was, I cannot imagine. And I will answer no more questions on the subject.'

'I thought you might have some idea where a man like Papa would go at dead of night, dressed like a vagrant.'

'Like a vagrant.' She should not encourage the girl, but she was so surprised the words were out before she could stop them.

'Yes. I saw him. I would not have recognised him but for his walk. There is something havey-cavey going on...'

Frances pulled herself together. 'Lavinia, you should not be talking to me about it.'

'But you are the only one I *can* talk to.'

'Fustian! Now, please put it from your mind. We will leave off the sitting and look at that exercise I gave you to do.'

It was a drawing of a large building, a mansion, meant to test the girl's line and perspective, but she had added two horses in the park in front of it and a tiny rabbit in the foreground which brought the picture to life. They were standing with their heads together, going over it when the Duke was announced. Before

Frances could collect her wits, he was in the room, bowing to her.

In his brown frockcoat and well-cut pantaloons, he looked nothing like the ne'er-do-well Lavinia had described. She could only surmise that the girl had seen him setting off for one of the many masked balls that were taking place that Season. She was suddenly confronted by a mental image of the Duke dressed in rags, bowing and dancing with a queen or a columbine and it made her smile.

'My lady.' He greeted her perfectly seriously, but her smile had made his own lips twitch.

'Your Grace. We were just finishing.'

'Let me see.' He took Lavinia's drawing from her and studied it. 'Is this all your work, Vinny?'

'Yes, Papa.' Her previous animation had left her and once again she was the uncommunicative child.

'Good. Well done.' He turned to Frances, smiling urbanely. She could detect no sign of the passionate man who had kissed her in his coach. 'She is showing promise, my lady?'

She was obliged to clear her throat before she could speak and then her voice was husky. 'Indeed, she is. I shall have a rival in a few years' time.'

'Oh, no, I do not think so,' he said. 'I do not think Lavinia will ever need to worry about earning a living.'

'No, but that does not preclude her from using the talents she has,' she said sharply.

'There are many husbands who do not like talented wives.'

'Do they not?' She had been prepared to put their animosity on one side for the sake of his daughter, but his superior attitude was the outside of enough. 'Well, I can tell you that mine was most supportive. And since his demise I have been glad of my talent. I paint and teach to keep myself busy, to prove to myself I am not useless simply because I am a widow, and to help provide for the orphans, not to earn a living.' She was not sure, but she thought she heard Lavinia give a little chuckle.

He smiled. '*Touché*, my lady. I beg your pardon. Tell me, how is the portrait coming along?'

'Well enough, my lord.'

He chuckled. 'A guarded answer. No doubt you had a problem persuading my daughter to sit still.'

'Problems are made to be overcome, sir. It was simply a matter of engaging her attention in something that interests her.'

'And how did you do that?'

'With the rabbit,' Lavinia put in. 'The one we found in the garden.'

'Rabbit?' Marcus queried, turning to Frances. 'Do you mean you kept it?'

'Of course. I promised Andrew I would. And I never break a promise.'

Was there a barb in those innocent words, a reminder that he had not always kept his promises? He was not used to being called to account and it annoyed him. 'And you have allowed Lavinia to handle it?'

'Yes, why not? It is part of the picture. It helps to portray her ladyship's character.'

He frowned. It was difficult enough controlling Lavinia without Frances Corringham encouraging her to defy him, but he must not let Lavinia see it had put his bristles up. 'May I see it?'

'The rabbit?' Frances queried in surprise.

'No, of course not. I meant the picture.'

'No,' she said firmly. 'I never show my work before it is finished.'

Now Lavinia really did giggle. 'I do not think anyone has ever told Papa no before.'

'Well, they have now.'

He took a deep breath to control his anger. 'I shall look forward to seeing the finished picture when it is convenient to you, my lady,' he said stiffly. 'Now, Vinny, we must go. Your dancing master is due at Stanmore House in half an hour.'

Frances led the way downstairs to see them out herself. 'I will see you on Monday, if that is convenient to your papa,' she said, kissing the girl's cheek. She did not know why she did it, except that she wanted to show the child some affection and was surprised when the girl hugged her and kissed her back.

'Lavinia, wait for me in the carriage,' he said. 'I want to speak privately with Lady Corringham.'

Frances wondered what was coming; a mention perhaps of that kiss, an explanation, even an apology, though his attitude since coming to fetch Lavinia was not one of penitence.

As soon as Lavinia was out of earshot, he turned to Frances. 'My lady, could you not have found some other means to persuade Lavinia to sit still?'

'Not one that came immediately to mind and, knowing how fond she is of animals, it seemed the perfect solution. You surely do not object?'

'I told her she could not have it.'

'She does not have it. It is in a box in my kitchen and when it has fully recovered, I shall see that it is set free.'

'That is nothing to the point. Did it not occur to you

that encouraging my daughter in her silliness would undermine my authority with her?'

'I did not think your authority was so fragile, sir, that a little thing like a rabbit could break it.' Far from wishing to express regret for his behaviour the night before, he was even more arrogant than usual. 'In truth, I am persuaded that Lady Lavinia is more than a little in awe of you.'

'Fustian! I have never laid a finger on her in my life…'

'Oh, I can readily believe that, when I understand you have hardly spent any time with her as a child.' She should not have said that, she knew, but she wanted a fight, needed it to give vent to her anger, anger with him for making her feel of so little consequence that he could kiss her without so much as a by your leave, anger with herself for allowing it. 'Children need both parents; from what I have gleaned, Lady Lavinia and her brother were often left to their own devices…'

'Has she told you that?'

'No,' she said hastily. 'I deduced it.'

'Did your extraordinary powers of deduction also tell you the reason?'

'No, your Grace,' she answered evenly, refusing to rise to his sarcasm. 'But if there is a reason, then surely you should have explained it to your daughter…'

'Oh, so now you are presuming to tell me how to deal with my daughter. I collect you are an expert on bringing up children.'

'That was a low blow and unworthy of you.'

He was chagrined but his pride would not allow him to admit it to her. 'So we are sparring, are we?'

'If it is the only way to make you see…'

'See what?'

'That children thrive on kindness and that if things are explained to them so that they understand, they will behave.'

'I am unkind to my daughter? I am unkind simply because I refuse to allow her to have a wild animal in the house?'

'No, of course not, but...'

'Then, my lady, I suggest you leave my daughter to me.'

It was all very well for her to ring a peal over him about his daughter, but she had no idea of the true state of affairs and he had no intention of telling her. His wife had not been interested in him as a person, only as the provider of a title. She had said more than once after Lavinia's birth that she wished the girl had been a boy, so that she might not be troubled by him again. And after Duncan was born two years later, she told him she had provided him with his heir and as far as she was concerned her duty was done. From then on they had led separate lives, publicly blaming it on her ill health.

He had seen his children only occasionally and now he found he hardly knew them and did not know how to deal with them. Were they still children or young adults? But he resented being lectured. He turned and took his hat from Creeley and clamped it on his head. 'I bid you good day, my lady.'

Frances watched him go, then turned back inside and went into the dining room for her own light repast. But she could not eat. Her throat seemed to be closed by her swiftly beating heart. Oh, it was too bad of him to look down his aristocratic nose at her and dictate to her as if she were a servant at his beck and call. Was that how he looked upon her? No, she told herself, if that kiss was anything to go by he had other ideas for her. He would soon learn his mistake. *If* he ever came again after today's brangle. Would he even allow Lavinia to come again? If he did not, she would miss her. And it was Lavinia who would be the loser.

She was still sitting at the table, the untouched food in front of her, when Percy was announced. He did not wait to be shown into the drawing room but followed Creeley into the dining room and, removing his hat, sat down at the table with her. 'You are eating late, Fanny. Had you forgot we were going out in my new phaeton this afternoon?'

'Goodness, yes, I had. Oh, Percy I am so sorry. Wait, while I change, it will not take me long.' She abandoned her meal and hurried to her room. It was the work of only a few minutes to change into a full skirt of soft green wool and a matching jacket, nipped in at the waist and fastened with silver frogging. Cramming a small green hat on to her dark curls, she hurried to rejoin her escort.

'Very fetching,' he said, offering her his arm.

The phaeton, standing at the gate, was painted butter yellow and was picked out in lines of red and black. Harnessed to it were two matching greys. She stopped to admire them. 'Percy, are they new too?'

'Yes, bought them off Lord Graham,' he said, helping her up to the high seat, before climbing up after her. 'Seems he's pinched in the pocket and about to swallow a spider.'

'Bankrupt? Goodness, how did that come about?'

'Gambling, my dear,' He flicked the reins and the huge red-painted wheels began to turn. 'He can't seem to resist it. I heard he was in to the tune of ten thousand.'

'Oh, his poor wife!'

'Yes, indeed. You need bottomless pockets to speculate that recklessly.' He paused. 'Talking about chance, I heard young James was in pretty deep…'

'Oh, chicken feed.' So that was what this talk of Lord Graham was leading up to, a jobation about James's irresponsibility, or hers in not curbing the young man, but it must mean James's debts were already the subject of gossip and she did not like that. 'I have dealt with it.'

'You should not be obliged to do so, my dear.'

'I am his stepmother.'

'Yes, but I know you, you will not go to the trustees for the blunt, but find it yourself. You cannot keep doing it, Fanny. He is not a child, he has to learn to stand on his own feet.'

'I know. You do not need to ring a peel over me. I have talked to him and he has promised to reform.'

'And will he?'

'Of course.' She spoke firmly, but both knew it was unlikely.

'Shall I speak to him?'

'No, please do not. He would be mortified if he knew I had mentioned the matter to you. Now, shall we change the subject? What other *on dit* have you heard?'

'Mrs Harcourt has bought a new house in Park Place, not a stone's throw from Stanmore House. They say she is determined to shackle the Duke of Loscoe.'

'Then she will come home by weeping cross.'

'How do you know that?' he asked, looking sideways at her. 'The lady, I have heard, can be very tenacious.'

'So she may be, but I still think she will fail.'

'Twenty pounds says she will have him rivetted by the end of the Season.'

'The orphans could find a good use for twenty pounds, but I cannot take your money, Percy. Mrs Harcourt has tried to engage the Duke's attention before and failed and, besides, there is another with a prior claim.'

He looked startled. 'Has he offered?'

'I doubt it. He has told me he is not contemplating matrimony…'

'Surely you would not agree to *carte blanche*?'

'*Me?*' she queried in surprise. 'You thought *I* was the prior claim?'

'Why not? Any one with half an eye can see he is dangling after you.'

She laughed, but it was not her usual happy chuckle but a rough sound that was alien to his ears. 'Oh, Percy, the great Duke of Loscoe *dangling*! I am quite sure he would not cast himself so low as to *dangle*.'

'Perhaps not, but you know what I mean.' He smiled, as they entered the gates of the park and joined the cavalcade.

'I assure you he holds me in aversion. I have had the temerity to criticise his handling of his daughter.'

'You do say! But if it is not you he wishes for a *chère amie*, it must be Mrs Poole…'

'Mrs Poole is her name, is it? I have heard the gossip. They say there is a child.'

'Yes. I wish you had not learned of it.'

'James told me.'

'James should learn to keep his tongue between his teeth.'

'Why? You did not think it would hurt me, did you?'

'Does it not?'

'No, of course it does not. Percy, it is seventeen years since I clapped eyes on the man; he could have had a dozen mistresses in that time, probably has, if the gossip about his marriage is true. Why should that concern me?'

'If it does not, then I am truly thankful.'

'Do you think we could talk about something else? The love life of the Duke of Loscoe is beginning to bore me.'

He inclined his head towards her. 'As you wish. Did you know Lady Willoughby is planning a masked ball for Felicity?' He chuckled suddenly. 'I suppose she hopes that if everyone is masked, she can more easily fire her off.'

'Percy, that is unkind in you.'

'Well, you must admit, the chit is definitely plain.'

'I do not think so. She is young and a little gawky, but she will blossom, especially if she finds a nice young man to offer for her...'

'Not the Duke of Loscoe?'

'I thought we had agreed to dispense with that subject,' she said sharply. Why was his name on everyone's lips? Why was everything he said and did a subject for tattle? Why could she not escape, not even with Percy, whom she thought she could trust to avoid talking of him?

'Sorry,' he said. 'I forgot.'

To Frances's immense relief, the conversation was brought to an end by the approach of a barouche carrying Lady Graham and her daughter, Constance. The two carriages pulled up to one side so that the ladies could exchange greetings, and though naturally nothing was said of Lord Graham's financial worries, her ladyship did look rather longingly at the greys.

'I feel so sorry for her,' Frances said, as they moved off afterwards. 'This is Constance's come-out Season and, if his lordship really is in deep, it will not help.'

'No. Undoubtedly the daughter will be expected to haul her papa out of the mire with a good marriage.'

'Do you think so?'

'Probably. But who among this Season's eligibles is well breeched enough to do it? Apart from the Duke of Loscoe, that is, since we are forbidden to speak of him.'

She laughed and thumped him on the shoulder, which jerked the hand that held the reins and for a minute or two his whole attention was given to controlling the spirited horses who, confused by the unexpected signal to ginger up, could not find the room to do so in the confines of the carriageway and were set on running everyone else down.

'You nearly had us over,' he said, when they were once more trotting towards the exit. 'These high-perch affairs can be unstable, you know.'

'Yes, I am sorry.'

They continued in silence for some minutes until he suddenly spoke again. 'If we are forbidden to speak of Stanmore, what are we to do when we come face to face with him?'

'What do you mean?'

'Only that he has just come through the gate and is riding towards us. Unless you wish to give him the cut direct, we shall have to acknowledge him.'

She looked in the direction he was pointing and saw Marcus, riding a huge black stallion. The other gentleman, on a grey, she did not know. 'I have no wish to cut him, Percy. That would make him more insufferable than ever, thinking I was in a quake over him.'

'And we cannot have that, can we?' he retorted, pulling the carriage to one side as the two men drew rein.

'Good afternoon, your Grace,' she said, as coolly as she could manage, considering her heart was beating nineteen to the dozen and her hands were shaking.

'My lady, your obedient. May I present my friend, Major Donald Greenaway. Donald, this is the Countess of Corringham.'

'Major.' She inclined her head towards him.

'How do you do, my lady?' he said, doffing his curly-brimmed hat. He was a big, burly man, dressed in a drab riding coat and biscuit-coloured breeches tucked into polished riding boots, by no means elegant, but neat enough. 'I believe you are teaching Lady Lavinia.'

She gave a short laugh. 'Yes, along with a dancing master and a good many other talented people.'

'Ah, but there is only one Countess of Corringham and I collect she is above compare.' His broad smile was enough to counter any offence she might have felt at his familiarity so soon after meeting. It was as if they were old friends.

Guessing it had been Marcus who had told him about her, she risked a sideways glance at him and was surprised to find him looking at her, an expression of acute discomfort on his face. She smiled and returned her attention to his companion. 'Gammon, Major,' she said.

'Oh, do not be so modest, my lady. The Duke has told me how you are bringing Lady Lavinia on by leaps and bounds.'

'His Grace is biased.'

'Oh, undoubtedly. But he is not the only one to say it. I collect all London is vying to send their daughters to you.'

'Fie, Major, I would not have expected a military

man like you to deal in flummery. And I am too old to be taken in by it.'

'Old, my lady? On the contrary, you are in your prime.' His laugh was a cheerful boom and startled a couple of riders who were passing by. 'Stanmore,' he said. 'Bear me out, do.'

Marcus smiled. 'I am sure the Countess knows her own worth.'

'An enigmatic answer, if ever I heard one,' Percy put in.

'Oh, the Duke is too much the gentleman to say outright that he does not always agree with my methods,' Frances said, thoroughly embarrassed, but determined to have the last word and a cool one too. 'But we have agreed a truce. Is that not so, your Grace?'

'Indeed it is,' he said, equally determined not to quarrel publicly with her. She was smiling at him, her violet eyes bright with laughter. It unnerved him. Had she forgotten that he had kissed her, that he had been so ill-advised as to tell her how he had been longing to do so for years? Judging by her behaviour she had not set much store by it and had put it from her mind. Why did he feel like a boy when in her presence?

'Sir Percival, I do think we should be going,' she said. She had acted the part of the imperturbable matron to the best of her ability, but she ought to retire from the arena while she still had her wits about her and before the Duke brought fresh guns to bear. 'Your Grace, I shall look forward to seeing Lady Lavinia on Monday. Major, it has been a pleasure to make your acquaintance.'

'And I yours, my lady.' He bowed, Marcus touched his hat, Percy bade them a brief goodbye and the phaeton bowled away.

'A beautiful woman,' Donald said, watching the colourful equipage disappear through the gate.

'Yes.'

'Have you really had a falling-out over Lady Lavinia?'

'It was nothing of consequence.'

'Oh, come on, man, don't be so close. Tell me about it.'

They turned and walked their horses along the Row. 'It was only a little thing but it made me think she is too easy going and allows Vinny too much sail.'

'And you would have the chit close hauled?'

'Not at all. But I do not like having my authority countered.'

Donald laughed. 'Oh, I am sure you do not. But methinks her ladyship has the measure of you.'

'How so? She will toe the line because she knows I can withdraw Lavinia from her at any time and she needs the money.'

'Does she? She did not give me that impression. Top of the trees, to say the least.'

'Oh, not for herself. For her stepson. He's deep in dun territory and is always applying to her to fetch him out.'

'And you feel sorry for her…'

'No, I do not,' he said sharply. 'That's the last thing I feel for her. She is well able to look after herself. Sharp as a razor and cold as ice.' He paused before going on with a chuckle. 'But put a child in front of her and she is as soft as warm butter. Her stepchildren and grandchildren adore her and they are so easy with her. Even Vinny…'

Donald turned to look at him, one eyebrow raised in

a query. 'Oh, I see. Caught you on a tender spot, has she?'

'What do you mean?'

'Oh, come on, old friend, you have been struggling with your daughter for years…'

'That is not altogether my fault.'

'I did not say it was. But if the Countess has unlocked the secret to Lady Lavinia's affections, perhaps you should listen to her, even if it does mean admitting you were wrong.'

'She does not make it easy.'

'You mean you do not. You can be very stiff-rumped at times, Stanmore.'

Marcus gave a wry smile. 'If you were anyone but the friend you are, I would tap your claret for that remark.'

'Do it if it makes you feel any better. We can always go to Jackson's and strip off.'

'No. And if I am to make any headway with my daughter, I must go home and have tea with her. I left her trying to master the steps of the minuet, but the dancing master does not have the patience of Fa—the Countess.'

'Oh, so you admit, her ladyship has patience.'

'I never said anything to the contrary.'

'I do believe you have fallen in love with her.'

'Fustian! We cannot spend half an hour together without falling out.'

'What is that to the point? I would say that is a sign of affection rather than otherwise. She would make an admirable duchess.'

'And I am not thinking of remarrying. I had enough of being leg-shackled the first time ever to welcome a second shot at it. Besides, she is perfectly content with her life…'

'Has she told you so?'

'As good as. And do not give me a jobation over it, for I will not listen. Let us cut across the grass and have a gallop. Demon needs the exercise and so do I.' And suiting action to words, he spurred his horse and sped away. He did not feel like justifying himself to Donald.

He pulled up on the other side of the park and together the two men walked their horses out of the Stanhope Gate, down Park Lane and along Piccadilly towards St James's. They spoke very little; Marcus was deep in thought.

He could not get Donald's words out of his head. Could not get Frances Corringham out of his head. She was there, plaguing his waking thoughts, disturbing his dreams, making him behave like a clodpole. And she made him feel inadequate when it came to his daughter, who seemed to have made a friend of her. Fanny had kissed her affectionately, just as if they were allies against him, and Vinny had returned it. Vinny never kissed him. As far as he could remember, she never had.

It was remarkable, Frances told herself, that on the next few occasions when Marcus brought Lavinia to her lesson or for a portrait sitting, he stayed to watch, not saying very much, but sitting thoughtfully on the other side of the room. Frances was encouraged to suggest he might escort them on a tour of the city looking at its architecture and he agreed without demur. It might, of course, mean that he did not trust her with his daughter, that he was afraid she would encourage Lavinia's wilful behaviour, or perhaps that Lavinia might confide more than she ought to of their family life. Or it might mean that he had taken her criticism to heart and was anxious to make amends.

Whatever it was, Lavinia blossomed. She behaved more pleasantly when she was introduced to new people and her conversation with Frances was more animated. She was still a little subdued when with her father, but the surliness seemed to have vanished. Marcus could not fail to notice and he knew the change had been wrought by Frances. She treated her like an adult and never talked down to her, so that they behaved like friends who had known each other all their lives.

It wrenched his heart to think that if he had married Frances when they were young she would have been the mother of his children and this wonderful affectionate interplay between the two people he loved most in the world would have been Lavinia's from birth. Frances would have brought his children up to value themselves. They would not have needed to misbehave to be noticed. Why had he not been stronger? Why had he not stood up to his parents and insisted on marrying Frances?

Oh, he knew the reason. He had been in awe of his noble father, just as Frances said Lavinia was in awe of him. Because he had been told that opposing his ailing mother would kill her and he had loved his mother. That had been moral blackmail of the worst kind; his mother had outlived both his father and his wife and died peacefully only a year previously. Did he want to exert the same sort of influence over his daughter? He could not bear for her to be as unhappy as he had been. Neither could he stand by and watch her come to grief for want of parental guidance. Why was being a father so difficult? He would be glad when his sister arrived to take over. Or would he, if it meant he saw less of Frances Corringham?

Marcus and Lavinia were riding together along Rotten Row early one morning when they met Frances, accompanied by her stepson, riding toward them. Frances looked every inch the aristocrat in her dark blue taffeta habit, cut to fit her neat waist. Its neckline was filled with a lace jabot, tied like a man's cravat. On her head was a copy of a man's riding hat, except that it was decked with a tiny veil and a sweeping peacock feather. She was riding a tall dappled grey, which he thought a trifle too powerful for her, but she controlled it easily, as they drew up to greet each other.

'Your Grace.' She was, as usual politeness itself, but nothing more. There was no warmth in her smile until she turned to Lavinia, when her face lit up with pleasure. 'Lavinia, how charming you look. That forest green suits you. Perhaps I should have painted you on a horse, after all.'

'You can always do another, my lady,' Lavinia said, laughing and making the feather on her riding hat dance. Then she turned to James, who seemed to be mesmerised by her. 'My lord. How do you do?'

'All the better for having met you, my lady.'

Marcus frowned and looked at Frances, who met his gaze unflinchingly. James was only paying the girl a pretty compliment and, as he had already given his assurance that he had no designs on her, she was not going to let herself be cowed by black looks from Marcus Stanmore.

'Papa, can we not all ride together?' Lavinia asked.

'That is, if you would like it, my lady,' she added to Frances.

'I should like that very much.' She wheeled her horse about to draw abreast of Lavinia, but James beat her to it. Reluctantly she fell in beside a brooding Marcus to follow them.

'Is the Earl staying with you, my lady?' he asked in a low voice, so that the two young people could not hear.

She knew his reason for asking very well. He did not like the idea of Lavinia becoming infatuated with the young man, which to her mind was very unreasonable of him. True, Lavinia was very young and James was something of a scapegrace, but he was by no means ineligible and who was not to say he would not settle down and make a good husband, especially when he came into control of his inheritance? 'No, your Grace, he lives in chambers in Albany when he is in Town.'

'But he visits?'

'Naturally, he visits. I should be sad if he did not. But if you are uneasy about Lavinia, I beg you not to be. I assure you, she is always chaperoned.'

'Thank you. She is too young to be able to deal with young rakes.'

'James is not a rake,' she said sharply. 'And do you not think it would be better to allow her to meet a few young men so that she may learn how to deal with them?'

'Time enough for that next year.'

'And next year, no doubt, she will be thrown in among all manner of men, old and young, eligible and otherwise, and be expected to choose a husband. It is not easy for a young lady of seventeen to separate the honourable from the dishonourable. It is all too easy for her to be taken in by a flattering tongue.' She paused and added heavily, 'Believe me, I know.'

'That, my lady, was as low a blow as ever I have dealt.'

She smiled in spite of herself. 'Then I beg your pardon. I will aim higher next time.'

He sighed. 'The trouble is that Vinny thinks she knows it all…'

'A failing of most young people, as you must know. Can you not remember what it was like to be young?'

'Only too well. I would not have my children make my mistakes.'

She laughed. 'Your errors belong to you, sir. The younger generation will make their own and learn by them too, as we all have to do.'

He wanted to ask her if she had learned by her mistakes, but decided not to risk a put-down. Instead he said, 'That is a very liberated doctrine, my lady, and I am not at all sure I can subscribe to it. Already Lavinia is getting above herself. She thinks I should allow her to go to Lady Willoughby's masked ball. Did you put the idea into her head?'

'No, I did not. A masked ball is not suitable for a young lady of sixteen, not yet out. I doubt Lady Willoughby will invite her.'

'No, but she has invited me and Vinny thinks I could persuade her. Which, of course, I will not.'

A little shiver of dread, of anticipation, of she knew not what, coursed through Frances at the news that he had been invited. She had received her own invitation and it was taken for granted she would accept, but would he go? 'You are right, my lord, Lady Lavinia must wait until she has come out before attending such a function, but I can imagine her disappointment.' She paused. 'I have an idea. I have been thinking of having a soirée at my home, just a few friends, young and old, with some music and a little country dancing. Would you allow Lady Lavinia to attend that? It might recompense her a little.'

'It is very kind of you, my lady.'

'Not at all. I have become very fond of Lavinia.'

'So I have noticed,' he said laconically. 'I believe the feeling is reciprocated.'

'You do not mind?'

'Not in the least. It pleases me.' His sombre eyes became two shades lighter as he allowed his smile to reach his eyes and illuminate his face. When he looked at her like that, her heart turned over and she had to remind herself he had always been a rake, that if the rumour was true, he kept a mistress and had had a child by her. She must not allow herself to be taken in by him a second time.

'Then I shall make the arrangements. Perhaps you would allow Lavinia to help me, if she wishes to, that is.'

'Yes, of course.'

The young couple were drawing a little too far ahead and they hastened to catch them. A few minutes later they reached the gate where they parted company. James bade Lavinia goodbye with great civility and she blushed prettily before riding off beside her father. Frances watched them go, then turned for home, knowing she was becoming more and more involved with the Duke of Loscoe and all because of his pretty daughter.

Her emotions rode a seesaw; being in his company was both pleasure and pain and yet she could not walk away from it. It was her destiny to love him until the day she died, but that was something she would keep to herself.

* * *

Lavinia was enthusiastic about the soirée; her very own dance, she called it and spent more time than usual at Corringham House helping Frances to make the arrangements. Marcus left them to it, which was just as well, Frances told herself, she did not want him fussing around telling her what she should and should not do.

They were writing out the invitations one morning when a message arrived from Mrs Thomas that there was a problem at the orphanage and Mrs Randall was needed. Frances laid down her pen and sent Creeley to ask for the tilbury to be harnessed and brought to the door.

'We will have to finish these tomorrow,' she told Lavinia. 'I must go up and change and then I will take you home before I go on.'

'May I come with you to the orphanage?' Lavinia asked, when they were seated in the tilbury and weaving their way in and out of the traffic in Piccadilly. 'I should like to see the children.'

'I am not sure your papa would approve, Lavinia.'

'Why not? He subscribes to the orphanage and I cannot see what harm it would do. Oh, please, Countess.'

In the event, the decision was taken out of Frances's hands for when they reached Stanmore House, the Duke was out and Miss Hastings had gone to the library; there was no one into whose hands she could deliver her charge. They rode on to Monmouth Street. 'You will notice that I am known as Mrs Randall at the home,' she told Lavinia. 'They believe I am the Countess's companion. So please keep my secret.'

'Even from Papa?'

'Oh, I do not think he would be interested, my dear. But the people at the home might be embarrassed and

behave awkwardly if they knew my real identity. They
behave more naturally if they think of me as their un-
pretentious friend. And that's how I like it.'

When they arrived, one of the little boys ran out to
hold the horses and Frances took Lavinia inside where
Mrs Thomas came forward to greet them. 'I am glad
you came, ma'am. I am afraid we have been robbed and
I suspect one of the children. He denies it, of course…'

'I will speak to him. Lavinia, wait here for me.'

She followed the matron into the tiny room which
was used as an office to find herself confronted by a
boy of about seven, with grubby blond curls and an
impudent smile. It was all she could do not to smile
back. She turned from him to the plump matron beside
her. 'What has he stolen?'

'Cheese, ma'am. A good pound of it. And half a
loaf.'

Frances squatted down beside the boy. 'Were you
hungry?'

He shook his head. 'No. Not me. Ma…'

'Your mother?' Frances queried. 'Do you mean you
are not an orphan?'

He did not know what she meant and did not answer.
After a little gentle prodding, he told her that his
mother, a widow, had sent him to the orphanage with
instructions to say he had no parents because then he
would be clothed and fed. The only trouble was, she
could not turn her back on her son and so she had taken
to hanging around outside the house in the hope of seeing him. And when she did, she asked him to bring her
food.

Matron was all for having him charged, saying to let
him off would set the others off and there would be no
end to the pilfering, but Frances could not do it. She

decided to send for the child's mother and offer her a job cleaning the orphanage, but Mrs Thomas had to be persuaded it was the right course to take and the lady herself had to be found, which meant that it was long past Lavinia's usual time for going home when Frances went in search of her.

She found her sitting on the garden wall of the home, sketching some of the children in the street. She jumped up when she saw Frances. 'Is everything all right, my lady?'

'Yes, perfectly. Now, let's get you home.'

She was not at all surprised when, drawing the tilbury up at the door of Stanmore House, she was confronted by an irate Marcus.

'Come inside, my lady,' he said, tight-lipped. 'I wish for an explanation.'

Frances had no intention of leaving Lavinia to face his wrath alone and, leaving one of his grooms to see to the horses, she followed him inside.

Chapter Eight

'Now, my lady,' he said, once they were in the drawing room. 'You will oblige me by telling me where you have been and why you have kept my daughter out so late.'

'Naturally, I will tell you,' she said coolly. 'You do not have to shout.'

'I am not shouting,' he said, though, realising there was some truth in what she said, lowered his tone. But that did not mean he was any less angry; the low controlled voice was even more ominous. 'But if I were, there would be some justification. I trusted you to take care of my daughter...'

'Which I have done. She has come to no harm.'

'I was not to know that.' He had been worried half to death and his relief at seeing both of them safe was tempered with anger that she could have put him through such anxiety. 'How do you think I felt when I went to fetch her from your house at the time prescribed, only to find neither of you at home? Gone out urgently, I was told. What was so urgent you could not deliver my child to me before you went on whatever errand it was?'

'I did. Or I tried to, but there was no one at home,' she said, determined to keep calm. 'You were out and so was Miss Hastings. The only people in the house were male servants. I promised you that Lady Lavinia would always be chaperoned, so I decided to take her with me.'

'Where?' He looked down at her plain grey gown and recognised it as the one she had worn when he had rescued her from the crowd in Covent Garden. Had she introduced Lavinia, his sheltered aristocratic daughter, to the seamier side of London life?

'The Countess took me to the orphanage,' Lavinia put in, unaware that she was exacerbating the situation. 'It was very enlightening. I had no idea…'

'Nor should you have,' he said angrily. 'It is not a proper place for you to go.'

'Why not? If it is proper for the Countess of Corringham, surely there is no harm in my accompanying her? I made some sketches like the ones her ladyship has in her studio. Do you know there was a little boy there, who reminded me of someone, though I could not, for the life of me, think who.'

'Nonsense, Lavinia! You cannot possibly know anyone in those environs. Now go to your room. I will decide what to do after I have spoken to Lady Corringham.'

She was instantly subdued and laying the sketchbook on the table, left the room, stopping only to bob a curtsy to Frances.

'It was not Lady Lavinia's fault,' Frances said, as evenly as she could. 'You did not need to speak so sharply to her.'

'I shall speak to my own daughter exactly as I please, madam.' Knowing she was right did not make him feel any less like taking her shoulders in his hands and shaking her until her teeth rattled. And finishing that up by kissing her soundly. 'One thing is very certain, I was wrong to think you would show her a good example of how to behave. You have been too long independent and I begin to regret my decision to hand her into your care.'

'I have not behaved ill. The home for the orphans is not in a good area of town, I admit, but it is clean and the children are neat and well behaved. It showed her ladyship that there are those a great deal worse off than she is who deserve her sympathy. I believe it has done Lavinia no harm at all.' She paused to take stock of how he was receiving her plea, but he was flicking open the sketchbook and appeared not to be listening. 'But I am truly sorry for being so late back. There was a small problem with one of the children...'

'This one?' He held out the sketchbook for her to see.

She saw a very competent drawing of a tousle-haired three-year-old boy. He was dressed in rags, but he had an impish face, wide bright eyes framed by delicately shaped brows and a broad grin. 'No. It was one of the older boys. I don't think I have ever seen this child before, except...'

'Except what?' He seemed to have forgotten all about Lavinia and his whole attention was on her answer.

'He reminds me of someone.'

'He is perhaps one of the orphans?'

'No, I do not think so. Unless he has newly arrived. I did not have time to talk to Mrs Thomas about any newcomers. But the home is full to bursting, I do not think there is room to squeeze even a little one in.'

'Then how did Lavinia come to draw him?'

'There were some children hanging round the gate…' She paused, expecting him to begin a new diatribe over letting Lavinia as far as the gate unsupervised, but he seemed mesmerised by the sketch. 'Is it important?'

'No, no,' he said hurriedly. It was not the boy, it was simply a child that looked like him. But he would have to check; he had promised himself he would leave no stone unturned, nor would he. 'It is of no consequence.'

'Then if you will excuse me, I must go, I have an evening engagement.' She took a deep breath. 'I am sorry to have displeased you, your Grace. No doubt you will find someone else to instruct your daughter. In any case, she is too talented for me to teach, and needs someone more illustrious.'

'Fudge! I decide who teaches my daughter. You will continue as before, but be warned, I will not have her leave your house when she is with you, unless I accompany you both.' He could not tell her about Poole, not yet, but if the man was out there somewhere and had recognised Lavinia, could he, would he, use her to exact his vengeance? Had he already seen her?

'Marcus Stanmore, you are the outside of enough!' she said, so exasperated she could not hold her tongue. 'Duke you may be, but I never met anyone so top-lofty and full of his own importance. Did you never make a mistake? Did you never do something you regretted?'

'Oh, yes,' he said softly. 'Often.'

'And I suppose you never thought of making an apology?'

'When it was justified, of course. You think I should beg your pardon?'

'No, I am suggesting that you might accept an apology with a good grace when it is offered. I have said I am sorry, I am not going to grovel.'

He laughed suddenly. 'No, I did not expect you would. I do accept your apology, my lady, and for what it is worth, I offer you mine.' He paused and added softly, 'You once spoke of a truce. Let us have a truce.'

'Very well.'

'Then I shall bring Lavinia to you tomorrow.'

It was as she turned to go that she saw the picture above the hearth. It was of a woman whom she assumed by her dress to be the Duke's mother and standing at her knee was a three-year-old child—Marcus himself, she decided. What set her heart beating was the way the boy stood, leaning back a little, the left foot slightly ahead of the right, the laughing expression on his upturned face, his tousled hair. It was almost exactly mirrored by the sketch he held in his hand, except for the clothing. On one it was very fine and on the other ragged.

It meant nothing, she told herself as she journeyed home. Lavinia had seen that picture in her father's drawing room every day since coming to London; she must have subconsciously copied the pose. But Marcus had been shocked by it. Who was it who had said that the Stanmores had such distinctive features that the Duke could not fail to recognise his own child? Had Lavinia inadvertently sketched his love child?

But what was the boy doing in that horrible rundown area of London, dressed in rags? Surely Marcus had not been so unfeeling as to turn his *amour* away without making provision for her or his child? For all his arrogance, she could not believe that of him. Or had the woman left him? It was a mystery and for a few minutes it occupied her mind to the exclusion of everything else, including her own hurt. Marcus had also noticed the likeness, she was sure of it. Had he been struck by guilt?

What would he do about it? By the time she arrived home she had made up her mind to try and find out more. She needed to lay a ghost.

She was back in Monmouth Street the following morning, before the children had even finished their breakfasts. Rolling up her sleeves, she helped to serve them with nourishing gruel and bread and butter. She looked closely into the face of each one, but none resembled the child Lavinia had drawn.

'Are all the children here?' she asked Mrs Thomas. 'There are none ill and still in bed? I should not like to miss anyone out.'

'They are all here, ma'am.'

So the mystery child was not one of the orphans. Did he live nearby? Where was his mother?

'It is a strange thing, but there was a man here last night asking the selfsame question,' the good lady added. 'At least, not a gentleman, for he was dressed very ordinary, as if he was down on his luck. He had a drawing of a little boy and asked me if I knew him, which I didn't, but I don't think I would have told him if I had. It was all too havey-cavey.'

'Did he say who the child was?'

'No, ma'am. Nor who he was. He had another fellow with him, a big muscular brute who never opened his mouth. Gave me the creeps they did. Up to no good, I'll be bound.'

Frances knew it was the Duke. Lavinia had seen him leaving the house dressed like a labourer. So that was the reason for it. He was searching for his bastard son. How had he come to be lost? What did he mean to do when he found him? The questions plagued her. 'Mrs

Thomas, if you ever come across that child, find out where he lives and send for me, will you?'

She left the house and returned home. She only just had time to change into a yellow silk day-dress, tidy her hair and compose herself on a sofa in the drawing room before the Duke and Lavinia were announced.

'Your Grace,' she said, dropping him a curtsy.

'My lady, your obedient,' he said, with an inclination of his head. 'I hope I find you well?'

'Indeed, yes. And you?'

'In plump currant, as your little grandson would say.'

She smiled at his little joke. His ire of the evening before seemed to have vanished. He was urbane and smiling, but his eyes looked tired and there was a paleness about his complexion she had not noticed before, as if he were bowed down by worry. She found herself feeling sorry for him. 'Do sit down,' she said. Returning to the sofa, she sat down and patted the seat beside her. 'Lavinia, sit beside me.'

He flung up the skirt of his dove grey frockcoat and sat down on one of her gilded chairs, putting his hat on the floor beside him. Lavinia flopped down beside Frances and then, as if remembering a lecture delivered before they arrived, sat upright and folded her hands neatly in her lap. It was all so formal, so trite, so awkward that Frances wanted to laugh. She rang the bell and sent a footman to the kitchen with a message for refreshments to be provided.

'Now, my lord,' she said, deciding to take the bull by the horns. 'What have you decided?'

'Decided?'

'Yes, about Lady Lavinia's lessons.'

'They are to continue, of course. I said so yesterday.'

'And the portrait?'

'That too.'

She was not sure that she didn't prefer the bombastic dictatorial Marcus to this scrupulously polite man. He gave her nothing to fight and she wanted to fight. She had to have a contest in order to prove she was alive, that she was her own mistress. And not his, definitely not his. 'And I am free to proceed in my own way?'

'Subject to the provisions I outlined yesterday. Why do you ask?'

'It is best to have everything perfectly clear between us, don't you agree?'

'Of course.' He bowed very slightly, knowing there was more to what she was saying than appeared.

'And the soirée?'

'It is up to you whom you invite to your home, Countess.'

'Yes, but will you allow Lady Lavinia to attend?'

'I have said so.'

'Good. Then we will finish the invitations today.' She paused, smiling. 'There is no necessity for you to stay now. I promise you we will not venture out, except perhaps to the garden.'

His mouth twitched at that and he rose to leave them. 'I will return in two hours.'

As soon as he had gone, Frances, who had suddenly realised she had been holding her breath, let it out in a long sigh of relief. She had survived another encounter with him and she had not given herself away.

'Oh, he is comical when he is trying not to be rude,' Lavinia laughed, as they went upstairs to the boudoir where the half finished invitations were scattered across her escritoire.

'Was he very angry?'

'No, he rang a peal over me, but it was not so bad. And he can never be truly angry with you.'

'Goodness, he gave a very good impression of wrath yesterday afternoon.'

'Oh, that means nothing, he soon got over it. This morning he was all sunshine and ready to forgive and forget.'

'I am glad to hear it. Now, let us finish these invitations and send them out, then we had better get down to work, or he will be back before we have done.'

And with that she closed her mind to the Duke of Loscoe and the little boy and concentrated on the girl and the evening she was arranging for her a week hence.

When Frances visited the home in Monmouth Street the following day, she found Mrs Thomas flitting around in great excitement, picking things up and putting them down again, giving the children tasks and then changing her mind. It was so unlike the lady to be excitable, Frances supposed something very out of the ordinary had happened.

'Oh, Mrs Randall,' she said, on seeing her. 'Such news, such wonderful news. We have a mystery benefactor. A very generous man. He has bought a new home for us. A whole house, big enough for us to take care of all the orphans we have and more besides—what do you think of that?'

'My goodness, that is good news,' Frances said, realising immediately that a bigger house and more children would take more money to keep up and that meant working harder than ever. As soon as she had finished Lavinia's portrait, she must begin on *Spring* and *Summer* for the gentleman at the Royal Academy. How much dare she ask for them?

'Where is this house?' she asked, unwilling to spoil the matron's happiness by pointing out the drawbacks.

'Not too far away. In Maiden Lane. There is work to be done on it before we can move, but the older children will help and there are one or two ladies like yourself who do not mind rolling up their sleeves. We shall soon have everything set to rights.'

'You may count on me to do whatever I can. Mrs Thomas but, just at present, my time is limited.'

'Oh, ma'am, you already do so much, I did not mean…'

Frances laughed. 'I know you did not, but rest assured, any spare time I have is at your disposal.'

Balancing the two sides of her life was becoming more and more difficult, but she did not want to give up either and, besides, it kept her busy and left her no time to brood. She had done enough of that when she was seventeen and had soon discovered it did not help. It had not restored Marcus to her and it would not do so now. She went home to her other life, to finish the portrait and complete the preparations for the soirée.

Because it was Lavinia's debut in such company, Frances, with Marcus's consent, had helped her to choose her dress and very lovely she looked. The gown was white, as befitted a young lady not yet out, made of silk and gauze and decorated with tiny seed pearls. It had a high waist, little puffed sleeves and a decorous boat-shaped neckline.

In the last few weeks Lavinia had lost the gaucheness of the adolescent girl, the slight clumsiness when moving in a crowded room and was developing a poise which would have flattered a young lady two or three years older.

'I am proud of you,' Frances whispered to her when she arrived on the arm of her father.

'Thank you.' Lavinia dropped a deep curtsy.

Frances turned towards Marcus, who was dressed in a plum-coloured tailcoat, grey pantaloons tucked into polished black Hessians and a white brocade waistcoat. There was a diamond pin in his pristine white cravat and a pleasant smile on his face. A handsome devil, she decided, the picture of elegance. And unaccountably she found herself wondering what he looked like dressed as a vagrant in ragged fustian breeches and scuffed leather jerkin. Would she love him any the less? In which guise had Mrs Poole known him? Had she even known who he really was?

Convinced her expression would give her away, she bowed her head so that he could not properly see her face. She really must rid herself of this obsession with him, with Mrs Poole, whoever she was, with the mysterious child and pay attention to her duties. 'Welcome, your Grace.'

'My lady, your obedient,' he said, removing his hat and bowing to her, while appraising her openly. She was in a gown of deep blue silk. The full skirt, narrow sleeves and square neckline were edged in gold ribbon and more gold ribbon was twined through her hair, which was done in a Grecian style which showed off her long pale neck. A simple gold band adorned her neck. There was no doubt in his mind that she was the loveliest woman there and he was filled with a deep longing and even deeper regret for what had been lost.

A footman relieved him of his hat and cloak and Lavinia of her shoulder cape and they proceeded into the reception room. Because it was only a small informal gathering, Frances had decided not to use the ballroom, but to take the carpet out of the drawing room so that the young people could dance. There were hostesses who judged an evening by how much of a squeeze it was, but Frances preferred her guests to have room to move about freely and talk to each other in comfort so, though the room soon filled, it was not overcrowded.

Percy was there, in lemon silk trimmed with blue, Major Greenaway looking dashing in his regimentals, James in a black evening suit spoiled, in Frances's opinion, by a bright cerise waistcoat and a huge cravat, Augusta in pale green and Richard in dove grey. There was Mr and Mrs Butterworth, Lord and Lady Willoughby with Felicity, Lord and Lady Graham with Constance, and half a dozen other young ladies and a few hand-picked eligibles. Lavinia was soon besieged by young gentlemen wishing to dance with her.

'A lovely chit,' Percy drawled when Frances finally had time to talk to him.

'Yes, she is.' Lavinia was at that moment dancing with James, laughing up at him unselfconsciously.

'Over the tantrums, is she?'

'There have been no tantrums, Percy. Lady Lavinia and I deal very well together.'

'That I can believe. Everyone knows how good you are with young people. Loscoe must be relieved.'

'Why relieved?'

'I collect he was finding her a handful and she would have been an encumbrance to his plans for finding a second wife.'

'Surely you are not still backing Mrs Harcourt?'

'Oh, no, that is a lost cause. He gave her a sharp setdown the other day and now she is telling everyone that he asked her and she turned him down.'

She laughed. 'No doubt, to save her pride.'

'Oh, no doubt of it.' He smiled. 'But hell hath no fury like a woman scorned. She is determined to discredit him. Unfortunately she has dragged your name down along with his.'

'Mine?'

'Yes, my dear.'

'Go on.'

'I am not sure I should.'

'If you do not, I will never speak to you again. I must know so that I may deal with it.'

He sighed. 'The lady is saying that you are the Duke's paramour and have been ever since he married, possibly even before that. It is why her dear friend, the Duchess, was so ill. It killed her in the end.'

'Surely no one in their right mind would believe that?'

'Perhaps they would not if that were all, but unfortunately the old gabble-grinder has been often in the company of Lady Barber and they have put two and two together and made a dozen of it.'

'Now you have begun you had better tell me the whole,' she urged when he paused to search her face for signs of distress.

'You remember the talk of a child?'

'Yes, a rumour started by Sir Joshua,' she said, but in her heart she knew it was more than a rumour. Lavinia's drawing, the Duke's reaction and the painting at Stanmore House all pointed to it being the truth. 'What has that to do with me?'

'Why, my dear,' he said, with a mocking smile, '*It is yours*. Yours and the Duke's. Word is that, unwilling to face the scandal, you gave it away at birth, and now he is free to marry you, he is desperately searching for it.'

Her laughter rippled out. 'Oh, Percy, what a Banbury Tale to be sure. When am I supposed to have been *enceinte*? And why did no one notice it?'

'A good question, my dear, and one I found myself asking when the whispers reached me, but it seems you were out of Society for six or seven months about three years ago…'

'Was I?' she asked, mystified. Then, remembering, added, 'Oh, that was when Augusta was expecting Beth. She did not carry her well and was often sick. And as Andrew was still no more than a baby and needed constant attention, I looked after them at Twelvetrees.'

'According to Mrs Harcourt, two children were born at Twelvetrees that summer.'

'Oh, Percy, this is far too outrageous for anyone to believe.'

'They have been a little short on scandal, this Season,' he said laconically. 'And anything that comes along is hungrily lapped up. And you are a prime target.'

'Why?'

'Because you are who you are, wealthy, respectable, talented and because the lady is jealous of you. The Duke is often in your company.'

'With his daughter.'

'Oh, she says Lavinia is merely the means to the end.'

'Does the Duke know about this?' It might explain his strange ups and downs of behaviour towards her. 'Does Lady Lavinia? Oh, I could not bear it if she were to be upset by it. What should I do? Should I speak to Mar—the Duke?'

'No, my dear, unless you want him to bite your head off. I have offered you a solution before. Marry me. That would silence them.'

'No, it would not, they would say I had duped you to save myself. You are too good a friend to be treated you so shabbily.'

'I would deem it an honour.'

'No, Percy, it would not serve and you know it. You are a confirmed bachelor, always have been, and to change your ways now would result in misery for both of us.' She smiled and patted his hand. 'But I am very sensible of the great compliment you have paid me.'

'Oh, well,' he said, with a rueful smile. 'I tried.'

'Now I think we have been talking long enough and the musicians are beginning a country dance. Go and find yourself a partner, Percy, or there will be more rattling tongues.'

He drifted away, leaving her to stand watching the dancers from behind her fan and wondering at the vivid imaginations some people had. But feeling sad too. Being credited with a child when she could not have one was not only unjust, it was cruel. She would have liked more than anything to have had a child and especially a child with Marcus. As usual when thinking of babies, she felt very low and ready to weep, but as everyone about her seemed to be enjoying themselves, she forced herself to smile.

'May I share the joke, my lady?' said a voice at her elbow.

She did not need to turn to know who it was, so she did not look at him. It would have been her undoing if she had. 'Oh, I do not think you would be amused by it,' she said, but the hand that held her fan stopped suddenly and her whole body stiffened. She must not give the tattlers any more food for their gossip. She must get rid of him. 'Why are you not joining in the dance?'

'Oh, that is for the young and I no longer qualify.'

'Fustian!'

'Besides, I have not thanked you for arranging this evening for Lavinia. It is wonderful to see her so happy.'

'I have been pleased to do it,' she said. 'Now, if you do not mind, I can see Mrs Butterworth beckoning to me. Please excuse me.' And she was gone, leaving him staring after her, a puzzled frown on his face.

Just when he thought they had gone some way to mending the rift between them and he had decided she deserved an explanation for his abominable behaviour, she had turned her back on him. Was she really as uninterested as she appeared to be? He could have sworn, when he kissed her, that her passion had risen to meet his, that she not only liked being kissed by him but actively desired it.

But, apart from that kiss, what other evidence was there that she even liked him, let alone loved him? When she was not treating him with cool politeness, she was quarrelling with him. In the weeks since he had come to London, they had done nothing but fight. Most of it was his fault, he freely admitted, but if she would not let him near enough to explain, to show her the caring man he really was, how could he put matters right?

'You do not seem to be advancing your cause, my friend,' Donald said, coming to stand beside him. 'I think you may have met your match.'

'Oh, I am certain I have. The trouble is, she thinks it is a sparring match.'

Donald laughed. 'What are you going to do about it? You can hardly tap her claret.'

'Don't think I'm not tempted.'

'How much longer do you plan to stay in Town?'

'I do not know. I felt sure we would find the child after Vinny drew that picture, but no one seems to have seen him since then.'

'Unless they are lying. The matron at the orphanage was decidedly cagey. What do you say to having another shot at it?'

'I don't know. I can't even be sure it was the boy or that any of them are in London.'

'Poole is. I know he is. But whether he knows where his wife and the child are, I can't be sure. If he does…' He shrugged. 'You cannot abandon the search now.'

'No.' Marcus smiled thinly. 'Lavinia seems to be enjoying herself, it would be a pity to drag her away. And Duncan will finish school for the summer in two weeks. We will go home to Loscoe Court then.'

'With or without the delightful Countess?'

'With or without the Countess,' he confirmed.

'Then we both have two weeks' grace, me to find the elusive Mrs Poole, you to have your wicked way with the incomparable Countess of Corringham.' He laughed suddenly. 'Twenty pounds says I succeed first.'

Marcus smiled ruefully. 'If it only meant having my wicked way and being done with it, I would take your wager, my friend, but unfortunately there is more to it than that.'

'Oh, my God, I do believe you are serious.'

'Deadly serious.'

'Then I suggest you lay all before her and hope for the best.'

'I intend to, when she condescends to listen to me, but I cannot go blundering in without being sure—'

'Oh, give me patience!' his friend exclaimed. 'I took you for a gambler—how wrong I was.' And with that, he sauntered off to find himself a glass of something stronger than the innocuous cordial Frances had provided.

Marcus continued to watch the company, apparently with no other intent than to enjoy his daughter's happiness, but his eyes were as often on the Countess as on Lavinia. She was flitting from guest to guest, rejuvenating a flagging conversation here, bringing two people together there, dragging unwilling elders into joining the dancing and making sure everyone had refreshments. But whenever she looked in his direction she turned away quickly and would not meet his eye. He would have left, but for Lavinia.

It was gone midnight when the party broke up and everyone took their leave and there was no opportunity, in the flurry of departures at the door, to do more than thank her and take his daughter home. Frances Corringham was the most exasperating woman he had ever encountered. One minute she was laughing with him, as easy with him as he could have wished, the next she was treating him with cool disdain. What had happened in those few minutes this evening to make so swift a change?

Frances saw everyone off the premises, instructed Creeley to lock up and went up to her room, where Rose waited to help her undress. A few minutes later she was in bed and the maid had gone. She blew out the lamp and settled down to sleep, but her mind was still too active for that.

She may have laughed when Percy told her the gossip, but it was no laughing matter. She was torn between telling Marcus what she had heard and letting him find out for himself. He would be furious, she knew. Would he simply dismiss it as nonsense, tell her that under the circumstances he must sever all connection with her and take his daughter elsewhere for her instruction? He had almost done so last week and that was over something paltry compared to this.

Would he even think she had encouraged the rumours? But he did not know she knew about that child, did he? Had Mrs Thomas seen the little boy again? Would finding him solve anything? At least, if she could find the mother, Mrs Poole, it might disprove the theory that the child was hers. Tomorrow, she would do something about it.

When Frances arrived at Monmouth Street the next morning, she was told by the janitor that everyone had gone to the house in Maiden Lane to help make it ready for occupation and so she instructed Harker to take her there, before sending him back to Corringham House, telling him she would find a cab to take her home when she was ready.

There was certainly a great deal of work to be done on the house, most of it scrubbing. There were also doors and windows to mend, a few slates to replace on the roof and chimneys to sweep, but it was a sound building. There were two large rooms downstairs beside a kitchen and upstairs several small bedrooms. These had been knocked into two large dormitories. The rooms on the second storey were being furnished for Mrs Thomas and her small staff of paid helpers.

Everyone, even the children, worked with a will and Frances, coming upon all this industry, happily rolled up her sleeves and took a bucket of water to help scrub the floors in the bedrooms. There would be time to ask questions about the child later, when they returned to Monmouth Street at the end of the day.

She had just finished and was taking the bucket of dirty water and the mop downstairs when she came face to face with Marcus, in immaculate snuff-coloured frockcoat and matching inexpressibles, who had just been admitted through the front door. She stopped half-way down the stairs, her mouth open in surprise, followed by annoyance that now her true name and position would become known and would spoil the wonderful rapport she had with both children and staff. 'What are *you* doing here?'

He looked up and smiled at the sight of her. She was dressed in a brown cotton dress which she must have borrowed from one of her maids by the look of it, and over that a huge apron which had once been white but was now as grubby as the rest of her. Her arms, below the rolled-up sleeves, were streaked with dirty water and she had obviously brushed her hair out of her eyes with wet hands for her face too was streaked and the wayward hair was tucked behind her ears.

If he had not loved her before, he would have fallen in love with that apparition and wished he had her talent for drawing, for he would love to have had that image to keep for all time. He could not bow to her, it did not seem appropriate; instead he smiled. 'Hard at work, Fanny?'

She pulled herself together and finished descending the stairs, where she stood and faced him coolly, aware that Mrs Thomas, who had admitted him, was staring from one to the other. 'As you see. There is much to be done and most of it with voluntary labour.'

He laughed, took off his coat and hung it casually on

the newel post of the staircase, then began rolling up the pristine sleeves of his shirt. 'Then lead me to it.'

He was going to spoil it for her, she knew it. If she had dared to, she would have physically bundled him out of the door and told him not to make fun of her. 'You can't—'

'Why not?' He turned and smiled at Mrs Thomas. 'You could do with an extra pair of hands, could you not?'

'Indeed, yes, sir, but you have already been more help than we can ever thank you for.' If it had been Marcus who had shown her the sketch and questioned her, the lady obviously did not recognise him now.

'Nonsense!' he said briskly. 'We are wasting time.'

'Oh, thank you, sir, you will have your reward in heaven, for it is not in our power to reward you here, except with gratitude. Mrs Randall will show you what needs doing.'

'Mrs Randall?' he queried, one eyebrow raised.

'Oh,' the good lady appeared flustered. 'I assumed you were known to each other when you spoke. This is Mrs Randall.' Then to Fanny, 'Mr Marcus Stanmore, ma'am. He is the gentleman who has bought the house for us.'

Frances had already deduced that much, so she was able to answer calmly, 'Then we are in Mr Stanmore's debt. How do you do, sir?'

He gave her a broad, half-mocking smile and offered her his hand. 'Very well, ma'am. And you?'

For a second, she stared at the hand as if afraid to grasp it but, pulling herself together, took it and felt the warmth flow from him to her and knew she would never be able to get the better of him, although that did not prevent her from trying. 'I am well, sir,' she said. 'Now, what would you like to do? There is scrubbing or cleaning windows. Or perhaps mending doors is more in your line of work. Some of them fit very ill.'

'Mending doors, I think,' he said, solemnly.

'I will leave you to it,' Mrs Thomas said. 'I am needed in the kitchen.' And with that she disappeared down the hall into the back regions of the house.

'Are you trying to make fun of me?' Frances hissed as soon as she had gone.

'Not at all. I am full of admiration.'

'You have been very generous, your Grace...'

'Mr Stanmore,' he corrected her, smiling easily.

Her own lips twitched. 'Mr Stanmore, then. You have been more than generous in buying this house, that does not mean you need to work in it...'

'No, but it is easy to be generous with money when you have a great deal of it. Time is another matter.'

'And your time is valuable.'

'As yours is, so do not let us waste any more of it. Show me these broken doors and what tools you have.'

It was surprising how quickly he buckled down to work and how skilled he was. He seemed to be able to turn his hand to anything in the carpentry line and, by the middle of the afternoon, the doors all fitted, two new window frames had been installed, a broken tread on the stairs had been mended and he had even clambered on the roof and replaced the broken tiles, making Frances's heart jump into her mouth.

And all the time he kept up a flow of cheerful conversation, not only with her when he passed her, also hard at work, but with the children. He had a fund of funny stories and they soon warmed to him and were vying with each other to fetch and carry for him.

Frances could not understand it. He was so warm and

patient with them—why could he not be like that with Lavinia? If he was prepared to give up time to being with these orphans, why did he begrudge his daughter his time? Was it anything to do with that mystery child? Did he love the little bastard better than the children born to him in wedlock? It was an unworthy thought and she put it from her.

It was the middle of the afternoon, when he packed away the tools and sent one of the children to the stables round the corner to tell the ostler to bring his carriage to the door. 'May I offer you a ride home, Mrs Randall?' he asked, reaching for his coat.

She knew he would not allow her to take a cab when he had a conveyance at hand, nor would he agree to let her go back to Monmouth Street alone. Besides, she had been longer from home than she had intended when setting out and she was never one to subject her servants to unnecessary inconvenience, so, deciding the search for the boy and his mother must wait, she accepted graciously.

By the time she had washed her hands, taken off the apron and crammed her hair under an unbecoming bonnet, the phaeton was at the door.

'I wonder that you should want to be seen with such a dishclout,' she said as they bowled away.

'When the dishclout is as lovely as you are and as warm and caring as I have discovered you to be, then I am proud to have you by my side.'

'Flummery!'

'But tell me,' he added, 'why the disguise?'

'It is not a disguise, but I prefer not to be known as the Countess of Corringham when I am with the children. It is too formal and makes them uncomfortable with me.'

'And Mrs Thomas does not know?'

'She may do, but she respects my wishes.'

'And the ladies on the fund-raising committee, do they know you are two separate people?'

'No, they would not understand.'

He laughed. 'No, they would think you had run mad. A Countess should never stoop so low as to get her hands dirty.' He glanced down at her hands as he spoke. It was a warm day and she wore no gloves; her hands were wrinkled and the nails were discoloured and broken. 'How will you explain that?'

'Oh, a good soak and a trim and you will hardly notice. And, in Society, I wear gloves most of the time.'

'I will keep your secret, my lady, if you will keep mine.'

'Yours?' Was he about to tell her the truth? Did she really want to know?

'That I am plain Mr Marcus Stanmore.'

'You mean to go again, then?'

'Indeed, I do. I was never so happy as I was this morning.'

'Oh. But what I cannot understand is why you can be so easy with the children at the orphanage, when you are so stiff with your daughter.'

'Precisely because she is my daughter. I want everything for her, I want her to shine, to make a happy marriage. I want to be a good father and am terrified of failing. I suppose with those children back there, there is no such constraint.'

'Why should you fail?'

'It is difficult to explain. My own father failed me, though he was unaware of it.' He turned and smiled at her. 'Do you really want to hear this? It is ancient history now.'

'But history or not, it seems to have a bearing on what is happening in your life now and the sooner you acknowledge that, the sooner you will overcome it.'

'Wise Fanny. Why have you been able to direct your life in the way you wanted it, when I have been tossed about on the wind, doing what everyone expected of me and feeling so unfulfilled?'

'Have you?' she asked softly.

'Yes, from the day I was born. First I had to remember that I was a Duke's heir and must behave at all times with studious politeness to my equals and to look after those beneath me without once letting them forget they *were* beneath me. I may have my fun, but discreetly, and if I found myself in a coil, why then, I was to buy my way out of it. And above everything I was to make the right marriage. It was dinned into me from the time I was old enough to take an interest in the fair sex...' He chuckled. 'And that was at an early age, I can tell you.'

'That I can readily believe.' She smiled a little, guessing what was coming, but determined to accept it calmly. It was all she had left, her cool exterior.

'When I left Cambridge and went home to Loscoe Court to help my father run the estate, Margaret Connaught came with her parents to stay and we were thrown together. I liked her well enough but she was only a schoolgirl and I was only twenty and had no thought of marriage. But my parents and hers had decided between them that we should be married just as soon as she was old enough. The Duke made it very clear to me I was expected to obey and...' he shrugged his shoulders '...I had not then met you.'

'Marcus,' she said softly. 'What has this to do with you being a good father?'

'Everything. The marriage was to take place in the autumn of eighteen hundred. Margaret was to have a Season that summer, though her parents made it very plain to her that it was for appearances' sake only and that she was not to entertain anyone else. I decided to have one last fling before she arrived in London with her parents and I met you.'

'As you say, history,' she said.

'As the world knows it, perhaps, but there is more. I begged and pleaded with my father to be let off, but he was adamant. It was unthinkable for a gentleman to renege on an offer of marriage and if I disgraced the family in that way, he would cut me off without a penny and my younger brother, John, would inherit in my place. I said I did not care. He asked me how I would support a wife with no income, especially a wife who had been left without a feather to fly with.'

'I blustered, said I would manage, but then I thought of you and knew I could not do it to you. You did not deserve to be cast into poverty and I was quite sure your mama would not let it happen. Even then I hesitated, but my father said my mother was ailing, and if I defied them it would kill her. I loved my mother very dearly, so I capitulated.'

'And?'

'It was a miserable marriage. Poor Margaret was as imprisoned as I was. She had met someone else that summer too. She hated me and brought the children up to hate and despise me too.'

'Lavinia does not hate you.'

'No? She is afraid of me, you said so yourself. And that is the worst cut of all because I was terrified of my father. He was often cruel and any infringement of his rules would end in a beating. There was nothing out of the ordinary in that, I suppose, but he seemed to enjoy it. I have never chastised Lavinia and yet you still say she is afraid of me.'

'Because she does not know you. She has never seen your soft side. Marcus, she is a lovely girl, but she needs to know you love her and will support her whatever she does.'

'It is easy for you to say.'

'No, it is not easy, it has never been easy. I have had to gain the trust of my stepchildren. They thought I had been brought in to replace their mother and it took a great deal of patience to persuade them I had no desire to do so. I encouraged them to talk about her and asked them what she would have done, so that little by little they came to trust me.'

'I know. I envied that when I saw it.' He laughed a little shakily. He had not meant to tell her so much, to reveal his own insecurity like that. 'And now you have Vinny eating out of your hand.'

'Oh, I would not go so far as to say that. We have simply reached an understanding.'

'And may we, too, come to an understanding, my dear?'

They were drawing up at her door and she prepared to alight. The little word of endearment had almost undone her, but she forced herself to speak lightly. 'Why, we understand each other perfectly, your Grace,' she said.

He jumped down, opened the door and held out a hand to help her alight. 'If that is so, why are we now reverting to that formal title?'

'Because, your Grace,' she said, with a smile and a

twinkling eye, 'we are back in the real world. I am no longer Mrs Randall but the Countess of Corringham, and you have ceased to be Mr Stanmore and are once again his Grace, the Duke of Loscoe.'

'Then his Grace hopes to see her ladyship at Lady Willoughby's masquerade next Wednesday evening.'

'How shall I know you?' she asked, mischievously. 'Will you be the aristocrat or the vagabond?'

He laughed. 'Wait and see.' And with that he flicked the reins and was gone.

She went slowly indoors, the smile fading from her lips. Knowing he was vulnerable made her love him more than ever. And understanding a little more about what had happened seventeen years before made her want to cry for the wasted years. But had they been wasted?

She had not gone into a decline; she had had a full life with a husband who was generous and affectionate; she loved her stepchildren, even James at his most exasperating; and her step-grandchildren were a delight. She had a talent she could use for the good of others and was rewarded by their happiness and she had a great many friends. And if she could count Marcus Stanmore as one of those, she should be content.

It was only when she reached her bedroom and sank on to her bed with exhaustion, she realised he had said not a word about Mrs Poole or the child. He had confided some things to her, but by no means all. There were still things he did not trust her to know.

Chapter Nine

'A queen?' Rose suggested. 'Queen Elizabeth, perhaps? Or one of those Greek goddesses. I don't recall their names.'

'No, Rose, everyone does those. I want something different.'

Frances had been teaching a class most of the morning, but now her pupils had gone, she was trying to decide on her costume for the ball. Once decided, she and Rose were going shopping for the materials and whatever accessories were required.

'An animal, then?' Rose was not one easily discouraged. 'I believe very realistic costumes can be bought ready made.'

'So they may be, but I should be stifled in fur.' She laughed suddenly. 'Unless it was a rabbit.'

'A rabbit, my lady? Why a rabbit? It is still fur.'

'Yes, you are right, it would not serve. The Duke's sense of humour can be precarious at times. He will think I mean to ridicule him.'

It was as if mentioning the Duke had summoned him to her, for she had hardly uttered the words, than Creeley came to tell her the Duke of Loscoe was downstairs and wished to speak to her. 'I have conducted him to the drawing room to await your pleasure, my lady,' he said, then added meaningfully, 'I think you should know, my lady, he is up in the boughs about something.'

'When is he not?' Frances murmured under her breath. And then aloud, 'Tell him I will be down directly, Creeley, please.'

Frances was glad Creeley had forewarned her; the sight of Marcus's thunderous looks was almost enough to unnerve her. She had taken five minutes to smooth her dress and tidy her hair before going downstairs but it was evidently not long enough to calm him.

'My lord,' she said, 'is something wrong? It is not Lady Lavinia, is it?'

'No, what the devil should be wrong with Lavinia? I am come on another matter.'

'Oh.' He had heard the rumours. Now the sparks would fly. 'Would you like some refreshment before you tell me? Tea? Madeira? Something stronger?'

'Nothing, thank you.'

'Then please be seated.'

He did not immediately obey, but paced over to the window and then back again, before taking up a position facing her. 'My son has absented himself from school and finished up in a gambling hell that even I would hesitate to enter...'

'I am sorry for that, indeed I am, but what has that to do with me?'

'It was your stepson who took him there.'

'Oh, no, I am sure he would not.'

'Duncan is not a liar, madam. He says it was the Earl and I believe him.'

'I am very sorry if that is the case,' she said. 'But I

am sure it was only a prank. Fledglings do like to try their wings.'

'An apt metaphor, my lady. The rakeshame you call a son duped this fledgling into attempting to soar so high, he had his wings burnt and is left without a feather to fly with.'

She could not help laughing, which was the worst thing she could have done. 'An exaggeration, I am sure.'

'Is two thousand an exaggeration?'

She gasped and the laugh left her. 'As much as that? But surely the Marquis is a minor—such debts are not recognised in law?'

'Maybe not, but it is a debt of honour and must be paid…'

'Oh. You wish me to reimburse you? Is that why you have come?'

'No, my lady, it is not. The money was not owed to the Earl, but to his associates.' He paused, wondering just why he had come. Unable to bear his son's misery, he had stormed out of the house to call on James, intending he knew not what. But on being told the young man was not at home, he had wondered if he might be with his stepmother.

Creeley had told him the Earl was not here and he should have retreated—instead he had insisted on seeing her ladyship. To what purpose? Perhaps to ask her advice, perhaps to commiserate, perhaps because he simply needed to see her that they might console each other, none of which he could bring himself to tell her because she thought it was a joke and, even in her mirth, offered to reimburse him. Him, the Duke of Loscoe, one of the richest men in the kingdom! He could buy up her assets a dozen times over and still hardly notice the difference. She knew that and was mocking him.

'My purpose in coming here,' he said stiffly, 'was to appraise you of your stepson's reprehensible behaviour and to inform you that my daughter will not be coming here again. And for your own good, I advise you to take the Earl of Corringham in hand before he ruins you. Good day, Countess.' And before she could utter any sort of response, he had left the room.

Frances followed him to the drawing room door, where she stood, a little shakily, and watched him take his hat from Creeley and leave the house. The butler closed the door on him and it was like a door closing on her life. For the second time in her life he had walked away from her and for the second time in her life, she was appalled, disappointed and angry. Her wrath was enough to sustain her as she wrote a note to James, commanding him to call on her at his earliest convenience, sent it by a footman and went back to her room.

'We will not be going out, Rose,' she said, wearily. 'I am expecting the Earl.'

'What about your costume, my lady? There is so little time if we are to make something…'

'I do not need to make anything, Rose. I shall go as a maid. We are of a size—I shall borrow something of yours.'

'But, my lady,' Rose said, appalled, 'it is not fitting.'

'Oh, it is *very* fitting, Rose. The Duke of Loscoe thinks I am a servant, then I shall be one. *If* he comes to the ball, which I am beginning to doubt, we shall see what he makes of it.'

'Oh, my lady!' Rose cried.

*   *   *

Marcus strode back to Stanmore House. He might have known it would be a waste of time appealing to her; she had once again made him feel inadequate, like a gauche schoolboy. If Duncan had been her son, how would she have handled the situation? Laughed at it, as she had laughed at him, said boys who aspire to be men were often foolish and must be indulged? Would she have refused to pay his debts because he was not old enough to incur them? Was that how she had brought up her stepson? No wonder the young man was so irresponsible.

But even in his wrath, he knew he was being unjust. He had seen her with James and Augusta and it would have taken a blind man not to see the genuine affection in which they held each other and he envied it. He could bear all Duncan's pranks if only the boy felt he could come to him, talk to him freely about his concerns. They might even laugh about them together. And that was the rub; there was no laughter between them and that was his fault for allowing his wife to shut him out over the years when his children were growing up. As he walked his temper cooled, but not enough for him to turn back and offer an apology.

Duncan was sitting in the library exactly where he had left him an hour earlier. His head was bowed and his hands were dangling between his knees. Ordinarily he was a handsome boy with the typical hairline and brows of the Stanmores, but today he was even more subdued than Lavinia was wont to be, which was hardly surprising. The peal he had rung over him could have been heard a mile away.

He had not beaten him, though he had threatened it,

but he had an idea Duncan would have preferred that to the punishment he had decreed. 'You will repay me from your allowance,' he had roared. 'Not a penny will you have until it has been paid. And if that takes until you reach your majority and come into your inheritance from your mother, then so be it.'

'But Father, how can I exist on nothing?'

'Work for it.'

'But how? I am still at school. Do you wish me to leave and find employment?'

'The vacations start next week. You will go home to Risley and make yourself useful on the estate. I will decide on your future later.'

Duncan had burst into tears and that had brought Vinny, who had obviously been listening outside the door, rushing in to comfort him. 'We will find a way, dearest,' she had said, kneeling in front of him and taking his hands in her own. 'We will find a way.'

'Don't be so ridiculous! What the devil do you think you can do?' he had shouted in angry frustration, making Vinny look at him with quiet hatred in her eyes. It was more than he could bear and, leaving the two of them weeping together, he had left the house, stopping only to clamp his hat on his head.

Now, looking at his son, so beset by gloom, he longed to comfort him, to take back his anger. He imagined he could hear Frances speaking so clearly that for a moment he really thought she was in the room. 'If you impoverish your son, what do you think he will do? He will do what all gamblers have done before him, he will go back to the gaming table to try and recoup. Is that what you want, to make a lifelong gambler of him?'

He sat down beside him. 'I am sorry I shouted at you, Duncan, but you must understand—'

'Oh, do not start again,' Duncan said, looking round wildly for a means of escape. 'I have said I am sorry. I did not mean it to happen. If you are going to ring a peal over me about it every time we meet, I had as lief go to Risley this minute.'

'No, you will go back to school until I am ready to take you. And you will stay at school, do you hear?'

'Yes, sir.'

Marcus did not know what else he could have done; the boy had to be checked. Gambling had been the ruination of many a good man and he did not want his son to go down that road. His fury should really be directed at those who led him astray, but that was not Frances Corringham and he should not have given her a jobation over it. If only she would behave more like a woman, be a little meek, show she cared what he thought, instead of returning every blow of his with one of her own.

And now, thanks to Duncan and her stepson, he had cut himself off from her company, had spoiled any chance he might have had of becoming close to her again. And they had been doing so well lately! He ordered out the carriage and escorted Duncan back to school in almost total silence. He was unprepared for another battle when he returned home and summoned Lavinia to the library.

She received the news that her art lessons were to come to an end and she would not visit Corringham House again with floods of tears. 'It is not my fault if Duncan behaves like a ninny, is it? It is not fair! I liked going to Corringham House. I do not see why I should stop going, just because my brother falls into a bumblebath.'

He handed her his handkerchief. 'It was time the lessons came to an end, Lavinia. I never said they would go on indefinitely, and the Countess told me herself that she thought she had taught you as much as she could and you needed someone more illustrious—'

'More illustrious, Papa? Who can be more illustrious than Lady Corringham?'

'Her words, not mine, Lavinia.'

'No doubt she said it because you were up in the trees about something. Lady Corringham was kind to me. She wasn't forever flying into the boughs.'

'No, if anything she was too indulgent. As I have been.'

'You, indulgent! Papa, how can you say so?' she cried and went into peals of hysterical laughter.

He stood watching her, his hands clenched beside him. How had his daughter become so wilful? Who had taught her to answer back? 'Lavinia,' he said, through gritted teeth, 'that is enough. I have made my decision.'

She stopped crying suddenly and wiped her eyes. 'You know in your heart, *if* you have one, that none of this was Lady Corringham's fault,' she sniffed. 'And it was not the Earl's either. If anyone is to blame it is Benedict Willoughby.'

'Young Willoughby? What makes you say so?'

'Duncan told me. We always tell each other things, always have, ever since we were little. The whole thing was Benedict's idea. He wanted a night out of school and he persuaded Duncan to tell the master you wanted him home for a few days and that he could bring a friend.'

'That much the master told me. You had better go on.'

'Benedict always has a pocketful of money—more than you allow Duncan—and he wanted to go to a gambling hell, but they were not allowed in. Then they came upon the Earl of Corringham and asked him to vouch for them. He was against it, but Benedict knew that the Earl had promised her ladyship he would not gamble again and so he said he would tell her if his lordship did not get them in. His lordship was very worried about displeasing his stepmother and so he agreed. But he truly did not mean to get Duncan into trouble.'

'Oh, you are privy to his lordship's intentions, are you?'

'He called while you were taking Duncan back to school.'

'And you received him?' Marcus could hardly believe his ears. 'Don't you know better than that?'

'It did no harm. Miss Hastings was present, I did not see him alone.'

'What else did he say?'

'He wanted to be sure Duncan would keep his word about not ratting on him. I assured him he had, but you had found out by other means...'

Marcus smiled grimly. Unfortunately for the young man, he had been seen with the boys by one of the proctors from the school whose task it was to keep an eye on miscreants and root them out from undesirable places. He had also spoken to others who were there and the full extent of Duncan's debts had come to light. In view of that, he had been brought home for his father to punish him. He was lucky he had not been expelled. 'And no doubt he will by now be facing his stepmother.'

'Yes, but Papa,' she went on, 'will you not own you have misjudged her ladyship and allow to me visit her again?'

He had been unjust, he knew that. And he was punishing himself as much as everyone else. 'I will certainly speak to her ladyship, but as for you resuming your lessons, I do not think so...'

'But, Papa, why not?'

'Lavinia, I have said my last word on the subject. Now go to your room and find something useful to do.'

Sulkily she went. He paced up and down for a few minutes and then changed into riding clothes and went to the mews to have his horse saddled. A good ride to clear his head and then another visit to Corringham House. Apologising did not come easy to him, as Frances had not been slow to point out, but he was truly sorry for bursting in on her and accusing her of...what had he said? He could not altogether recall, he had been so angry.

He was not usually governed by his temper. He was known as a level-headed fair-minded man who listened before making judgements. Why had he suddenly changed? It had happened since coming to London and seeing Frances again, of learning that she had not gone into a decline over him, that she had been managing very well without him all these years. And seeing what a good mother she had been and how lost and inadequate he felt with his own children had only served to make matters worse.

Could it be that he was jealous? He laughed at himself as he turned his horse in at the park gates and set off across the grass at a gallop. Demon was a powerful horse and had not had much real exercise lately. Being out in the rookeries with Donald for nights on end meant he was rarely up early enough to go riding and later in the day, he had been occupied with social engagements and escorting Lavinia back and forth to Corringham House. Which brought his thoughts back to Frances.

What did he want to say to her? Was sorry enough? Donald had advised him to lay all before her and he had almost decided to do that, but Duncan's escapade had intervened.

Could they recover the ground they had made after that visit to the orphanage which had been so enjoyable? He slowed his horse to a walk and regained the bridle-way.

'Stanmore! Here you are!'

He looked up from his reverie to find Donald wheeling his horse to ride beside him. 'Hallo, my friend.'

'Why so downpin? Lost a fortune, have you?'

'Not money, no.'

'Then she turned you down?'

'Who?'

'The fair Countess, of course.'

'Haven't asked her.'

'Marcus, I despair of you. If anyone had told me that the Duke of Loscoë would become tongue-tied over a lady, I would have wagered my best evening coat they were drawing a bow at a venture.'

'I am not tongue-tied. The opposite is true. I have said too much.'

'Oh, you told her about the bantling and she is not in the mood to forgive?'

'I never got as far as that.'

'Oh, I see.' It was said knowingly. 'You have perhaps heard the latest *on dit*?'

'What latest? You mean about me being always on the Countess of Corringham's doorstep?'

'Worse.'

'You had better tell me,' he said grimly. 'I shall hear it sooner or later.'

'I was going into a tobacconist's in Bond Street the

other day, when who should draw up in a barouche but Lady Barbour and Mrs Harcourt. They had the top down and were talking quite loudly, no doubt for my benefit, for I know they had seen me. I was about to turn and doff my hat, but their words stayed me.'

'Go on.'

'They have heard about the child. And, according to Mrs Harcourt, it belongs to you and…' he hesitated, knowing his lordship's uncertain temper '…the Countess of Corringham. It appears you and she have been lovers for years, even before you married your late wife, and though the child was put out for adoption, now you are single again, you are trying to find it and are intent on setting up home with her.'

'My God! Is there no limit to that woman's malice?' The words were said quietly but that didn't mean he was sanguine about it. Far from it. He was on his way to visit Frances, to make his peace with her, but how could he go after this? What could he say? He could not tell her that malicious tattlers were tearing her reputation to shreds and all because of him. He wondered how long before she heard it and what she would do. There would be no more mocking laughter, but misery. The fact that it was all a tissue of lies made no difference, the damage had been done. His plans for telling her he loved her, had always loved her and wanted her to be his wife, had been blown away on the wind.

But somehow he must let her know how sorry he was, sorry for everything, the rumours, blaming her for Duncan's scrape, stopping Lavinia going to her, all of it. He could not leave her again with the words unsaid. He would wait until the night of the ball, when everyone would be in costume. Somehow he would find a way of having a private conversation with her.

'What are you going to do about it?' Donald's voice broke into his reverie.

'I do not know. If Lord Barber had not been so old and infirm, I might be tempted to call him out but since we are dealing with women, they must be made to eat their words, and finding that child and his mother is the only solution. Have you made any headway at all?'

'None. I think I must have shown that picture to every inhabitant of London outside the *ton*. The lady might, of course, be masquerading in high Society, a demi-rep or someone's light o' love...'

'No. That child is in the rookeries, I know it. Poole might already have found them and if that is so, heaven help them.'

'I don't think so. That was why I was looking for you. If my informant is correct, Poole is going to Derbyshire and means to lead the framework knitters in an attack on Loscoe Court. You have one of the hated mills on your land...'

'It is rented, man, I don't work it.'

'They won't care about that, not if Poole tells them differently.'

'When is this to happen?'

'On the ninth of June, two days hence. We'd best be there.'

'But I am engaged to go to the Willoughby ball on the eleventh.'

'Seems to me, the trouble at Risley is more important than dancing with your *belle amie*. Besides, with luck we could have it all sewn up right and tight and be back in time, if we rode post haste. You might be late, but these affairs go on all night, don't they?'

It was all very well for Donald to roast him, but if the frameworkers were intent on causing trouble at

Risley, he ought to go. He had intended to go home after the ball, after he had put things right with Frances, knowing it would be the last time he would see her for how long—another seventeen years? Now, even that was to be denied to him. He cursed loudly and fluently and returned to Stanmore House to make his preparations.

It took Frances and Sir Percival, who had volunteered to be her escort, twenty minutes to get through the crush at the entrance to the Willoughby mansion in Piccadilly. It seemed as though the whole *haut monde* was intent on squeezing through the door at once, though some were so heavily disguised beneath cloaks and masks and extraordinary headgear that they were unrecognisable. Frances, waiting her turn in the line for admittance, was sure that many had come without invitations.

'This is the worst squeeze I have ever encountered,' she whispered to her companion. 'Hold on to your hat.'

His hat was a vast tricorne which went with the much-decorated uniform of Napoleon Bonaparte. She had laughed when he arrived at Corringham House with his carriage. 'I do hope the Duke of Wellington does not put in an appearance or you will start another war.'

'And if he sees you, he will take you for a serving wench and order you to fetch him a bumper of brandy before settling you on his knee. What mad whim persuaded you to dress like that? You will be sent hither and thither all evening, fetching and carrying.'

'Do you think I can carry it off that well?'

'You do everything well, my dear,' he had said, escorting her out to his carriage.

He was a perfect gentleman and very attentive and she wished, in some perverse way, that she could love him enough to marry him. But she did not and never could and so they continued to be the best of friends. Knowing the ways of the *ton*, she wondered that the gossips had never breathed a whisper about their friendship, but then it would not be scandalous enough for them. Two mature people free to marry if they wished, but choosing not to, had little in it to interest them, not when there were juicier morsels to chew on.

On the other hand, the *amours* of the Duke of Loscoe were meat and drink to the tattlers. A man of mystery, a superior, arrogant man, a widower who was, according to them, in want of a wife. Whom would he choose? Why could she not stop thinking about him? Why did every mundane thought and gesture bring him to mind, as if he lived inside her head? Had she not decided that the Duke of Loscoe was a lost cause and that, if he was intent on being objectionable, she was better off without him? Why could she not make herself believe it?

'At last,' Percy murmured, as they reached the head of the stairs where Lady Willoughby stood beside her husband, waiting to greet them.

Her ladyship was dressed in a bottle green satin tunic, baggy trousers and a matching turban, meant to indicate something of Indian origin. Her husband had eschewed costume and was wearing his usual black evening suit. On his other side, Felicity stood demurely dressed in a diaphanous white gown over a white satin slip. It was decorated with swathes of greenery meant to represent a wood nymph. It would have been a good choice for a young lady's come-out ball except that Felicity was far from nymphlike.

Beside Felicity stood a tall youth of perhaps seventeen, in what was obviously his first suit of evening clothes and very uncomfortable he looked too. Frances assumed that this was Benedict. If James was to be believed, he had been the ringleader in the escapade at the gaming hell and Duncan Stanmore, being two years younger, was no more than his willing accomplice. Why Marcus had not been able to see that, she did not know.

All she did know was that she had not seen him or Lavinia since that uncomfortable confrontation. Would he come tonight? Did it matter? She had completed the portrait and sent it round to Stanmore House, telling herself she was glad to see the last of it. But it had been good—even in modesty she realised that. She had succeeded in catching the mood of her subject, pensive and defiant at the same time. The mouth was determined, yet the eyes held a faraway, dreamy expression. Telling her to think of something pleasant had certainly worked.

'Countess, how charming you look,' Lady Willoughby exclaimed, as the couple in front passed into the ballroom and Frances found herself face to face with her hostess. 'But I am glad you are not masked; you might have been taken for one of my servants.' And she went into peals of nervous laughter.

'Her ladyship's demeanour will soon disabuse anyone of that idea,' Percy said pompously. 'Servility is not to be found among her attributes.'

'Good evening, Sir Percival,' her ladyship said, choosing to ignore his put-down.

He doffed his hat and swept her an elegant leg. 'My lady, your obedient.' And then, passing on. 'Good evening, Willoughby. Miss Willoughby. And young Willoughby.'

The greetings returned, they went into the ballroom, to be met by a cacophony of sound. The dancing had not yet begun and the musicians were still tuning their instruments to the accompaniment of loud voices trying to be heard one above the other, calling each other, making jokes, commenting on each other's costumes. This, if Lady Willoughby had anything to do with it, was going to be the event of the Season.

Frances and Percy joined in, talking to acquaintances and catching up on the latest news, though Frances was alert for whispers behind fans which might suggest she was the subject of gossip. She found herself glancing now and again towards the door to catch sight of new arrivals. Some were easily recognised, but others were well disguised. Could Marcus be one of those? Why was she looking for him? They had surely said all there was to be said to each other and any more discourse would only add to the hurt.

When the orchestra struck up the first country dance, she still had not seen him and allowed herself to be led on to the floor by Percy, who then relinquished her to Lord Graham for the next dance. And then she stood up with Mr Butterworth who, unlike his wife, was as thin as a pole, and after that more partners for a full hour and a half, until she called a halt through exhaustion.

She was sitting out a gavotte, talking to Richard and Augusta, when Augusta laughed. 'Mama, just look who has arrived. What does he look like?'

She turned and beheld James, dressed as a Cavalier in pale blue and lemon silk, sauntering into the room with two friends similarly attired. Seeing his sister and stepmother, he came over to speak to them.

'Mama, your obedient,' he said, sweeping off a huge hat with a long feather. 'Gussie. Richard. May I present Sir Giles Forrester and Mr Arthur Harriman.'

The introductions effected, Frances turned back to her stepson and looked him up and down. 'You look very fine, James, but I am surprised Lord Willoughby has made you welcome...'

'Oh, he don't bear a grudge,' he said airily. 'Done and dusted. Which is more than can be said for another I could name. Poor Risley, a Marquis no less, and not allowed out until the end of term.'

'How do you know that?'

'The little filly told me.'

'You mean Lady Lavinia. When did you see her?'

'At Stanmore House, went to see how Risley did. She said they were all going back to Loscoe Court.'

'When?' The question was out before she had time to think.

'Almost immediately, I believe. Did the Duke not tell you?'

'No, why should he?' So, he would not be coming tonight. Disappointment mixed with a strange feeling of relief swept over her. They would not meet again. There would be no more sparring matches, no more opportunities to hurt each other—for she was sure she had been as guilty in that respect as he had—no more sitting in companionable silence while she painted. The gossip would die down when it was realised he had left town, just as she had predicted it would. She would go back to being what she was before he had arrived. Was that only a few short weeks ago?

The gavotte had finished and another dance was beginning. She became aware that James was bowing again, a broad smile on his handsome face. 'My lady, may I have the pleasure of this minuet?'

'Oh, you are an impossible child,' she said, laughing.

'Well, do I have to fight your suitors to dance with you?'

'No, of course not.' She laid her hand on his shiny

satin sleeve and allowed him to lead her on to the floor.
'But I do not doubt your friends will find it amusing.'

'No, for they are consumed with jealousy. Their mamas are not so young or so lovely.'

'Fie on you, James!' she said as they made their way down the ballroom in the stately dance. 'Save your compliments for those more deserving.'

'None is more deserving,' he said seriously. 'You know I adore you, don't you?'

'Do you?'

'Yes, and I would do anything for your happiness, and if anyone has made you sad, then I will call him out, be he never so lofty.'

'Oh, James, you are a goose. Who is supposed to have made me sad?'

'His Grace, the Duke of Loscoe.'

'His Grace?' she said sharply. 'Whatever makes you say that?'

'A little bird told me you have quarrelled. And that same little bird is convinced you are miserable over it.'

'Does this little bird have a name?'

'Now, do you suppose I should be such a gudgeon as to tell you that. Good God! Lady Lavinia!' This last remark was uttered, not in answer to her question—though it could easily have been—but because he had looked up and seen an apparition.

Frances turned in the direction in which he was gazing and beheld a witch. She was dressed in a black skirt, a long black cloak and a pointed hat. The bottom half of her face was covered by a wax mask with impossibly pointed nose and chin. Only the laughing eyes and the finely drawn brows were revealed, but they were enough to make Lavinia recognisable to those who knew her. She was dancing with Benedict Willoughby.

'Oh, dear,' Frances said. 'Do you suppose her father knows she is here?'

'I doubt it.'

'What do you think we should do? He might arrive at any moment.'

'I hope, for her sake, he does not. But it is a capital rig, don't you think?'

'No, I do not. She is not yet come out; it will cause no end of a stir if she is discovered. The Duke has enough gossip to contend with without Lady Lavinia adding to it.'

'We shall certainly add to it if we confront her, Mama.'

'Then let us manoeuvre to be near her when the dance ends so that we can shield her and persuade her to leave.'

But before they could do anything at all, the dance came to an end and Frances watched in horror as Benedict took Lavinia by the hand and led her from the room. 'I am going after them,' she said, making for the door. James shrugged his shoulders and followed.

When they finally pushed their way through the crowd and gained the upper gallery, the young couple were nowhere to be seen. Rows of doors led to other rooms, but they were all firmly shut. Could they have gone into one of those? Or downstairs? The dining room was on the lower floor, as were the library and the rooms set aside for the ladies to rest and refresh their toilettes.

'There!' James said, leaning over the banister and catching sight of a black cloak and hat disappearing down a corridor. Frances, trying not to give the appearance of haste, started down. She had no idea what she would say to Lavinia when she caught up with her, but somehow she must be persuaded to go home. And knowing how wilful she was, that was not going to be easy. And in the back of her mind was the conviction that if Marcus ever found out about it, he would somehow lay the blame at her door.

There were few people on the ground floor except those either coming or going from the rest rooms. No one paid any attention to the two hurrying figures, any more than they had noticed the earlier couple, who had disappeared into the conservatory. James pulled open the door for Frances to enter.

In the half-light from the lanterns in the garden, they saw Lavinia, whose mask lay on the floor, silently struggling with Benedict. He had his arms around her, but she was fighting him off, kicking and scratching, but making no more noise than an occasional grunt.

James and Frances ran forward but before either could intervene she had delivered a telling punch to his stomach with one hand and slapped his face so hard with the other, her ring cut his cheek. He swore and clapped his hand to it, at the same moment as he saw James bearing down on him. He did not wait to find out what fate was in store for him, but fled across the tiled floor and through the outer door into the night.

'My, that was a spirited defence,' James said, admiringly. 'Another minute and you would have had him floored.'

She turned and looked at him, then at Frances and burst into tears. Frances took her in her arms to comfort her. 'James, go and find a hackney. Do it quietly. We will wait for you in the ladies' room.' Then to Lavinia, 'Come, we will tidy you up and no one will be the wiser.' She picked up the mask. 'Better put that back on and pull your cloak round you.'

'You won't tell Papa?'

'No, though that is not to say I shouldn't.'

'I didn't mean…I didn't think…' she began as James put his head out of the door to make sure there was no one about before beckoning them forward.

'No, of course you did not,' Frances said and, with a nod to James to be gone, ushered her charge into the ladies' room which was, to her relief, empty.

There was a washstand with water, soap and towels, several small tables, some comfortable chairs and a sofa, a looking glass and sundry combs and brushes.

'Now,' she said, sitting on the sofa and pulling the girl down beside her, 'let us see the extent of the damage.' She took the girl's face in her hands; it was blotched with weeping, but otherwise unmarked. 'Nothing to be seen there. Did he hurt you anywhere else?'

'No.' Lavinia grinned suddenly. 'I gave a good account of myself, didn't I?'

'Yes, my dear, you did, but you know it should not have come to such a pass. Whatever were you thinking of?'

'I was mad as anything with Papa. He said I was not to come and see you again…'

'I know,' she said softly, fetching a cloth wrung out in cold water and setting about bathing the girl's face. 'But coming here like this would not incline him to change his mind, would it?'

'It wasn't fair. It wasn't your fault that Duncan got himself in a coil, nor mine either, and so I told Papa.'

'Oh, I am sure that made him see the error of his ways and retract,' Frances said with gentle irony.

'No, it made him angrier than ever. It was Benedict Willoughby's fault. He has always been a bad influence on Duncan and I did not see why he should go unpunished. I hit on the idea of confronting him and making him confess to Papa that he was the one at fault.' She smiled suddenly. 'And then I thought of the masquerade and I prevailed on Felicity to give me an invitation…'

'So she knows you are here?' Frances was trying to tidy Lavinia's tangled hair as she spoke, and though she appeared calm, her mind was busy with the problem of how to spirit Lavinia out of the house and back home safely without Marcus finding out.

'Yes, but I swore her to secrecy.'

'Apart from coming to the ball where you should never be, why did you allow Benedict Willoughby to take you out of the room like that? It is to be hoped that no one else recognised you, for it looked very bad.'

'I was giving him a jobation about leaving Duncan to take the blame for what happened and he didn't like it. I didn't want to make a scene in front of everyone, but I was determined he should recognise his fault and admit it to Papa…'

'So you agreed to go somewhere private. Oh, Lavinia, how foolish of you.'

'He said he had something important to tell me and I thought…' And she burst into tears again, undoing all Frances's good work on her face.

'Oh, my dear, please do not upset yourself. There is no harm done, if we can get you safely home.'

'Oh, but there is. It is dreadful. He told me…he said I had no right to be Miss Goody Twoshoes when my father was a rakeshame of the worst kind. He said Papa had…had fathered a child on his groom's wife…'

Frances's heart gave an uncomfortable lurch but she answered evenly, 'I am sure that is nonsense, Lavinia. Benedict was just trying to frighten you.'

'So I told him, but then I remembered. Mrs Poole did

have a baby when her husband was away at the war, but she disappeared with the child before he came back.' She gave Frances a lopsided grin. 'Even I am not such a wet goose as to think it could be her husband's.'

No, Frances decided, Lavinia who had been educated alongside her brother, with the freedom of the countryside and its animals for her textbook, would know facts that were kept from more gently nurtured young ladies. 'But that doesn't prove it was the Duke's, does it?'

'But I remembered something else. That drawing I did of the little boy. I said he reminded me of someone...'

'And so you have put two and two together. Lavinia, had it not occurred to you that you saw some small thing in the child's face or posture that made you recall that picture in the drawing room at Stanmore House and you exaggerated the likeness without realising you were doing it? It is possible, you know.'

'Then why did Papa take it away? And where did Benedict hear the tale?'

'Lavinia, there are some nasty malicious people in the world and some of them have been denigrating your papa, but we do not have to believe them, do we? Benedict Willoughby was simply making mischief. Now dry your eyes, James will be back soon and I will take you home and we must contrive to get you up to your room without the Duke seeing you.'

'He has gone to Risley and though he said he would not be gone above two days, he has not come back or I would not have risked coming.'

Before Frances could comment on this, there was a tap at the door. 'It's me. Open the door.'

Frances went to obey and James slipped inside. 'There is a hackney at the door.'

'Good. I will take Lavinia home. Tell Sir Percy I have the headache and have gone home, will you?'

'Yes, but there is a problem. The Duke rolled up just as I arrived with the cab and he accosted me. Wanted to know if you were here. I told him yes, but you were unwell and had desired me to fetch you a cab to take you home.' He grinned ruefully. 'He says he has his carriage here which is infinitely more comfortable than a dirty cab and insists on taking you home himself.'

'Oh, no. Did you not try to dissuade him?'

'Naturally I did. I said I would not put him to the trouble, that I was ready to leave myself anyway, but he would have none of it. It seems he has come expressly to see you and…'

'Oh, dear. I really do not think I can abide another jobation from him.'

'I do not think he means to give you a jobation. He said to tell you he will not speak unless you give him leave, but he will see you safely home.'

'Oh, what are we to do?' wailed Lavinia. 'He will see me and…oh, I wish I had never come.'

'You do not wish it any more heartily than I do, my lady,' Frances said with some asperity. 'Now, let me think. James, I think I must go and speak to the Duke and allow him to take me home. Once we have gone, you smuggle Lady Lavinia out to the hackney and see her safely to Stanmore House. It is not an ideal solution, for she should not be with you without a chaperon—'

'No, she should not. His Grace will have my hide for it.'

'We will just have to risk it, we can't involve anyone else. Wait until we have gone before you come out.'

She stooped to kiss Lavinia's cheek. 'Do not worry, child, all will yet be well. Now I must go.'

She was mad, she told herself, as she found her cloak among the others deposited there, slipped from the room and made her way to the entrance hall, where Marcus stood waiting. Not only had she teased him about Duncan, she had exacerbated her crime by condoning his daughter's mischief. If he ever found out about it, his fury would know no bounds. And to top it all, she had landed herself with his saturnine company for a journey home which would be fraught with tension.

Chapter Ten

He turned when he heard her step behind him and was
momentarily taken aback by the costume she had chosen to wear. It was almost Puritan in its simplicity: a
plain wool skirt of a colour like dark tobacco with a
cream cotton blouse, over which was a white starched
apron. On her lovely head she wore a mob cap, though
it was not big enough to hide the gleaming coils of her
dark hair.

Far from making her look common, the costume
served to enhance her natural poise; she did not need
expensive clothes to display her beauty. It was there, in
the lines of her face, the soft curves of her body and
the light in her eyes. He wore no hat, so he could not
sweep it off, but he touched his forelock in the manner
of a yokel and grinned. 'At your service, my pretty
wench.'

Notwithstanding the trepidation she was feeling, she
smiled. In spite of the fustian coat and the thick
breeches and leggings, he made a very poor peasant,
being upright and proud and having clean well-
manicured fingernails and hair professionally trimmed.
But she was reminded of Lavinia's tale of seeing him

going out dressed like a labourer. If the idea was to deceive, she doubted he had been very successful. 'La, sir, you flatter me,' she said, adopting the simpering manner of a serving girl.

'No.' He was serious now. 'No flattery was intended. But I am told you are unwell and would go home.'

'It is nothing but a slight headache, but the party is very noisy and I have had enough of it.'

'My barouche is at the gate, I did not send it away. Will you do me the inestimable honour of allowing me to conduct you home?'

How formal he had suddenly become. And there was about him a kind of intensity which was almost frightening. But she could never be afraid of him; she knew him too well, loved him too well. Angry, yes, disappointed, yes, but never fearful, except perhaps on Lavinia's behalf. 'Thank you.'

She hardly dare glance behind her as the flunkey by the door opened it for them and Marcus escorted her out, but she hoped James was watching and would give them ample time to leave before emerging. The hired carriage stood a little way off; its driver, muffled in a caped overcoat for all it was a warm night, sat on the box waiting patiently for his fare to emerge. She pretended not to notice it.

Marcus handed her up and, once she had settled, climbed up beside her, bidding his coachman take them to Corringham House. 'Handsome over the bricks,' he told him. 'Her ladyship has the headache and we must convey her smoothly.'

Though time in his company was exquisite torture, she knew that the longer they took, the longer James would have to see Lavinia safe home, and so she smiled a little wanly and sat back in the corner of the carriage and exhibited every appearance of someone in the throes of a dreadful megrim.

'My poor Fanny,' he said, turning to look at her, though he could see little in the gloomy interior, not even her lustrous eyes, for she had shut them. 'If I have in any way contributed to your indisposition, then I am truly sorry for it. I would not for the world hurt you or have anyone else hurt you…'

Her eyes opened and she stared at him across the carriage. 'Your Grace—'

'No,' he interrupted her, 'you must not call me that. Look at me.' He tugged at his rough coat. 'Do you see a duke before you?'

She smiled. They must not quarrel again, she simply could not go on giving blow for blow because, sooner or later, she would miss her aim and he would see what was really in her heart and, for her pride's sake, she could not allow that. 'No, I cannot say that I do. But I truly do not know what I see.'

'A man,' he said. 'I hope you see a man. And his name is Marcus Stanmore.'

'Very well, I see Marcus Stanmore,' she murmured, confused by this change in him. Where was his arrogance, where his fiery temper?

'Whom you once loved.'

'Did I?' she queried.

'Oh, Fanny, have done with this teasing, I must speak seriously to you, if your headache can stand it.'

'I am not sure that it can.'

'Then I will call on you tomorrow.' It was a disappointing blow after riding hell for leather to be back in London in time to see her, but he supposed what he had to say could wait one more day.

'I wonder at your risking it,' she said pertly. 'Your

name has already been linked to mine. Always on my doorstep, so they say.'

'Oh, you have heard it then?'

'The latest *on dit*? Who has not? Is that not the reason you have withdrawn your daughter from my corrupting influence? And forbidden your son to associate with mine.' She realised as soon as she spoke she was on dangerous ground, but she hoped Lavinia was well on the way home by now.

'No, it is not. And believe me, I am sorry. I should not have blamed you for my own inadequacy as a parent. Will you forgive me?'

'I forgive you.'

'But can you also forgive me for the slander which has been heaped upon you? I have only just heard the full extent of it and it has appalled me.'

'Oh, it is nothing but malicious gossip. I take no note of it.'

'Do you not? But supposing I do? Supposing it is of the utmost importance to me, that you should understand the truth.'

'Why? You do not have to explain it to me, Marcus. The tattlers will soon find something else on which to exercise their tongues.'

'No doubt they will, but I will have them retract.'

'How will you do that?'

'Prove they are wrong.' He paused and reached out to take her hand in his. She did not withdraw it. 'Fanny, have you, by chance, heard something about a lost child?'

'Yes, but you do not need to tell me...'

'Oh, but I do. That child is not my mine.'

'Not yours? But Lavinia's drawing was so like... You saw it too...'

'Oh, he is a Stanmore, no doubt of that, but he is my brother's offspring, not mine.'

'Lord John's?'

'Yes, you met him once, that summer of your come-out, do you remember? He was the bran-faced youth who was forever getting in my way. I had to throw him off more than once in order to meet you alone. I used to swear he did it on purpose.'

'I remember.'

'How is your headache? Is it too much to listen to this?'

She had forgotten she was supposed to be in pain and smiled. 'Go on.'

'John had just left Cambridge and had not yet decided what he wanted to do with himself, and he was at home when the news came that the man who had been my head groom, Joseph Poole, had been killed in Spain. I had promised to look after the wives of any of my men who were lost as a result of serving their country and I was foolish enough to ask John to call on her to see if she needed anything. Margaret was very ill at the time and I had been summoned to her bedside and could think of little else or I might have wondered why he needed to go so often. He was a sympathetic sort and I think he only meant to comfort her, but the result was a child...'

'Oh, I see. But how did the child become lost?'

'I did not turn her off, if that is what you are thinking. In fact, I considered insisting on John marrying her, but I knew that would not serve. He was not yet ready for that commitment, even if she agreed, which I knew she would not; at every level they were poles apart. It is well I did not, for it would have been bigamy. I sent John on the Grand Tour which is where he is now and gave her a pension, for all her husband's years of service, I told her, and she seemed perfectly settled with her child.

'At the end of the war, her husband was reported alive and well and on his way home. He had apparently been a prisoner. Unable to face him, Mrs Poole fled with her child.'

They had drawn up outside Corringham House, but neither made a move to alight. She maintained her serious attention, but inside she was singing with joy, not only because he was not the rake he was reputed to be, but a caring gentleman who worried about his people, and because it was important to him that she should know the truth. 'And you are concerned for their welfare?'

'Yes. Poole arrived home, expecting to find his wife waiting for him; instead, he learned about the child and swore revenge, not only on her, but the man who had ruined her. I tried to reason with him. He demanded to know the name of the father, but I would not tell him. He left the area and I assumed he meant to find his wife and punish her.'

'And you must find her first?'

'Yes.'

'Oh, Marcus, I am so very, very sorry. Have you no idea where she can be?'

'No, but Vinny drew the child, I am sure of it, though no one has seen him since.'

'Have you told Lavinia about this?'

'No.'

'Don't you think you should? I think she may have heard some of the gossip and she understands it very well. She deserves to know the truth.'

'I will tell her tomorrow. But that is not all. I believe

Poole has seen the child and assumed, like everyone else, that I am its father. I am not afraid for myself, but I fear for Mrs Poole and the child.'

'Oh, dear, no wonder you have been distracted.'

'It is not the only thing I have been distracted about.'

'There is more?'

'Much more. And it concerns you.' He smiled rue-fully in the darkness. 'In a way the gossips were right about one thing. I did ask you to instruct Lavinia so that I might see you more often...'

'In order to spar with me and look down your aristocratic nose and tell me where I was going wrong.'

'No. If I did that, then I regret it.' He paused, then deciding he might as well jump in with both feet, added, 'Because I love you, I have never ceased to love you, all the years we have been apart. And though I dared not hope you had nursed fond memories of me—I had, after all, treated you shabbily, for which I beg your forgiveness—I wanted to see you again, to talk to you. In a way I wanted to prove to myself that my dreams of you had been built on nothing but air, that when we met again, I would see how foolish they had been. Instead, I found myself ensnared all over again.'

'I set no trap for you.'

'Oh, no, that was of my own making. I struggled a little at first, telling myself I would not risk marriage a second time, but the struggles were so feeble, I realised I did not want to escape. Fanny, tell me you understand. Tell me you forgive my boorishness, my bad temper, everything you found so abominable and that you will allow me to try and make it up to you. I love you. I want you to be my wife. I have wanted it these seventeen years. Please tell me it is not too late. Say you will.'

Her heart was pounding in her throat and she could not speak. He had said he loved her once before and where had that led her? She was no longer a silly chit of a girl, but a mature woman, able to weigh up the consequences of anything she did. And one of the things she had done, only this evening, was to condone his daughter's prank and send her home in a cab with her stepson, unchaperoned.

Would his new-found contrition allow him to overlook that? And if she confessed, here and now, he would immediately conclude she had lured him into taking her home in order to accomplish it. He would say she had listened to him unburdening himself under false pretences. She allowed herself a secret, rueful smile in the darkness, imagining his anger and it would be far worse than any that had gone before.

'Marcus, you have taken me by surprise,' she said, though it cost her dear in self-control to speak calmly. 'I need time to consider...'

'What is there to consider?'

'Four days ago you were railing at me for my faults...'

'I have apologised for that. And I will not grumble at you again.'

'No? Marcus Stanmore, you should not make promises you cannot keep. You did it once before, you know.'

'I know. I cannot blame you for your hesitancy. Will you at least consider my proposal? If you do not trust my promises, then be assured I shall try not to fly into the boughs quite so often if we were married...'

'But I should often tempt you sorely.'

'I will bear it.'

She laughed then, very gently. 'Oh, Marcus, for seventeen years I have secretly dreamed you would come riding into my life again like a knight in shining armour and carry me off on your white charger, to some heavenly place where we had nothing to do but love each other. But, you know, life is not like that. We have both moved on. You are the Duke of Loscoe, aristocrat and landowner, with all the responsibility that entails, and I am Frances Corringham, portraitist and proxy mother, not only to my stepchildren but numerous orphans…'

'The functions are complementary, Fanny. They go hand in hand.' He lifted her hand to his lips as he spoke and kissed the palm. 'But I collect you have the headache and my importuning is not helping. I will be patient and call on you tomorrow.'

'Very well,' she said, wondering what the morrow would bring. She must send for James first thing in the morning, find out if all went well, before Marcus arrived. 'I shall expect you, but not before noon. I intend to sleep late.'

'Then, my darling, I must contain myself in patience.' He opened the door, jumped to the ground and turned to hold his arms out to her. She dropped into them as easily as a young girl and he set her feet on the ground, though he did not release her. He stood looking down at her upturned face, his hands round her slim waist, so close their bodies touched and almost melded into one. Then very gently, very tenderly, he lowered his mouth to hers.

Her arms flew wide, fluttered about as if she did not know what to do with them, and then wound themselves around his neck, lost to all propriety. She felt gloriously and wonderfully alive. And loved and, for the moment, that was enough.

The coachman sat upright on his seat, facing forward,

his hat pulled down over his eyes, but there was a smile on his face. If his master chose to dress and behave like a yokel and if the Countess found it easier to accept his advances as a serving wench, then why not?

'Until tomorrow,' Marcus murmured as he released her. He stood and watched until she was safely indoors then climbed back into the carriage and commanded the coachman to take him home and not to spare the horses.

He was back at a ridiculously early hour. Frances, who had slept very little and was therefore up and clad in a flowing undress gown of peach silk, was sitting at the desk in the library penning a note to James when Creeley announced him.

Flustered she rose to meet him. Although she had been awake half the night and although she loved him and wanted nothing so much as to be his wife, she had not yet decided how to answer his proposal. Before she could allow him to repeat it, she needed to know if he had found out about Lavinia's escapade and, if he had, did he know the manner in which his sixteen-year-old daughter had returned home? And if he appeared to know nothing, ought she to let sleeping dogs lie?

Her self-questioning was brought to an abrupt halt when he appeared before her. His clothing was as fashionable and well-tailored as always, and though she could not exactly say he was untidy, he had obviously dressed with less than his usual care. His cravat was crumpled and his whole demeanour a little wild.

'Marcus, whatever is the matter?'

'Is Lavinia here?'

'Here?' she repeated, mystified. 'Why would she come here without you?'

'I don't know. It was all I could think of, that she

was still miffy that I had stopped the lessons and would come anyway.'

'She has not been here. Are you saying you do not know where she is?'

'That is exactly what I am saying.'

She sank back in her chair, her legs too rubbery to support her, her head full of wild imaginings. 'What happened?'

'I do not know. She did not come down to breakfast and as I wished to speak to her on the matter we were discussing last night, I sent for her to come down. She was not in her room and no one knew where she was.'

'You have searched for her?'

'Naturally we searched for her. She was not anywhere in the house. Nor in the garden.'

'But she was home last night?' She desperately needed to be reassured.

'I do not know. That ninnyhammer, Hastings, went to her own room straight after dinner and left Vinny alone in the library. No one has seen her since, not even her maid, for she gave the chit the evening off. If she has got herself into a coil…'

'Why do you think that?' Frances asked, her head in a whirl of half-formed questions, self-accusation and guilt.

'Because it is better to think that than to imagine someone has taken her.'

'Oh, surely not.'

'I would not put it past him.'

'Oh, he would never do that,' she said, thinking of James because she could not contemplate anything else but that James must know where Lavinia was. How soon could she get rid of Marcus to go and ask him?

'It would be a way of punishing me.'

'Why would he wish to punish you?'

'Fanny, did you not listen to a word I said last night? Joseph Poole is capable of anything…'

'Poole?'

'Yes, who did you think I meant?'

'No one,' she said quickly. 'Is there any evidence? Did someone break into the house?'

'There is not a shred of evidence of that, which is why I am inclined to think that she was up to some rig or other which has gone horribly wrong. Fanny, I beg of you, if she has hinted by any word or deed that she was planning something foolish, then pray tell me.'

'No, she said nothing to me.'

'What about that stepson of yours, do you think she would have confided in him?'

'James?' She could hardly breathe, let alone speak.

'They have had some discourse, I believe. In fact, they…'

'Oh, no, sir, I will not countenance that. Whatever his faults, James would never do anything to sully a young lady's reputation and especially one in whom I had an interest.'

'Notwithstanding I mean to go and ask him.'

'Please wait while I dress and I will come with you.'

'Then make haste, please. While we argue, she could be anywhere.'

Half an hour later, they were waiting in James's drawing room while he was fetched from his bed. Marcus paced the room in a fever of impatience, while Frances, no less impatient, sat on a straight-backed chair, wondering how she was to climb out of the bumblebath she had tumbled into without forever damning herself in Marcus's eyes. He would forget he had ever asked her to marry him and who could blame him?

When James arrived, it was obvious he had been awakened from sleep. He was wearing a burgundy dressing gown over his nightshirt and his hair was tousled. 'What is this?' he demanded. 'Can't a fellow be allowed a decent night's sleep?'

'Lavinia has disappeared,' Frances said, determined to have her say first. 'His Grace has some crazy notion she might have confided some mischief to you. I told him it was out of the question. Why, you hardly know her.'

James collapsed into a chair as if he needed its support. 'When did she disappear?'

'I don't know,' Marcus said. 'But if you know anything, then I beg you to tell me. There will be no recriminations, I promise you....'

James glanced at Frances. She was imperceptibly shaking her head. 'I know nothing, sir. I was at the ball with Mama last night—you saw me yourself. That is, if it was last night Lady Lavinia disappeared. Could she not have decided to go for an early ride this morning?'

'Alone?'

'It was only a suggestion. You know your daughter best.'

'I'll send to the stables where I hire her hack and check the coaching inns, in case she has taken it into her head to go home to Risley, though why she would I cannot think. I told her I would be back...'

'Wait for me to dress and I will do that for you.'

'Thank you. Much appreciated.'

'I'll ask Miss Hastings to go to Hookham's library,' Marcus said, as he disappeared. 'And I think, just in case Poole is at the bottom of it, I'll enlist the help of

'Major Greenaway. He can be trusted, but I would rather this did not become another piece of gossip to add to the rest.'

'You may rely on James,' Frances said, while Marcus continued to pace the room.

When James reappeared in riding clothes, they all left the house together. 'I'll be quicker on horseback,' he said, opening the carriage door for Frances to enter, while Marcus climbed on to the driving seat and picked up the reins.

'You saw her safely home?' she whispered.

'Indeed I did,' he whispered back, making a great play of helping to put her skirt into the carriage. 'But I would not want to be in your shoes when Loscoe finds out about last night. I should confess all, if I were you.'

'If we do not find her soon, I shall have to, but I would rather Lavinia told him herself.'

'Pray we find her quickly,' he said more audibly, as he shut the carriage door and stepped back.

They were soon back at Corringham House and Marcus jumped down to help her alight. 'I think I will pay a courtesy call on Lady Willoughby,' she told him. 'If I can contrive to speak to Felicity without alerting suspicion, she might know something. She and Lavinia often talked together, as girls will.'

'Not an elopement,' Marcus said. 'Dear God, not an elopement.'

'No, of course not,' Frances said briskly. 'Your daughter is far too sensible for that. And I am sure if there had been a young man, she would never have been able to keep it to herself. And these things have to be planned.'

'Then why mention it?' He paused. 'Frances, you have been on edge ever since I told you about this...'

'I am concerned, that is all.'

'Frances, I shall shake you, if you do not speak out. My daughter is missing, perhaps even hurt and you prevaricate.'

'I am sorry and I do not think it is relevant, truly I don't.'

'I shall decide what is relevant and what is not.'

He was right. She took a deep breath and faced him squarely, thankful that there were few people in the street. 'Lady Lavinia went to the Willoughby's ball last night.'

'She did what?' he asked, incredulously 'You took her...'

'No, I did not. She persuaded Felicity to invite her and arrived alone. She was dressed in costume and a mask. I do not think anyone recognised her, except...'

'Go on.' His voice was steely. 'You knew it was her, so who else did?'

'James recognised her. And Benedict Willoughby. I am afraid Benedict behaved rather badly...'

'That young scapegrace! Frances, get back in the carriage. We are both going to confront that young man and, on the way, you will tell me all.'

She could do nothing but obey and by the time they arrived at the Willoughby mansion he was in full possession of the facts. And very, very angry. Frances began to fear for young Benedict and was beginning to hope that no one would be at home.

But Marcus knew how to control his temper when in polite society and he gave no hint of the turmoil within him as he gave his hat to the footman and waited to be announced. Unfortunately a great many other people had also decided to pay their respects and offer congratulations for a very successful ball, and their silly nonsensical conversation drove him to demand an interview with Lord Willoughby in private.

This was done so loudly and forcibly that it stopped the conversation instantly and everyone turned to stare. Marcus, becoming aware of this, turned to the company. 'I beg your pardon, do carry on. I will not keep your host above a minute.'

The two men retired to the library, but they were there a great deal longer than a minute. First there were raised voices, then a servant was sent to fetch Frances and Lady Willoughby to join them. Frances was required to repeat what she had witnessed and did so with some reluctance.

'I do not know how you can accuse my poor boy of such a thing,' Lady Willoughby said at the end of it. 'After all I have done to help you, too. Why, if it hadn't been for me, you would never have got the Duke's commission at all.'

'That is nothing to the point,' Marcus said. 'I wish you to bring the boy before me and we shall see what he has to say for himself.'

'I am not sure he is at home,' Lady Willoughby said.

'He had better be. My daughter is missing and...'

'Missing?' repeated Lord Willoughby. 'And you suspect my son? Well, I can tell you straight, he had nothing to do with it. The girl is a hoyden, let run wild and that's the truth of it. There's no telling what mischief she has been up to. Run away, I shouldn't wonder.'

'She attacked my poor Benedict,' Lady Willoughby put in. 'All because he would not lie. She wanted him to say it was his fault your son went to that gaming hell and when he would not, she laid into him. If she had been a boy he would have been able to defend himself, but as it is he was obliged to keep his hands in his pockets and has sustained a nasty cut on his face and a bruised shin.'

Marcus allowed a faint smile to cross his face. 'Good for her,' he said. 'I hope it has taught him a lesson. Come, Countess, I think we are wasting time here.' He picked up his hat from the table where he had placed it and strode from the room, followed by Frances.

'I'll take you home and then I'm going to find Donald Greenaway,' he said. 'And alert the Runners. If some lowlife scum has got her…'

'Oh, no. Oh, Marcus, I am so very, very sorry. I feel…'

He turned to grin lopsidedly at her. 'Responsible?'

'In a way, yes. She is such a bright intelligent girl, one tends to forget how young she is and how sheltered she has been all her life.'

'I think we will defer any discussion on the way she has been raised until she is safely home again, don't you?'

'Very well.'

Neither spoke again until he stopped the carriage at her door, helped her to alight and bade her let him know if she thought of anything else that might help. And the next minute the barouche was bowling away, leaving her to make her way wearily indoors. That there was going to be a serious discussion, she did not doubt, and that it might develop into one of their acrimonious brangles, was not unlikely. Last night's joy seemed a million miles away, almost as if it had never happened.

He had offered her marriage and because he was an honourable man and bound by the conventions of society, he could not withdraw it. It would be left to her to refuse him. And she must. She could not hold him to it, could not expect to live in harmony with him, when he so obviously felt he could not trust her with his daughter. She stood in the hall of her home and stared up the grand staircase, as if she could not bring herself to mount the stairs. Surely she should be doing something?

She ought to try and project herself into the mind of the girl. What would she be thinking and doing? Last night, she had been terribly upset by the gossip Benedict had repeated and inclined to believe it. James had taken her home, but who was to say she had gone to bed? Even if she had, would she have slept or would that nasty piece of tattle gone round and round in her head until she could stand it no more?

Supposing she had gone downstairs to look at that picture in the drawing room and that would have made her think of her own sketch. Then what? Would it have led to a burning desire to get at the truth?

Frances turned to Creeley who stood watching his mistress in puzzlement, waiting for instructions. 'Go and tell John Harker to bring the tilbury round right away,' she said. Then she went up to her room and changed into the plain clothes she wore for visiting the orphanage. By the time she returned downstairs the carriage was at the door.

Half an hour later, she alighted outside the new orphanage in Maiden Lane, hoping fervently that Lavinia was there.

'I was just going to send you a message by one of the boys,' Mrs Thomas said, as soon as she saw her.

'Oh, she is here?'

'She? It is a little boy, not a girl.'

They were obviously talking at cross-purposes and Frances began again. 'I meant the young lady who was here with me the other day. You know, the one who did that sketch of the little boy. I thought she might be here.'

'No, but the little boy is. He arrived last night, poor little mite. The Runners found him lying beside his poor dead mother in a hovel off Seven Dials. She had been bludgeoned to death.'

'Oh, the poor thing! Was he hurt?'

'No, but he is very thin and very hungry. I bathed him and fed him but he hasn't said a word about what happened, though he did say his name was Jack.'

There was no doubt in Frances's mind that Joseph Poole had carried out his threat and that was followed by the dreadful thought that there might be some connection between the murder of Mrs Poole and the disappearance of Lavinia. She had, until now, been inclined to discount Marcus's fears, but now she was filled with a dreadful sense of foreboding.

'Are you sure Lavinia was not here either last night or early this morning?'

'Not to my knowledge, but shall we ask the children? One of them might have seen her.'

The children were being given a reading lesson, but were ready enough to stop that and listen to her. 'You remember the young lady who came here the other day to help us?' she said. 'The one who was drawing. Have any of you see her since?'

One of the boys, a lad of about ten, said he had seen her at Covent Garden when he had been sent to buy some carrots for the orphanage. She had been talking to a man.

'Are you sure it was the same young lady?'

'Oh, yes, it were her all right.'

'Do you know who the man was?'

'No, never seen him afore.'

Frances was appalled. She ran out to her carriage and bade John Harker drive as fast as he could to fetch the Duke. Then she went back indoors and asked to talk to the little boy. As soon as he was brought into the room, she knew why everyone assumed he was Marcus's son. Although his face was paper white, the bone structure, the large eyes and the wing-shaped brows left no doubt in her mind that he was a Stanmore. If Marcus had not told her the truth, she would, on this evidence, have believed he was the father.

Although she was very gentle in speaking to the child, taking him on to her lap and cuddling him, he was too young to be able to tell her anything, except that his name was Jack. Unwilling to upset him by further questions, she relinquished him into the care of one of the older girls. 'Take good care of him, Mrs Thomas,' she said. 'He is very precious to someone I know and there are those who might wish to harm him as they have done his mother.'

'He is safe here.'

'Can you tell me precisely where he was found?'

'Not precisely, no. I was told it was a dreadful hovel off Monmouth Street, which I suppose is how he came to be outside the old orphanage when the young lady saw him.'

'Thank you. When the Du—Mr Stanmore arrives will you tell him that I have gone to Covent Garden.'

'Oh, ma'am, do you think you should? If there is danger…'

'The danger is not to me, Mrs Thomas, but to that young lady, and I must find her.'

Mrs Thomas tried to dissuade her but she could not stand by waiting for Marcus to arrive. John Harker might not be able to find him easily, especially if he was out searching himself, and in the meantime anything could have happened to Lavinia. She might have suffered the same fate as Mrs Poole. It did not bear thinking about.

In a matter of minutes, she was at the spot where Marcus had rescued her from the mob and here she stopped, not knowing quite what to do next and though she was plainly clad she was still far better dressed than anyone else in that rundown area. She was standing looking about her, trying to decide on her next move, when someone came up to her and leered into her face. 'Well, if it ain't that artist woman what pays people to let her draw them. My mate said you gave him a guinea for standin' doin' nothin'.'

'Yes, but I do not have my drawing materials with me today.'

'What you doin' 'ere then, fine lady like you?'

'I am looking for a young lady. She came to draw too.'

'Oh, that one wot was askin' all the questions?'

'You've seen her? Today, I mean.'

'Yes, she was talkin' to one o' them tub-thumpers wot goes around stirring up trouble. We ain't ag'in people askin' for justice, but it ain't our quarrel, though he says it is. I ain't agoin' to put my neck in a noose listenin' to his ranting...'

'Poole,' she said. 'Was his name Joseph Poole?'

'I don't recollect his name.'

'And the young lady?'

'If you ask me, ma'am, you'd be wise to keep a

tighter rein on that girl o' yours, she could get into trouble talkin' to men like that.'

'Yes, you are right. Did you see where they went?'

'Now, I ain't in the way of spyin' on people, mind my own business, I do.'

Frances produced her purse and extracted a guinea. 'Will this aid your memory?'

He took the coin and bit on it from force of habit, not because he expected her to given him counterfeit money, but you could never tell. 'Don't know where they went, but if you was to talk to him...'

'That is my intention.'

'Then you need to know where he's lodgin', don't you?'

Another guinea extracted the name of street and the information it was a tavern called the Magpie.

She hesitated only a moment before setting off in the direction his grubby forefinger pointed, and a few minutes later she found the dingy hovel which she would never have recognised as a tavern, but for the creaking sign over its door. Taking a deep breath, she passed inside.

The low-ceilinged room in which she found herself reeked of stale beer, unwashed bodies, cabbage water and sundry other scents she could not identify but which were equally obnoxious. She put her handkerchief to her mouth and advanced towards the man who was sweeping the floor. He looked up in surprise at the apparition in front of him and then his eyes narrowed with a gleam which was both malicious and avaricious.

'Well, well, what 'ave we 'ere?' he said, softly, leaning on his broom handle to survey her. 'Come to join the other chit, 'ave you?'

'Is she here?' she said eagerly. 'Take me to her at once.'

'Well, as to that, I ain't sure as I should. I'll 'ave to ask.'

She tapped her foot impatiently as he disappeared into the gloomy depths of the tavern. She was shaking with fear, wondering how long it would be before Marcus arrived and whether she or Lavinia would still be alive when he came. But she would not leave, could not leave without Lavinia.

'Now, who might you be?' a voice asked from the doorway at the back of the room.

The fear disappeared in a red surge of anger as she turned to face the speaker, a big roughly dressed man wearing a fustian jacket and breeches tucked into gaiters. 'Never mind who I am, what have you done with Lady Lavinia?'

'She is safe and well, though I tell you straight, if she were mine, I'd put her across my knee and dust her drawers. Such a wildcat as I never met, but what can you expect, with a father like hers.'

She was about to make some scathing comment about his own fatherhood and the murder of Mrs Poole, but wisely desisted. 'Where is she? I demand you take me to her.'

'Demand, my lady? Oh, I do not think *demands* serve. Now a polite request, that's a different matter.'

Frances swallowed hard. 'Then, may I see her please?'

'Certainly you may. Follow me.'

Reluctant as she was to venture any further into that depressing building, she felt she had no choice and followed him through the door against which he had been leaning, along a corridor and up some twisting stairs where he flung open a door and pushed her inside.

The tiny room was furnished with a truckle bed, a washstand, a table and a single chair. Lavinia was sitting on the bed, but sprang up when she saw Frances and threw herself into her arms. 'Oh, thank God you have come. I thought he would kill me.' She stopped suddenly when she saw Poole behind Frances and realised she had not been delivered but that Frances was to share her prison. 'Oh, what are we to do?'

'Do? Why, nothing,' the man said. 'Now his Grace has a double reason to pay up. You will excuse me, while I send to him with the glad tidings.' And with that he turned and left them, bolting the door from the outside.

Lavinia subsided onto the bed and burst into tears. 'I thought you had come... I thought Papa was with you...'

'I do not think he is very far behind,' Frances said, sitting down beside the girl and putting her arm about her. 'But there is no doubt that dreadful man will not give us up without a fight.'

'His name is Joseph Poole. He used to be Papa's head groom. I recognised him straight away when he spoke to me. He said he had something to show me and I thought he was going to take me to the little boy. Only there was no little boy and he brought me here and locked me in. I told him my father would punish him, but he just laughed and said, his luck must be in for a ripe plum had fallen into his lap and he wasn't going to waste it.'

'But what were you thinking of, to come out here by yourself? Surely you knew it was dangerous. Your papa is distraught with worry at your disappearance...'

'Oh, I do not think so. He is far more concerned with searching for his... his...' She did not know what to call him.

'The little boy is not his love child,' Frances explained. 'He belongs to your Uncle John. Your papa promised his brother he would look after the child and when Mrs Poole disappeared with him, why, he had to find them, didn't he?'

'Oh.' She was silent for a moment, digesting this, and then added, 'He should have told me. I am not a child.'

'To him, you are. And he wished to protect you, but—' She stopped to hug the girl. 'I think he has seen his mistake. Now, I think we must do what we can to free ourselves.'

'But you said Papa was coming.'

'He should be, but he cannot know exactly where we are, so we must at least get away from here or make such a commotion he cannot fail to hear us.'

'Shout for help, you mean?'

Frances smiled. 'Perhaps, but not yet, or Poole or his friends will gag us and tie us up. We must pretend to be helpless creatures, waiting for rescue. Then he will perhaps drop his guard.'

'Even if he does, we cannot rush past him and escape. We have to go down the stairs and through the taproom to reach the street and there is the tavernkeeper...'

'Yes, I know.' She rose and went over to the window. It was not a great drop to the street, but it was a very busy one, with people coming and going, women gossiping on doorsteps and ragged children playing in the gutter.

'Do you suppose he is one of those?' Lavinia asked, nodding towards the children.

'No, he is safely at the orphanage, taken there last night.'

'Oh, if only I had gone there first, but they said they had not seen him when I showed them that drawing. Does Papa know?'

'I think he does by now.' She was wrestling with the catch of the window, but it would not open. 'I shouldn't think this has been opened in years. It's jammed solid.'

She was wondering whether to risk trying to break the glass when Poole returned carrying paper, pen and ink.

'I think a letter from you, my lady, would do more to persuade the Duke than any words of mine,' he said. 'So you will please sit down and write what I dictate.'

Frances turned from the window to face him. 'And if I don't choose to?'

'Then it will take something else to convince him I have you. A lock of hair, or a finger perhaps. Yes, a finger, that will do.'

She sat down at the table and he placed the writing things in front of her. 'Now write,' he said, dipping the pen in the ink and handing it to her.

Chapter Eleven

Marcus ran Donald Greenaway to earth at Manton's where he was examining a brace of new pistols. 'Thought we might be in for a scrap,' he explained. 'These are the very latest thing.'

'Never mind those now. I need you. Lavinia has disappeared.'

'Disappeared? How? When?'

'I don't know. The silly chit decided to take herself to the ball last night and that scapegrace, Benedict Willoughby, told her about the child, said it was mine. She may have been upset.'

'May have been! I should say she certainly was. But you think that was why she disappeared, ran away because she couldn't face up to it?'

'The Countess certainly thinks so.'

'The lady knows the truth now, does she?'

'Yes.' He was not inclined to elaborate. 'Now, I mean to organise a proper search. Get help from the Runners. If that madman…'

'Poole, you mean? You think he's back in London?'

When he and the Major had arrived in Derbyshire they discovered his erstwhile head groom had persuaded the framework knitters that they were in the van of a national revolution and that if they marched on London, thousands of working men and women would follow their lead. Some of them started out, but faced with a magistrate and a troop of cavalry they had turned tail. Poole had tried to rally them into marching on Loscoe Court, which had been his intention all along but, thanks to Donald's informant, they had forestalled him and persuaded the marchers to disperse. Unfortunately Poole had slipped away in the confusion.

'He would still want his revenge, wouldn't he? If Lavinia was wandering about town on her own, he might very well have picked her up. Do you have any idea where the man might be lodging?'

'None, my friend. Our best course is to go to where we saw him at that first meeting, someone there might know, though persuading them to tell us might be more difficult.' He paused. 'But are you sure there isn't some more simple explanation. Could she have gone visiting friends, or shopping?'

'No, I've been everywhere she might be and no one has seen her. I thought she might have gone back to Risley on her own, but Corringham has checked all the coaching inns she might have left from. And Frances doesn't think she has eloped to Gretna Green or anything like that because as far as anyone is aware her affections have not been engaged by any of the young bloods in town this year and she could not have done it without involving someone else to help her. Besides, she has taken no baggage. She never meant to be away more than an hour or two.'

'If Poole has her, he won't harm her, he'll demand a ransom. It will be his passport out of the country.'

'I can't wait for that. Anything could have happened. Are you going to help me or not?'

'Of course I am, you don't have to ask.' He turned to tell the gunsmith he would take the pistols and the account should be sent to his lodgings before picking up the box that contained them and following Marcus out to his curricle. 'When was the last time you were at home?'

'Hours ago. I have been combing the streets looking for her and you too. No one at your lodgings knew where you were.'

'I suggest we go back to Stanmore House before we do anything else. She may have returned or there may be a ransom demand waiting for you…'

They clambered into the curricle and set off as fast as the traffic would allow which was not fast enough for Marcus who swore at a dray which impeded them and a phaeton being driven by some young blade in a many-caped driving coat and the yellow and black striped waistcoat of the Hellfire Club.

'Paying a ransom would not necessarily ensure her safe return,' Donald said calmly as Marcus negotiated a hackney carriage which had moved out to overtake a slower vehicle and suddenly blocked the road. 'And I do not fancy being thrown into the road and trampled to death by flying hooves, so go handsomely over the bricks, will you?'

Marcus smiled grimly, remembering that he had used that phrase the evening before, hoping to prolong his tête à tête with Frances in the carriage. And all the time she was listening to his explanations, his declaration of love, his proposal of marriage, she had been keeping from him the fact that his daughter had gone out on her own and she had condoned it by covering up for her.

And because of that Vinny thought she could do as she pleased and go out when she pleased. According to Frances, James Corringham had seen her home, but supposing he had left her at the door and not watched her go in? Supposing Poole had been lying in wait?

As soon as his daughter was safe, Frances Corringham would learn from him that he was displeased, more than displeased, he was angry. And after yet another confrontation, she would turn down his offer. Why, in heaven's name, had he ever made it? He must have been mad.

They were approaching the house when he noticed James standing beside his horse on the road by the door. He jumped down almost before the curricle came to a halt. 'Have you news, Corringham? Is she found?'

'No, but the Countess had disappeared too.'

His heart missed a beat. 'You can't mean it? She has just gone off on some errand of her own. You know she would not think it necessary to tell anyone where she was going.'

'I know she could never sit at home doing nothing, waiting for news, even though she said she would,' James said, ignoring the implied criticism. 'And I was right. John Harker—he's her groom, you know—came to me in a great panic. He'd come from the orphanage where he'd taken her. She told him to tell you where she had gone but he couldn't find you and so he came to me. The message was that Lady Lavinia had been seen talking to a man in Covent Garden and her ladyship was of the opinion it was a man called Poole—'

'I knew it,' Marcus said. 'And I suppose the silly ninny set off to look for them.'

'Something like that. She also said to tell you that the child was safe in the orphanage.'

'It appears her ladyship is better at finding people than we are,' Donald said laconically, as he came to stand beside the two men.

'And losing herself into the bargain,' Marcus snapped. 'They are a pair, those two. Was ever a man so plagued with independent women!'

The independent women were busy trying to open the window of their prison. Frances had taken a dirty blanket off the bed to help deaden the sound and protect their hands and faces from broken glass as she hit it with her shoe. One pane shattered and they could hear the broken glass falling into the street with a clatter which could not fail to be noticed by the people going about their business down there. But the window itself remained obstinately shut and removing one small pane did not help. The wooden frames were rotten and she might be able to break them, but it would take time and make a great deal of noise.

'I'll have to hit it with something heavier and break the frame as well,' Frances said.

'Even if you could, we couldn't climb down; if we jumped, we'd break our necks. And if we didn't do that and landed safely, we wouldn't get far considering the street is full of people and they'd set up a hue and cry. Mr Poole is bound to have left the tavernkeeper on guard.'

'They might help us.'

'Do you think so? Do you really think those people down there care a fig for us? They'd strip us bare as soon as look at us and you know it.'

Frances was well aware of the truth of that, but she had to do something, she could not sit and meekly await their fate. She dropped the blanket on the floor, scattering broken glass, and tugged ineffectually at the window frame. 'Considering these buildings are all but tumbling down with neglect,' she said angrily, 'you'd think the windows would fall apart at the least breath of wind. Instead they are as tight as any prison bars. Oh, damnation, now I've cut my hand.' She turned suddenly and caught the sleeve of her gown on a splinter of wood. 'And now I've torn my gown as well.'

Lavinia grabbed the bleeding hand and wrapped her own handkerchief about it. 'Countess, leave off, do. Come and sit down and we will think of something else.'

Frances smiled as she went to sit on the edge of the bed beside the girl. 'You know, Lavinia, you are very cool. I expected to find you in a quake.'

'When I was alone I was very near it, I confess, but now you have come and you say Papa is on his way, I am not at all troubled.' She laughed suddenly. 'Though we shall both have to have an extra long bath and burn our clothes, for I very much fear this mattress is full of ticks. Papa will undoubtedly not allow us into his carriage and we will have to go home in a cab.'

Frances was glad the girl could joke about it, but then Lavinia did not know that Mrs Poole had been brutally murdered. What Poole had done once he could do again. She smiled. 'At least we now have some fresh air, and if we watch out we shall perhaps see your papa approaching and can shout out to him.'

But that was not to be, for a few minutes later Poole returned with the tavernkeeper, whom he called Mullet, and informed them they were being moved.

'Why?' Frances demanded.

'To keep the Duke and his minions guessing. If you

could find me, so can they and I don't choose to let them, not yet.'

He grabbed Frances by the arm and, helped by the tavernkeeper, swiftly tied her hands behind her back and gagged her, before turning to do the same to Lavinia who had tried pummelling him on the back and been unceremoniously thrust aside. Then each man picked up a struggling female and flung her over his shoulder and in that way they were carried downstairs, through the taproom and out of the door where they were deposited in a dilapidated closed carriage.

They travelled for hours, first over cobbles with the sounds of the busy streets ringing in their ears, and then over rougher ground when all they could hear was the creaking of harness, the clop of hooves and the soughing of the wind, until suddenly they stopped. Frances, who had sat up and was doing her best to work her wrists free, looked up as Poole opened the door. 'Out!' he commanded.

When she did not obey quickly enough, he grabbed her arm and hauled her out. She stood unsteadily, looking about her while Lavinia received the same treatment. They had drawn up outside an isolated cottage. There was nothing to be seen but the narrow path over which they had just come, winding its way over flat uneven ground which she was sure was marshland and very unstable. The path continued towards what she took to be the sea or perhaps the Thames estuary, for the air had a salt-laden tang. In the opposite direction she could see a church on the distant horizon. There were no other buildings.

'Inside,' Poole commanded, pointing to the cottage.

They stumbled inside. They found themselves in a

tiny room with a bare earth floor and very little in the way of furniture. There was a table, four upright chairs, a sagging horsehair sofa and a dresser. The grate spilled cold white ash.

'You'll be tight enough here and Mullet will look after you,' Poole said, pulling off their gags. 'No use shouting, there's no one to hear and no point in trying to cut and run, there's nowhere to go.'

'You are going to leave us here with him?' Frances demanded, nodding in the direction of the tavernkeeper.

'I am. But you had better pray it won't be for long. When I come back, if the Duke has been disposed to be generous, then I might set you free.'

'You expect him to pay a ransom for us?' Lavinia asked.

'Oh, he will pay. Even if he were glad to be free of your troublesome self he would never acknowledge it; he cannot be seen to cut off his own daughter, can he? Not his *legitimate* offspring. Now his *bastard*, that's another matter, he can throw him off with impunity...'

'That child is not his Grace's son, whatever you may think,' Frances said. 'You are mistaken if you imagine an honourable man like he is, who had promised to look after his people, would do such a thing.'

'Oh, ho, methinks I smell a romance here. The tales of you and he were not so far abroad after all. I am doubly blessed with two such fine specimens for barter. If you are good, friend Mullet will untie your hands, but you had better behave, because I have to tell you he has a very short temper and there's no telling what he'll do if you cut up rough.' And with a last instruction to his accomplice to watch them carefully, he returned to the coach and drove away.

For the next hour Frances and Lavinia sat side by

side on the sagging sofa, while Mullet relit the fire and set a pot on to boil into which he threw some meat and vegetables. This they knew would be their supper, but though they were very hungry, neither of them could eat any of it when it was served to them on two cracked plates taken from the dresser.

'Starve, then,' he said, taking their plates and scraping the contents on to his own. 'You'll get nothing else.'

'I need to relieve myself,' Frances said.

'There's a privy out the back.' He stood up and opened the back door for her. 'There.' He pointed. 'And don't shut the door.'

'Why? Do you think I can disappear from there? And if I could, where would I go? Mr Poole is expecting to release us unharmed. Should I not believe him? And would I go anywhere without my young friend?'

He went back inside and slammed the door, though she knew he was watching from the window. She went into the reeking privy which was nothing more than a little wooden shed with a hole in the ground which stank so badly she thought she would be sick. She shut the door firmly and relieved herself because she had to, and then went back into the house, deep in thought.

Mr Mullet had found a small cask of brandy in the bottom of the dresser and was busy sampling it when she returned. 'Best French cognac, left behind by the smugglers,' he said, holding out a glass of the liquid to Frances. 'Try it.'

'No, thank you,' she said coldly.

'Please yourself.' Mullet was evidently very fond of a tipple because, with nothing else to do and the company not to his liking, he sat down before the dying fire and proceeded to do justice to his find.

'Do you think he will drink himself insensible?'

Lavinia whispered when Frances rejoined her on the sofa.

'No, he's too wily for that and, being a publican, I have no doubt he can hold his liquour.' She smiled suddenly. 'He'll have to go out to the privy some time. Be ready.' Aloud she said, 'Why don't you try and sleep, my dear? It will help the time pass.'

Lavinia stretched out on the sofa and shut her eyes. Frances went to the grate and picked up a piece of charcoal, which she took to the table and began sketching on its bare surface.

'What you doin?' Mullet demanded.

'Amusing myself drawing.'

He came and stood behind her chair. 'Why, that's me to the life, ain't it?' He sounded inordinately pleased.

'Yes. Go and sit down again. I can't finish it if you stand over me.'

He returned to his seat and adopted a stiff pose. 'No, no,' she said. 'That's no good. Carry on with what you were doing, it's more natural.' He relaxed and Frances continued to draw. If Marcus arrived and they had gone, taken elsewhere or even killed, at least she would have left a clue and the man would pay for his crime. She wrote 'Mullet of the Magpie' at the bottom of the picture and then pretended to put her head in her arms to sleep, covering the words. Mullet poured himself yet another glass of cognac. And another.

A few minutes later, he got up and staggered to the door, turning to make sure both his captives were asleep before going out into the dusk. Frances got up and shook Lavinia. 'Shh, be quiet and follow me.'

They crept outside. Mullet could be heard in the privy, singing a bawdy song at the top of his powerful lungs. Frances picked up a stout piece of wood she had noticed earlier and silently propped it at an angle against the door, so that he was effectively imprisoned. 'Now,' she whispered. 'Let's be away, as far and as fast as we can before he realises what's happened.'

There was only one way they could go and that was back along the road by which they had arrived. Crossing the marsh would be foolhardy. 'We'll make for the church,' she went on. 'Thank goodness it's nearly dark, but be careful not to stray off the road or we'll be lost for certain.'

Hand in hand they ran. They ran until their breath was spent and they could run no more. The little cottage disappeared beneath a fold in the land behind them, but the church seemed no nearer. It was probably several miles away, but at least they had left the marshes behind and the terrain on either side of them was now scrubby pasture, dotted with bushes and brambles and an occasional cow, lying down for the night.

'Do you think he's got out by now?' Lavinia asked as they stood panting for breath and listening for sounds of pursuit.

'Probably. We must keep going.'

They had been walking for several more minutes when they heard the sound of a carriage approaching very fast. In a moment they had dived into the ditch beside the road and lay, hardly daring to breathe as an old coach passed them going towards the cottage. 'Poole,' Frances said, lifting her head slightly. 'He wasn't alone.' She scrambled up to stare after it. 'Now we'd best make haste because as soon as he sees Mullet, he'll turn right round and come back.'

She had hardly spoken before the carriage came to a halt. 'They've seen us! Run!'

They left the road and ran across the grass, stumbling

in their haste as two men left the carriage to run after
them. They could hear them shouting, but kept going,
tearing their clothes on the brambles and muddying
their shoes..

'Vinny! Fanny! For God's sake, stop running, will
you?'

Frances came to a sudden stop. She knew the owner
of that voice, even though he was shouting at the top
of his lungs.

'Papa!' Lavinia, too, had at last understood what they
were saying. She turned and ran back, straight into the
arms of her father. Frances followed more slowly and
stood facing him, panting for breath. 'Thank God, you
are both safe,' he said. 'Are you hurt, Vinny? Did those
men hurt you?'

'No, they would not dare while her ladyship was with
me.' Lavinia laughed, lifting her face from his chest.
'You should have seen her, Papa, she was so brave, like
a lioness. And when that dreadful man Mullet went out
to the privy, she shut him in so that we could make a
dash for it. He'll be raging by now, even if he has got
out.'

He smiled and reached across his daughter to take
Frances by the hand and draw her towards him. 'Then
I am indebted to her.' He conveyed her hand to his lips,
looking at her over it with an expression she could not
fathom. Tenderness? Sorrow? Or was there just a gleam
of wry amusement? Could he be laughing at her? 'For
everything.' The last two words were said with heavy
emphasis, confusing her all the more.

'But why did you come in that awful coach?' Lavinia
asked him, 'It is Mr Poole's. We thought…'

'Come, let us go back to it and you shall hear the
story.'

With Lavinia on one side of him and Frances on the
other they went back to the stationary coach from which
had emerged Donald Greenaway and James. They were
standing in the road watching them approach, while
John Harker sat on the driving seat, smiling from ear to
ear. James hugged his stepmother and bowed to
Lavinia, his eyes alight with pleasure. 'Thank God we
were in time.'

Frances had noticed Poole sitting in the coach, sul-
lenly staring out at them. 'What is he doing there?'

'Oh, do not be alarmed, he is securely trussed,'
Donald said. 'Now all we have to do is wait for the
Runners who are not far behind and then we can go.'

He had hardly spoken when they heard the sound of
another vehicle arriving. A huge prison van, drawn by
two great draught horses, hove into view and drew up.
Three Runners emerged, carrying bludgeons and pistols
and they soon manhandled the silent Poole into the van.
'There's another man back there,' Donald told them.

'You can safely leave him to us, Major. You be on
your way. I dare say the ladies will be glad to bathe
and rest.'

'We are not far from Twelvetrees,' James said, as he
and Marcus joined Frances and Lavinia in the coach,
leaving Donald to climb up beside Harker. 'We will go
there for you both to recuperate, before returning to
London.'

As soon as they were on their way, Lavinia began a
long account of exactly what had happened to them,
which made her father smile. He knew, as the others
did, that the sudden relief from tension had made her
talkative and she just could not stop.

Frances remained silent. Now all danger was past, she
did not know what to say, even if Lavinia had paused

long enough to allow her to say anything. When the euphoria of the rescue died down and Marcus contemplated what might have happened and where to lay the blame, he would turn to her, and although she did not think she had encouraged Lavinia in her wilfulness, she had not curbed her as she ought.

She dreaded the end of the journey, when he would insist on speaking to her alone and would coldly repeat his proposal in such a way that she would be under no illusion that he meant her to refuse him. Oh, how difficult that was going to be!

Lavinia, having come at last to the end of her narrative, demanded to know how he had known where they were. 'Lady Corringham said you would come, but when they moved us, we thought you would never find us. Mr Poole seemed very sure you would not.'

'Once we had John Harker's message, we were well on the way. From the lad at the orphanage we followed the trail to the man who had given Lady Corringham her directions.'

'But that would only lead you to the tavern,' Frances put in.

'So it did and we searched it, but all we found was a piece of cloth snagged on a broken window and several spots of blood.' He did not tell her what had gone through his mind, seeing that piece of cloth which he had recognised as coming from the gown Frances had been wearing the day he helped at the orphanage. And the spots of blood had set him in a fever of impatience to find who had been hurt. 'We feared you may have tried to escape and one of you had been injured but everyone in the neighbourhood denied all knowledge of you, even when offered money.

'We thought we had come to an impasse, but we

decided to leave a guard watching the place while we looked elsewhere. I went home and found the ransom note pushed under the door. It told me where to leave the money.'

'In a sack in the kitchen of the old orphanage in Monmouth Street,' Frances put in. 'Poole made me write it. Did you see the tiny magpie I drew in the middle of my signature?'

He smiled. 'Yes, I saw it and very cleverly done it was, but we had already searched there and knew you were gone. The only way was to catch Poole when he came to collect the ransom. I kept watch with the Major from across the street, but it wasn't Poole who arrived, but another man. We arrested him and inveigled him into telling us where he was meeting Poole. We told him to go ahead and followed him; when Poole arrived we arrested him.'

He made it sound easy, but there had been a desperate struggle and several times Poole had almost escaped before the Runners had arrived to help and the man had eventually been overcome.

'Are you going to charge him with the murder of Mrs Poole?'

'Very probably. Along with incitement to riot. He tried to get the framework knitters to march on Loscoe Court, but Major Greenaway and I had been forewarned and arrived ahead of them.'

'That was why you went back to Risley?'

'Yes, I talked to the men and explained that Poole was using them for his own ends and they went away peaceably enough. Unfortunately Poole slipped through our fingers and came back to London.'

'And being thwarted, killed his wife?'

'Yes. For which he will surely hang.'

'And what about little Jack?'

'His name is Jack, is it?' Lavinia put in. 'Is he named for Uncle John?'

'You know the truth?' her father queried.

'I do now, her ladyship told me, but I do think it was despicable of Benedict Willoughby to repeat that awful gossip. Do you think we shall ever live it down?'

'Of course we will.' He hugged her to him, while smiling at Frances over her head. 'Gossip comes and goes, the gabble-grinders will soon find something else to get their teeth into.'

They had been passing through cultivated countryside while they had been travelling and now they entered a village and, a few minutes later, rattled through the wrought-iron gates of Twelvetrees. 'Home,' James said.

Although the housekeeper had not been expecting them, the ladies were soon stripping off their filthy clothes in their respective rooms and enjoying a hot bath, while down in the kitchen a meal was prepared for everyone.

Lavinia had been right; everything they had been wearing had to be destroyed, but fortunately Frances had left some clothes at the house when she moved to London and thus it was that Lavinia emerged in a blue spotted muslin which, though slightly too big, was soon taken in, and Frances found a green jaconet, slightly old-fashioned, but still a good fit. Without a maid to arrange her hair, she had brushed it and left it loose, held back by a simple ribbon.

The meal was a noisy and cheerful affair with everyone adding to the enjoyment, but at the end of it Lavinia pleaded fatigue and retired to bed, leaving Frances to make her way to the drawing room alone. She had not been there five minutes when Marcus joined her.

'You did not spend long over the port,' she said, looking past him for the other two.

'No.' He shut the door behind him and came to sit next to her. 'I prefer the company in here.'

'Oh.'

'Is that all you have to say?'

'What would you have me say? That I am sorry?'

'You are sorry that I prefer your company?'

She realised he was teasing her, but she dare not turn to look at him and kept her face obstinately forward. 'No, I did not mean that.'

'What did you mean, then? What have you to regret which I do not regret even more?'

'Yes, I thought you might. But have no fear, I shall tell no one.'

'Now you are talking in riddles and I am not in the mood for conundrums, so please explain what it is you are not about to tell.'

She turned to face him. He was looking down at her with such intensity, his eyes seemed to burn into her. His mouth, which she knew could be soft and gentle, looked hard, as if he dare not relax. She took a deep breath to steady herself. 'I shall tell no one of our interview last night and that you offered me marriage.'

'Why not?'

'I would not wish to embarrass you in Society when the marriage does not take place.'

'It is not to take place?'

'No, and you need not sound so relieved, you should know that I would never hold you to it.'

'Why not?' His tone, which until then had been gently mocking, was suddenly hard.

'You know very well, Marcus Stanmore,' she retorted angrily. 'I have been a thorn in your side ever since you came to London. Not that I intended to be, for I did not know you were come and I dare say we would never have been more than polite acquaintances if you had not brought Lavinia to be taught by me. So do not blame me for it.'

'Blame you for what?'

'The way Lavinia has behaved, for condoning her mischief, taking her to the orphanage, sending her home in a cab with James…'

'Do you think I should blame you?'

'No, but I know you do.'

'I see you still imagine you can read my mind.'

'So I can.'

'Then tell me what I am thinking now.'

She smiled wanly. 'You are thinking what a lucky escape *you* have had…'

'No, what a lucky escape *you* have had.'

'That too, of course, and it is polite of you to say so, but…'

'No, it was not luck for it was down to your courage. You could have been killed, as Mrs Poole was. Lavinia could have…'

'Oh, you blame me for that too.'

He took her shoulders in his hands and turned her to face him, shaking her gentle. 'Fanny, my love, I shall have to spank you if you do not stop this nonsense. Don't you know that I blame you for nothing? Nothing except making me see sense. If you had not taught my daughter more than how to draw a line and brought her out of the sullen mood she has been ever since I brought her to London, I would never have come anywhere close to understanding her. Nor understanding myself either.

'I know I love you. I thought I did when we were

both so young, but now I am not so sure it was love. Youthful infatuation, if you like, passion, perhaps, love, in a way, but not the enduring love I feel for you now. I came to London a month ago, a lonely and embittered man, determined to do my best for my wilful children but with no more idea of what that best was than that teapot there. And when I saw you with your own step-children…' He chuckled. 'I was jealous, I admit it.'

'Marcus, how can you say that? I own they are not my flesh and blood, but they are my children and I would do anything for them.'

'Don't I know it! But do you not think you could spare a little of that love for me?'

She looked up at him and saw the soft gleam in his eyes and the wry twist to his mouth which told her that he was in earnest and no longer teasing her. 'It is not a question of sparing it, Marcus. The love I have for you, the love of a woman for a man, is very different from that of a parent to a child, as you very well know, having children of your own.'

'I know,' he said softly. 'But did I hear aright? You did say the love you have for me?'

'Yes.'

'And do you still mean to refuse my offer of marriage?'

'Do you wish me to?'

'No, by God, I do not. Nothing will make me happier than for you to say yes. And we can be married as soon as may be.'

She was suddenly as shy as a schoolgirl and looked down at her hands, one of which was bandaged. 'Very well, I accept.'

'Oh, Fanny!' He laughed aloud, seized her hands and turned her to face him. 'Oh, thank heavens! You can be so inscrutable at times, I began to wonder if I would ever break the ice.'

She laughed as he took her into his arms and kissed her soundly. This led to another and another, until Donald and James, having consumed the better part of a bottle of port between them, decided they had been left out in the cold long enough and joined them, making as much of a noise about it as they could to give the lovers time to break apart.

'I can see felicitations are in order,' James said, crossing the room to kiss a flustered Frances on the cheek. 'I wish you happy.' Then he turned to shake Marcus by the hand. 'Congratulations, sir.' He grinned teasingly. 'But as head of the family, I would expect my approval to be sought...'

Marcus laughed. 'And do I have it?'

'If you make my darling stepmother happy, then you do.'

Donald came forward and added his congratulations, a toast was suggested and drunk and the hilarity brought Lavinia down in her dressing gown, saying they had woken her. 'Not that I mind,' she said. 'For I was having a dreadful nightmare.'

'Of a wicked stepmother, I shouldn't wonder,' James said, with a laugh.

'No,' she answered, puzzled. 'Why do you say that?'

Marcus went to her and put his arm about her shoulders. 'Would you mind very much having a stepmother?'

'If she is as nice as mine?' James added.

Lavinia looked from one to the other and then a broad smile creased her face. 'Oh, you haven't...you aren't...'

'Lady Corringham,' Marcus said, almost pompously,

though with a touch of pride, 'has consented to become the Duchess of Loscoe.'

Lavinia flew to Frances and hugged her. 'Oh, I am so pleased. I thought I had spoiled it all, being so naughty.'

'You very nearly did,' her father said. 'Now, I think it is time we all retired, if we are to be back in Town tomorrow. There is much to do.'

She went dutifully and was followed by James and Donald. Alone once again, with all the things that had divided them safely disposed of, Frances and Marcus spent a few delectable moments in each other's arms before they reluctantly drew apart. They had waited seventeen years and though they were impatient to consummate their love, both knew it would not do, not with James and Lavinia in the house. 'Three weeks,' he said, kissing her goodnight outside her bedroom door. 'Not a moment longer.'

May 1818

Stanmore House was a very different home from the one Frances had entered the year before. It had been refurbished; the old dark wallpaper had gone, along with the heavy oak furniture. Now the rooms were light and airy and it was possible to see some of the fine pictures which hung on the gallery wall. Frances had cleaned them so that their true colours had been revealed. Among them was a set of four new ones, named *Spring*, *Summer*, *Autumn* and *Winter*.

She had been surprised, on the day she had gone there as Marcus's bride, to find *Autumn* and *Winter* on the wall of the library. 'You were the one who bought them?' she queried in surprise.

'Why not? They are good. But I am still waiting for their companions.'

And so, in the weeks that followed, whenever she had time from her new status as the Duchess of Loscoe, entertaining their many friends, the refurbishment of the house and visits to Loscoe Court, not to mention spending time with her children, grandchildren and the orphans, she had completed the commission.

Her portrait of Lavinia with the rabbit had pride of place beside one of Jack with a toy monkey. No longer a ragged urchin, the child had been adopted by Marcus and had been absorbed into the extended family. John had agreed to this and had set up home in the Scottish castle which Marcus had gifted to him. 'What do I want with a castle in Scotland,' Marcus had said, echoing Frances's thoughts of eighteen years before.

Tonight every chandelier in the place had been lit. There were flowers and greenery everywhere and the great ballroom floor had been polished within an inch of its life for tonight was to be Lavinia's come-out ball and Frances wanted everything to be perfect for her.

'I have just been to see Lavinia in her gown,' she told Marcus when he came into her room to watch her being dressed. Rose disapproved, but there was nothing she could do about it as he sat down to watch his lovely wife sitting in her shift having her hair brushed. 'She looks so radiant. Every buck in Town will be mooning over her.'

'Then let us hope it will not go to her head,' he said laconically, taking the hairbrush from her maid's hand and indicating with a turn of his head that she should leave them. He was already dressed in a black evening suit of the best superfine, his cravat a piece of art in itself, so precisely was it tied.

She looked up at him, marvelling at the way his hair curled, the way the little lines creased his eyes when he smiled, the firm line of his jaw and the love in his eyes when he looked at her, a love mirrored by her own. 'Marcus, you should not send Rose away like that. You will make me late.'

'There is plenty of time and you know I like to brush your hair,' he said, suiting action to words. 'If we had the time…'

She laughed. 'But we haven't.'

He sighed. 'I suppose you want me to fetch Rose back?'

'Yes, but not until you have heard my news…'

'More *on dit*? Tell me then, though why you should think I would be in the least interested I do not know.'

'Oh, but I know you will. And it isn't exactly *on dit* yet, but it will be. You see…' She paused and laughed. 'Marcus, a miracle has happened. I am…I am in what the prudish among us call an interesting condition.'

'You mean you are pregnant?' He dropped the brush and seized her hands, pulling her to her feet. 'Oh, my darling, I am so pleased. But I thought…'

'So did I, but it appears there was nothing wrong with me that a good man could not cure.'

That was what the doctor had told her; she was not barren, it had been her elderly husband who could not have more children. At last, at long last, she was to be a mother. And what made it even better was that her child would also be Marcus's.

'Oh, my love, my dearest one, this child of ours will be loved so much…'

'And indulged.'

'Oh, yes, but not over-indulged, I think.'

'Certainly not,' she said. 'Now, will you go and fetch Rose?'

He did, but not until he had kissed her several times, laughing and swinging her round until she was quite giddy and had to beg him to stop.

* * * * *

The *Regency*

LORDS & LADIES
COLLECTION

More Glittering Regency Love Affairs

VOLUME TWENTY

Prudence by **Elizabeth Bailey**

Governess Prudence Hursley was well aware of her lowly
position in life and expected to see little of her new
employer, Mr Julius Rookham. However, his wilful nieces
continually threw Prue into his path, and the more she got to
know the confirmed bachelor, the more she found
herself wishing for the impossible!

∾

Lady Lavinia's Match by **Mary Nichols**

When their parents married, James, Earl of Corringham,
and Lady Lavinia Stanmore became as close as brother and
sister. Now, years later, James has outgrown his rakish ways
and is burning with a love for her that he longs to reveal.
However, he faces a rival in the shape of the mysterious
Lord Wincote…

On sale 4th April 2008

**If you've missed any of the volumes in the
Regency Lords & Ladies Collection, you can
have them delivered straight to your door**

**Please add 99p postage & packing
per book**

DELIVERY TO UK ONLY

**Post to: End Page Offer,
PO Box 1780,
Croydon, CR9 3UH**

E-mail: customer.relations@hmb.co.uk

Just fill in the attached form and ensure that you
include full postal address details.
Please pay by cheque or postal order
(payable to 'Reader Service'). Prices and
availability subject to change without notice.

Order online at: www.millsandboon.co.uk

Allow 28 days for delivery

Volume	Authors	ISBN & Price	Quantity
1	Nicola Cornick & Anne Ashley	978 0263 84570 9 £5.99	
2	Ann Elizabeth Cree & Anne Ashley	978 0263 84571 6 £5.99	
3	Paula Marshall & Meg Alexander	978 0263 84572 3 £5.99	
4	Francesca Shaw & Meg Alexander	978 0263 84573 0 £5.99	
5	Joanna Maitland & Mary Brendan	978 0263 84574 7 £5.99	
6	Elizabeth Rolls & Mary Brendan	978 0263 84575 4 £5.99	
7	Anne Herries & Anne Ashley	978 0263 84423 8 £5.99	
8	Elizabeth Bailey & Anne Ashley	978 0263 84424 5 £5.99	
9	Sylvia Andrew & Claire Thornton	978 0263 84425 2 £5.99	
10	Meg Alexander & Claire Thornton	978 0263 84426 9 £5.99	
11	Mary Nichols & Paula Marshall	978 0263 84427 6 £5.99	
12	Anne Gracie & Paula Marshall	978 0263 84428 3 £5.99	
13	Helen Dickson & Joanna Maitland	978 0263 85105 2 £5.99	
14	Julia Justiss & Joanna Maitland	978 0263 85106 9 £5.99	
15	Claire Thornton & Georgina Devon	978 0263 85107 6 £5.99	
16	Gayle Wilson & Georgina Devon	978 0263 85108 3 £5.99	